Praise for Laura Drake's previous novel, *The Road to Me*:

"An unforgettable story of self-discovery and survival, reconciliation and redemption."
– Barbara Claypole White, author of *The Perfect Son*

"In *The Road to Me*, Laura Drake takes on the complexities of one family's struggle to get over a lifetime of mistakes and misunderstandings, expertly blending the heartbreak of a grandmother's past and a granddaughter's reluctance to trust her. *The Road to Me* offers a fresh and entrancing take on reconciliation and forgiveness, a truly captivating story filled with wit, wisdom and a whole lot of heart."
– Donna Everhart, author of *The Education of Dixie Dupree*

"A heart warming tale that many will identify with in so many ways."
– *Bookanon*

"I'd love to read another story in this vein penned by Ms. Drake. If you like emotional reads where families reconnect, this might be a story you'd enjoy."
– *Novels Alive*

Amazing Gracie

Amazing Gracie

Laura Drake

THE
ST●RY
PLANT

The Story Plant
1270 Caroline Street
Suite D120-381
Atlanta, GA 30307

Copyright © 2023 by Laura Drake

The Library of Congress Cataloguing-in-Publication Data is available upon request.

Story Plant paperback ISBN-13: 978-1-61188-352-7
Story Plant E-book ISBN: 978-1-945839-73-3

Visit our website at www.TheStoryPlant.com

First Gramarye Printing: April 2023
Printed in the United States of America
0 9 8 7 6 5 4 3 2 1

Dedication:

To all those who have served, my deepest gratitude.

"The soldier above all others prays for peace, for it's the soldier who must suffer and bear the deepest wounds and scars of war."– Douglas MacArthur

Grace is when God gives us what we don't deserve.
Mercy is when God doesn't give us what we do deserve.
– Dan Roberts

Chapter 1

Released from hell-hole duty overseas, most soldiers raced home. 'CJ' Maxwell trudged. She'd kept a low profile, but the flight was commercial and she had to be in uniform. If one more person had thanked her for her service, she'd have hurled.

Heroes deserved a welcome, not fuck ups. A Less Than Honorable discharge was a fly's weight compared to the elephant of remorse sitting on her soul. She hadn't known there were mistakes you couldn't come back from. The faces of her three friends flitted through her mind. Faces their families would never see again. Faces *she'd* never see again. And it was her fault. Eyes downcast, she scuttled through the airport, ducked into the first bathroom, and changed to a different camouflage—one that let her hide in *this* environment.

On her way out, she dropped the purple heart in its velvet-lined box into the trash and walked into the Southern California sunshine.

Hours later, in the sunbaked street outside Victorville, California, she stepped from the rental car to stand before the dusty, stuccoed crackerbox her memory had led her to. Sweat gathered in her armpits, luring her back into the cool car and the siren call of the interstate. After all, if they were still here after six years it would be a world record. What was that old saying? Home was the place they had to let you in? "Close enough for government work," she mumbled.

Not that she'd ever see government work again.

She was almost to the cracked cement walk when a shirtless guy came out of the battered one-car garage, confirming she was in the right place. He had the stamp of all her mother's boyfriends: long, lean, and hungry as a desert coyote.

He swiped oily hair out of his face and turned that hungry look on her — up, then down. "Hey, pretty lady. You lost?"

"Nope." Not lost. Not pretty. Not a lady. She turned at the sidewalk and took the broken steps to bang on the storm door.

Her mother opened it. The years had not been kind to Patsy: frizzy red hair, a sallow complexion, skinny freckled legs, and a barfly's paunch. Named for Patsy Cline, she'd always aspired to be a singer, but the closest she'd gotten was warming a barstool on karaoke night.

Jaded? Sure. But CJ had survived too many moves, too many boyfriends, and way too many let downs for a tearfilled family reunion. "Hi, Patsy." She forced a smile that only made it to one side of her mouth.

"Well, I'll be damned." The door squealed open.

They stood eyeing each other.

"You comin' in, Cora Jean, or you gonna stand on the porch gawking all day?" Patsy turned and walked into the shadowy interior.

CJ caught the door and stepped in, inhaling the miasma of old grease, cigarettes, and failed dreams of home. *This* was the price she'd pay to see her sister. She followed her mother to the kitchen. "The landlord still hasn't changed this nasty carpet?"

"Cheap bastard. But if he did, he'd probably raise the rent, so…" Patsy's lighter clicked. "You want tea?" The words trailed on a cloud of smoke.

"Sure." The Formica table was the same one she'd done her homework at in high school. The chairs didn't match; when one fell apart, they found another at the Trade-a-Ra-ma.

Patsy opened the fridge and took out the same stained plastic iced tea pitcher. "How long you on leave for?"

CJ's stomach squirmed, but she wasn't going to lie. "Forever."

"What?" She took glasses from the cupboard and turned, cigarette dangling from her lips. "You said the Army was your career. You said—"

"Plans change, okay?" When her words bounced off the too-close walls, she dialed back the volume. She didn't want more questions. "Can I stay a couple days?"

"This is still your home." Patsy took a deep hit on her cigarette, set it in the ashtray on the table, then carried over the glasses of tea. "You'll have to bunk with Gracie, though, unless you want the couch."

CJ glanced to the flowered, butt-sprung monstrosity, trying not to imagine what the stains were from. "If she'll have me."

"Oh, she'll be delighted. She's told all the kids at school about her sister, the soldier-super-hero."

Great. The weight she carried dug into her shoulders. How do you explain to a nine-year-old that her hero was the opposite?

"Well, I'm glad you're outta that shithole. You were in danger over there."

"Mom, I fixed trucks. I didn't ride them into battle." Except for that last time, and that sure wasn't on purpose.

"What are you going to do now?"

Her mother's interest in anyone outside herself was less than skin-deep, and for once CJ was grateful for it. "I'm buying a motorcycle and touring the U.S. for the summer. After that, we'll see."

13

"Wow." She leaned forward, a familiar glint in her eye. "You must have made serious money over there."

CJ knew a plea for a 'loan' wouldn't be far away. "Not really. I just saved it all. I've been planning this for a while." She took a sip of the too-sweet tea. "I just need a couple days to buy a bike and everything I'll need, then I'll be out of your hair."

The back door opened and the hungry coyote stepped in, greasy jeans sagging on bony hips.

"This is Blade." Patsy waved her cigarette. "This is my oldest, Cora Jean."

CJ swallowed a smile. "Is your name really Blade?"

"It's what they call me. And for good reason." He stuck out his scraggly-haired chin and tried to look bad.

He looked about as scary as an anorexic scarecrow. "I'll take your word for it."

Patsy gave CJ a 'don't start' look. "She's staying a couple days."

He wiped his greasy hands on a dishtowel. "I about got that piece of shit car fixed."

"I dry dishes with that!" Patsy lurched from her chair, snatching at the towel he held over her head. "Were you raised by wolves?" Her screech reached glass-shattering level.

"What, is the queen coming for tea? Jesus, woman, quit bitching at me." He dropped the towel on the floor, stomped to the living room, and flopped onto the couch, exposing an ankle bracelet care of the county. He aimed the clicker at the TV and a game show's canned applause came on.

"Doesn't he work?" CJ whispered.

Patsy took another drag. "He's fixing your old car so he can go on interviews."

You don't interview for the kind of jobs this guy was qualified for. Another loser in a long string of her mom's poor choices. God knows CJ'd met enough of them to be a judge.

14

Patsy stubbed out her cigarette. "Well, I gotta get to work. You hang out. Gracie will be home from school by four." She stood and grabbed the red apron emblazoned with the FoodTown Grocery logo and her slouch purse from the floor by the back door. "Hey, Blade," she called to the couch. "Don't forget, you gotta call that guy about my gig."

He waved a dismissive hand.

CJ wiped surprise from her face. Her mother wasn't a bad singer. She'd even had a couple singing dates in the past, but that was dog-years ago. "You got a gig?"

"Hope to. I'll be home by 5:30. Hey, can you fix dinner? There's shit in the fridge."

"Sure."

Patsy glanced to Blade, who ignored her. A flick of pain crossed her face before she turned and opened the door.

Why? The unanswerable question of CJ's childhood. Her mother could do better. Why did she always choose the ones who used — her house, her money, her body — and gave nothing in return? CJ dumped her iced tea in the sink and walked out to her car to grab a change of clothes and her shower stuff. She didn't want to move in on her half-sister until she had permission, even if the room had been CJ's first. Though when she walked into it, that was hard to imagine. The ceiling was painted black, with glow-in-the-dark stars and planets stuck all over it. CJ's band posters had been replaced by pictures of rocks, gems, and the cosmos. The bed and the ratty chenille bedspread were the same, but particle-board bookcases lined every wall, filled with reference books about geology, archaeology, and astronomy. Rocks covered the windowsill, dresser, and every other flat surface.

Amazing Grace Newsome. Her name was the only vestige of Patsy's brief hippie phase. CJ had never met the father — she'd gotten a scholarship to a running camp that summer, and by the time she got home Patsy was preggers and the sperm-donor long gone. But CJ had fallen for the baby, and from her birth until CJ left for the army her sister belonged more her than her mother. Everyone called her Grace, but to CJ she'd always been Mazey. A sweet, quiet child who had matured to a smart one, from the looks. Of course, they'd Facetimed once a week, but seeing this room told her more about Mazey than all those overseas calls.

Photos she'd sent home were tucked into the edges of the mirror over the dresser: her wrenching on a troop carrier, her standing in fatigues, arms around her buds... memories exploded like a land mine, tearing fresh holes. She turned away from The Land of Before.

In the hallway, a courtroom show competed with snores from the couch. She walked out, closing the front door behind her, and pulled the address she'd researched from that back pocket of her jeans.

Twenty miles up the road the Indian Motorcycle show-room floor was packed with inventory, both new and used. An electric current shot through her. This is what had sustained her in the desert. The friends' trip had turned into a memorial ride, but she was determined to go. To see it for the guys who couldn't.

"Can I help you find something, miss?" A salesman with 'Syd' embroidered on his denim shirt walked up.

"I'm looking for a current model Roadmaster Trike in Indian signature red, chromed out, with cream upholstery, ABS, independent suspension, reverse, and a raked tree." Her fingers caressed the handlebar of the bike next to her.

He stood, mouth open a bit.

"Oh, and if you have a new model from last-year's inventory I'd be good with that, too."

"You've done your research."

Only four years' worth. She'd first thought about two wheels, but figured it would take too long to learn and she was too antsy to wait. She scanned the showroom. "Do you have one?"

"I have a used aftermarket trike. Let me show you." He turned and took a few steps, but stopped when he realized she wasn't following.

"Not interested. Can you get me what I want, Syd? Or should I call the dealer in Bakersfield?" She crossed her arms and leaned her weight on one hip. If he thought she was an easy mark to pawn off dead inventory, he'd find out different.

"No, no. I can get you one. Let me make a couple of calls."

"Okay. I'll be in the gear department." She walked to the back and picked out a skull-cap helmet, riding gloves, motorcycle boots, chrome polish, and wax. She checked the items off her list and stuffed it back in her pocket.

The salesman found her ten minutes later. "I can have the exact bike you want here Friday."

"Good."

"Do you want to come to my office and we'll talk price?"

"Lead on." She probably knew more about a fair price for this bike than he did. And she expected a good discount for cash.

~~~

CJ slid the meat loaf and potatoes into the oven to bake, then looked up at the rattle of the storm door closing. Mazey still had that 'all in' smile. Even as a toddler, she smiled with her whole face.

"You're home!" She ran and flung herself into her sister's arms.

CJ's butt hit the counter. "Hey, punk." She tried to squeeze her sister but got mostly backpack. *This* was who she'd come seventy-five hundred miles to see. She squeezed tight despite hard edges of books biting into the inside of her arms.

"I'm so glad you're here." Mazey's voice was muffled in CJ's armpit.

"Me too." She slipped the straps off Mazey's arms and dropped it with a clunk. "What do you have in here, rocks?"

"Of course." Mazey shot her a 'duh' look.

She held her sister at arm's length. Tall for her age and the kind of skinny that comes from a growth spurt that made her all coltish legs and long, bony elbows. Black hair parted in the middle hung to her shoulders without a bend or wave. Oversized black-rimmed glasses made her eyes big, her face small. She wore the worn, mismatched clothes CJ remembered from her own back-to-school shopping trips at the Goodwill store. The soft spot she'd always had for her sister throbbed. "Man, I missed you, punk."

The wattage on Mazey's smile cranked up. "You used to call me that when I was little."

CJ ruffled her hair. "Well, you still are."

"How long are you home for?"

"Just a couple days. Can I bunk with you?"

"That'd be awesome!" She grabbed her backpack, and CJ's hand. "Come on, I'll show you." She led CJ around the room, showing off her treasures. "And here," she picked up a nondescript rock ball, "is a Mexican geode I bought with my birthday money."

Her sister didn't buy new clothes, she bought rocks. "Don't you have to break it open to see the crystals?"

"Yep."

"And…"

"I'm waiting for something special to happen. Then I'll open it to celebrate." She said it like she held the very best Christmas present under the tree.

"Why do you like rocks so much?"

Mazey set the geode gently on the windowsill, crossed to the bed and fell on it, hands behind her head. "I put the stars up in the same configuration they are in our hemisphere."

CJ wondered why Mazey didn't want to talk about what clearly meant a lot to her but wasn't going to push. She flopped beside her sister, taking in the innocent sweat and bubble-gum scent of childhood.

"See the Big Dipper?" She pointed.

She'd rather look at her sister. "I'm so proud of you. You're the brightest, coolest kid I know."

Maizie studied the ceiling. "I'm the only kid you know."

"That does not detract from your amazingness."

Her mouth curled a bit at that.

"How's school? What're you in, fourth grade?"

"Yeah. It's okay. Kinda boring, but the school librarian is amazing."

"But you told me you're in the gifted program."

"Geek Squad. That's what the kids call it."

She fingered the bedspread nubs in a self-soothing motion CJ remembered from her own stint in this house. "Only because they're jealous that they're not The Amazing Gracie."

She shrugged. "School's out Friday. Can I hang out with you after that?"

CJ slid her arm under Mazey's neck and hugged her. "For as long as I'm here, it's you and me, kid."

Dinner hadn't changed a bit in six years. Her mother chatted with her boyfriend du jour, pretty much ignoring the byproducts of her loins.

"This is good, CJ," Mazey said, poking at her plate.

"If you want to convince me, you're going to have to eat more of it." She gave her sister an encouraging smile.

"Seriously?" Patsy screeched. "He wants me to sing? If you are shitting me, Blade, I'll scratch your eyes out."

"Hey, that's what the man said."

Her mother squealed and launched herself into Blade's lap, bumping the table.

CJ steadied it before the beer bottles fell over, while her mother went full-on make out session right at the dinner table. His hands roamed over the tats exposed by her Walmart cami, the spaghetti straps sliding down her scrawny arms.

CJ caught her sister's wince out of the corner of her eye. "Hey!" she yelled.

They looked up.

"There's a minor in the room." She didn't bother to hide her disgust.

Her mother giggled, wriggling out of Blade's arms and back to her chair. "You don't know how great this is. I'm gonna headline at the Honky Donk Bar!"

"I didn't say headline." Blade shoveled in a forkful of meatloaf. "I said he's gonna try you out on Monday night." He talked around a mouthful.

CJ looked away, appetite gone.

"Yeah, but I'll be headliner by the end of the summer, you just see if I'm not." She stuck her hands into her orange rat's-nest hair. "I've gotta get to the beauty shop and get my hair fixed. And clothes! I've gotta have a new outfit for the gig." She looked across the tiny table.

CJ knew that look — like a puppy at the pound. She'd seen it a lot in high school, once she started earning money from her part-time job.

"CJ, hon, could I borrow some money? Just enough to make me presentable for my opening. I sure can't go like this. And there's extra expenses with you staying here..."

She studied her plate to avoid Patsy's hopeful face and block the sting of the fact that her mother just suggested charging her rent for the few days she'd be here. "Yeah, no problem."

The hungry coyote had the same green tint in his eye. "Whoa, you didn't tell me you had a high-roller there, Babe."

"CJ's a good girl." Her mother's syrupy tone might have sounded sincere to someone who didn't know her. "She's a sweetie."

Yeah, an easy mark always was around here. But beneath the disappointment in her mother was a small but persistent pocket of pity.

"I'm done. Can I go?" Maizie sat shredding her paper-towel-napkin onto her plate.

Ignoring her youngest, Patsy leaned over and laid an open-mouth kiss on Blade.

Jesus. Six years gone, and exactly zero had changed — like a ghetto Groundhog Day. "You go. I'll be there in a few."

She scooted out and CJ carried dishes to the sink. Her mother nattered on to Blade, stitching old dreams into a worn-thin king-sized quilt—one she would never own.

By the time CJ got a shower and stepped into the darkened bedroom, Mazey was already in bed. "You asleep?" she whispered.

"No."

How could one word sound so sad? CJ felt her way to the bed and slid in beside her sister. The clicking fan in the window pushed hot air over them. CJ looked up at the soft glow from fake stars above her. "You really put all these stars in the right place?"

Her sister flipped onto her back. "I could only put the closest ones in. They don't make them small enough to fit in the ones more than five light years away."

"You're the smartest of us. You know that?"

"Maybe. But you're the bravest."

She held in a snort. "Nope. You're the bravest, too."

"How'm I brave?"

"You live here full time."

"It's not so bad. You survived."

"Long enough to know it's not easy." She felt bad, not staying and helping Mazey — somehow. But she had a trip to take. A promise to keep. They lay quietly for a time. Mazey's breathing evened out, and CJ thought she'd drifted off.

"You asked me why I like rocks."

"I did."

"Rocks don't leave." She flipped onto her side, away from CJ. "They never let you down."

Chapter 2

The next morning CJ pulled herself from the recurring nightmare, dressed, and slipped out of the sleeping house onto the front porch as the fireball sun edged over the horizon. Desert air was seldom crisp, but at least at dawn it wasn't recycled dragon's breath. She did a couple stretches, then took off down the broken sidewalk.

She may suck at truck repair and life in general, but one thing she knew how to do was run. She started in junior high to escape the domestic drama, but when the gym teacher noticed, he told the cross-country coach and CJ ended up on the team. She loved it. It was a competitive, but solitary sport. What it came down to was you, your willingness to bear pain, and the cadence of your shoes slapping the dirt.

But outrunning her past was proving as impossible as outrunning her shadow.

The scars on her stomach throbbing, she turned right at Mammoth and jogged past her old high school. It hadn't changed a bit, crouching in the gravel landscape, worn and dusty as the land around it.

The Army had never been a second choice for her. With no money and only average grades, college was out. When she enlisted she hoped to be trained as a medic, then planned to use the G.I. bill to get her EMT certificate. But the Army's aptitude test said she'd make a better truck mechanic than a people one. One more thing they got wrong.

She was so damned tired. No, more than tired. It was as if her soul was on empty. The well of hope and optimism that she'd taken for granted all her life had dried up in the desert. She'd tried. She'd keep trying. But late at night, awake in the dark, she was starting to wonder why.

The jury was still out on if it was too late for her, but Mazey… Her sister's words of last night drifted through her mind. Why couldn't little Mazey have been born to a middle-class family, one who would recognize her big brain, her wonder and her passion, and see that she had the opportunity to make the most of it?

Well, Mazey didn't have that, but she had a big sister… who wouldn't be around long enough to help. But hey, her sister was smart enough to make it on her own. CJ sped up to leave the thought behind. She'd be fine.

After seven miles of pounding past her old haunts, she climbed the steps and opened the back door, sweat-covered and breathing hard.

Blade sat drinking coffee at the kitchen table in boxers and nothing else. He eyed her cut-off sweats and camo t-shirt. "You look good enough to lick, girl."

She walked by, not bothering to hide her shudder or a lip-curl of disgust.

When she stepped into the small bathroom, her shower kit called to her. *No. Not doing it.* She peeled off her clothes and made the mistake of looking in the full-length mirror on the back of the door. The crosshatch of small scars on her upper thighs pulled her fingers like a magnet. Some white, some pink, many more red and healing.

This is sick. You know it.

She pulled out her old-fashioned blade razor and shampoo then stepped into the shower. After washing everything, she put her foot on the edge of the tub to shave her legs. Ants crawled over her brain, whispering louder and faster as they went. Her gut churned, a toxic stew of conscience and compulsion. When shivers of need pulsed under her skin, her vow wavered. Again.

A twist to the bottom of the razor exposed the blade. She removed it, found a few inches of clear skin and made three quick, short, perfectly parallel cuts. The relief was immediate, as if the pressure spilled out with the ribbons of red running down her thigh. Somehow, the outside physical pain helped make the inside pain bearable. This was wrong, but was the only relief she'd been able to find since the accident in the desert.

By the time she stepped out of the shower, a pad of folded toilet paper and some medical tape blotted the bleeding.

Five minutes later, she stepped into her sister's room and tickled her awake.

Mazey squirmed and giggled. "Quit!"

She forced a lilt into her voice. "Last day of school. If you get ready fast, I'll make you breakfast. Pancakes okay?"

"Are you kidding? Anything more than dry cereal is way okay."

"Then get moving and I'll drive you to school, too."

Mazey bounded out of bed and hugged CJ around the waist. "I'm so glad you're home."

"Me too." She may only be able give her sister a one-day reprieve from the brutal hierarchy of the school bus, but it was better than nothing.

Blade was gone when she walked into the kitchen. Whistling, she made peanut butter pancakes with whipped-cream happy faces.

An hour later she eased the rental car into the drop-off lane of the elementary school. The stuccoed building hadn't been hers; she'd gone to school in Idaho, Arizona, then Nevada before coming here. "I'll be back to pick you up this afternoon."

"Thanks, CJ." Mazey slammed the car door and strode for the front doors, a smile on her face. Kids swarmed, but no one called out to Mazey. It was like there was an invisible force-field around her. No one came close.

A small group of bitches-in-training whispered and pointed at Mazey.

The car door was open and CJ's foot was on the ground before she thought better of it. She'd be seen as the bad guy, picking on a couple of kids.

Little shits.

But Mazey took no notice of them. Her narrow shoulders and slender back seemed so vulnerable stepping into the school's shadowy interior. CJ wanted to save her from the bullies, from her mother, from her life. "She'll be fine." She nodded to convince herself and pulled away from the curb.

~~~

Her new bike reclined in front of the showroom window like a Hollywood starlet — shiny, showy, and drawing a crowd.

"I didn't know Indian even made a trike."

"Love how they kept it retro. Cool leather bags, too. All it needs is leather tassels on the handlebars."

"Only if you wanna look girly."

She smiled and walked by the guys clustered around the window. Tassels. Good idea.

While the service department installed the tassels and temporary plates, Syd the salesman followed her in his car to drop off her rental.

On the way back, he glanced over. "You mentioned you're taking a long trip. You going alone?"

"Yeah. Why?"

He raised an eyebrow. "You got something to protect yourself with?"

"I can outrun trouble."

His profile looked dubious. "I'm not trying to scare you—"

"Like you could."

"Hey, I'm not trying to insult you. I'd say this to a guy traveling alone. You never know what you'll run into out there."

She shot him a side-eye, still not sure he wasn't talking down to her. "What do you suggest?"

"This." He reached across her, flipped open the glove compartment and pulled out a red plastic thing that looked like a box-opener, right down to the slide on the side.

She reached for it, but he snatched it back. "Not till you know how it works." He touched the slide embedded on the side and a wicked five-inch blade snicked out, quick as a snake's tongue.

"Jesus."

"Yeah. It's spring-loaded." He touched the slide again and the blade was gone in a blur.

"You gotta admit, it would intimidate an attacker." He handed it to her.

It was weighty and solid. She felt safer just holding it. Well, safe and a little scared. "What if it comes out accidentally?"

"It won't. That's why the trigger is recessed. See?" He turned into the dealer parking lot.

"Is this legal?"

"Depends on what state you're in. California? No. But would you rather need it and not have it? You'd have to be alive to be charged with owning it."

"Good point. Do you know where I can get one?"

"Through the mail."

"Well, I'll have to pick one up in another state then. I'm leaving Sunday."

He parked behind the dealership, turned off the ignition, and turned to her. "I can sell you that one if you want."

She flipped the blade out and back. "I want."

~~~

After Syd gave her operational instructions on the bike, it took her a while to load all her purchases into the side bags. Then she strapped on the skullcap helmet, threw a leg over, and fired it up. No worry about a clutch, the shift was at the touch of a lever. A brake pedal rested under her right foot, turn signals on the left handlebar. Tach and speedometer on the dash in front of her. The purpose of rest of the dials and buttons was fuzzy, but she had the essentials down.

She hit reverse and backed up, turned the handlebars, and thumbed it into first. Heart racing faster than the engine, she rolled to the exit and waited for traffic to clear, then turned right. Thanks to her work with trucks, she knew from the sound of the winding engine when to shift. She hit the speed limit, knuckles white, cruising with the traffic.

The hot wind swirled around her, lifting her hair and her spirits. It had been so long since the black cloud that hung over her had lifted. She took a deep breath, almost giddy with freedom. The sign for the freeway came up, but she hesitated. Without the heavy metal cage she felt exposed, afraid.

Time to get over herself. These were only the first few miles leading to a cross-country trip. "Fuck fear," she laughed into the wind, merged onto the on ramp, geared up, and buried the throttle.

Two hours later she was sure that the bike was a good idea, and the trip was a good idea. Back when she'd come up with it, it had been just a dream in the desert — something to plan in the tedious hours between shifts — a motorcycle trip to see the beauty of America. But after she told her friends, as their friendship deepened it became more than a dream. It became a plan. They mapped the route, researched the bikes, Googled the places they'd see. They committed to saving up their money and their leaves for the trip.

She learned young, as the almost-forgotten caboose on Patsy's train-wreck life, that nothing was easy. CJ'd thought the Army would change things — that she'd finally get a piece the 'good life' everyone talked about. What she saw instead was a ravaged Middle eastern country, and people in such dire straits it made her life back home seem like the Yellow Brick Road.

She slowed and pulled off at the exit that led to Mazey's school. She scored a place right out front of the line of mommymobiles, thanks to the bike's short wheelbase and a mini-van that didn't pull up fast enough. She got odd looks when she pulled off her helmet. She'd get used to those after a few days on the road.

The bell rang, and seconds later kids burst through the double doors — running, laughing, talking. Seeing the bike, several walked over to admire.

"Wow, that's pretty. Will you take me for a ride?"

"Aren't you afraid? I'd be afraid."

"Is it hard to ride?"

"How old do you have to be to drive one?"

She did her best to answer the machine-gun questions while watching for her sister.

Mazey came out the way she went in, smiling with her force-field intact. When she recognized CJ on the bike, a look of wonder crossed her face. She stepped around the gawkers into CJ's hug.

"Wait, *this* is your sister? The soldier?"

She beamed. "Yep."

"Wow, who knew The Mouse was telling the truth?"

CJ frowned, but before she could say anything Mazey rounded on the boy.

"I don't lie. And I'm not a mouse." She pointed to the bike. "I'm riding this motorcycle home, so all of you can just be jealous."

CJ hid a smile and handed her sister the skull-cap helmet. "Strap this on and let's blow this pop stand, Amazing Gracie."

The kids trailed off in clumps, whispering.

She showed Mazey how to buckle the helmet's strap, whispering, "Ignore them. They suck."

Mazey giggled. "Believe me, I know."

"Okay, you're set." She patted the top of the helmet. "All you have to do is put your foot on the running board and swing your leg over. It'll be like riding in an armchair." She took her sister's heavy book bag and dropped in into the trip trunk on the back.

"But you don't have a helmet."

"Your head is worth a lot more than mine. It's only a few miles. I'll be fine." She mounted the bike and it fired with a throaty growl. Faces turned. The adults had frowns, the kids had a look of awe.

"Now hang on." When Mazey's arms came around her waist, CJ checked the mirror and pulled out.

"'Bye looooooooosers!" Mazey whooped.

CJ concentrated on the traffic. She had precious cargo aboard.

"Do we have to go right home?" Mazey yelled in her ear.

"Sorry, but we do." She was tired from being tense and hyper-alert all day, and she wasn't wearing a helmet. But she relished having her sister's arms around her, her body leaning trustingly against her back.

She pulled up in front of the house and shut it down. Mazey clambered off first. "That was the best! Can we go again? Maybe after dinner?"

CJ helped her undo the chin strap. "We'll see." She walked to the back and hefted the backpack out of the trip trunk.

Magnified by her glasses, Mazey's eyes were full of sadness. "You're not staying long, are you?"

"No, punk. I'm leaving Sunday."

"Would you take me with you?" Her voice was mouse-sized. "Just you and me, all summer. Think of the amazing things we'd see."

"Are you nuts? You're nine." CJ couldn't even be trusted with truck maintenance. She shuddered, imagining how she could wreck a kid.

Mazey snatched her backpack and threw it over her shoulder. "When will I be old enough to have a say in my own life?"

CJ had empathy. After all, Mazey's childhood mirrored her own. "What would you do if you did?"

"I'd climb on the bike with you, and we'd go find my dad." The corners of her mouth turned down in a little girl's pout, but the determination in her eyes was much older.

"Your *dad*?" She'd never considered the other half of her sister's DNA. "You never even met him."

"Yeah, but I know what he'd be like. He'd be nice, and good, and caring."

Blade came around the side of the house, beer in hand, and headed for the garage.

"And decent. And employed." She looked up at her sister with a tight-lip warning not to argue. "And he'd love me. More than anything."

CJ hated to kill the dream, but better that than living in denial. She knew where that road led. "Yeah, but he bailed, right?"

"Oh right, one more thing. He's smart. That's why he didn't stick around." She spun and marched for the door.

"You must've gotten your brains from that side of the family," she muttered, trotting to catch up. "You're officially on vacation. What are you going to do with your summer?"

Mazey opened the door and they walked in. "I'm going to try to get some babysitting jobs, and maybe mow lawns in the neighborhood."

Enterprising kid. "Here, sit." CJ tapped a kitchen chair. "I'll get us some tea and a snack. What are you saving up for?"

Mazey dropped the backpack and sank until her chin rested on her fist on the table. "For a P.I."

"Huh?" CJ pulled the tea jug from the fridge.

"Private investigator. To find my dad. I know his name. It's Beau Brown."

"Yeah, but Brown has got to be one of the most common names—"

"So *don't* help." Mazey bolted upright, crossing her arms around her waist as if it would ward off a stomach punch. "See if I care. I'll find him on my own. He's probably been looking for me all these years, and I just didn't know it." She nodded. "I'll find him."

CJ finished pouring and carried the glasses to the table. What an odd, determined kid. "Hey, if you say it, I believe it."

"Can I use your laptop to do a search?"

She didn't want to encourage Mazey's delusions, but she couldn't say no. Dreams were all her sister had. The kid didn't yet know that this house was where dreams went to die. "Sure. Password is 'Gear*ratio'."

"Thanks!" She streaked for the bedroom.

Two hours later, CJ carried the last dinner dish to the table.

"So, did you find a job today?" Patsy snuffed her cigarette in the ashtray Mazey held.

Blade took a swig from his beer bottle. "I'll have better luck tomorrow."

Yeah, probably. From the fumes drifting off him, he'd spent the afternoon covering a stool at a bar. CJ passed the homemade mac 'n cheese to Mazey.

Patsy eyed the corn dogs. "Dinner is a bit...kid-centric, don't you think?"

CJ nodded. "This is Mazey's gradution-from-fourth-grade celebration." God, how do you forget your kid's last day of school?

"Well, I'm a fan," Blade said through a mouthful of half-masticated hot dog.

Probably because he was mentally younger than Mazey.

"Oh, that's right. Today was your last day." Patsy patted Mazey's arm. "Don't have to worry if your grades are good enough to move on. I had a few scares with your sister, there."

"But thanks to all your brilliant support, I made it."

Patsy's smile proved her immunity to sarcasm.

Blade and Patsy chatted through dinner, ignoring the other two diners. CJ was carrying dishes to the sink when Patsy's voice came from behind her. "Hey, Cora Jean, would you babysit for us tonight? We're checking out the lounge where I'll be singing on Monday night."

Mazey rolled her eyes. "I'm nine, and you've been leaving me alone for *years.*"

"Sure. Mazey and I will have popcorn and play Jenga. How does that sound, Punk?"

~~~

The next morning after running, CJ grabbed a shower. Mazey had said she wanted to go shopping with her today. She'd let her sister sleep in until she got breakfast on the table.

But when she walked into the kitchen Mazey was already there, sitting at the table in her threadbare nightgown. CJ froze in the doorway as her guts went into freefall, plunging to her feet.

Blade, in his boxers, loomed over Mazey, whispering in her ear. She leaned away, her face twisted with worry.

"Hey!" Fury pushed CJ's blood back into circulation, throbbing in her face, pounding in her ears.

Blade jerked upright. She knew that look in his eye — *the* look. CJ should know.

And if looks could kill, he'd be a smoking corpse.

Mazey's brow smoothed. "Hey, CJ."

"Why don't you hop in the shower, Punk?" The words came out soft and calm, but with a fine shake to them.

33

"We're going shopping, right?" She bounced out of the chair.

CJ's stare didn't leave Blade. "You bet we are. Scoot, now."

Mazey skipped past and down the hallway to the bathroom.

CJ didn't remember moving but she was standing toe to toe with the slime, finger in his face. "If I *ever* get even a *hint* that you are messing with my sister…" She took a breath to clear the dark flecks from her vision. "I'll wait until you're asleep." Breathe. "And I will use rusty garden shears to cut your tiny dangling parts off."

His face paled and he backed a step away. After a moment, his lips quirked up in an oily smile. "But you're not gonna *be* here, remember?"

Chapter 3

CJ left the damned coyote in the kitchen and stalked to Mazey's room.

She was sitting on the bed in fresh jeans and wet hair, bouncing with impatience. "I'm ready, let's go."

"In a minute." CJ closed the door and crossed to sit beside her sister on the bed. "Does Blade bother you like that a lot?"

"I just ignore him. Today's the first time he ever got in my face."

"You, um…teachers have talked to you about people putting their hands on you, right? That you should tell someone?"

Behind her glasses, Mazey's eyes got huge. "You mean he's a moron *and* a perv?"

Wow. Her sister was naïve. Around Patsy, innocence died faster than the belief in the Tooth Fairy. How had she managed that? Glancing around the room, the answer came to her. Mazey lived on a different plane. Her focus was beneath her feet, for rocks and the sky above, searching the stars. The rest of her time was spent with her nose in a book. Her passions were the super-power that kept her from the crap all around her.

CJ had spent all her time in the real world. Maybe if she hadn't lived so much time there, she'd still have hope. That old Jackson Browne song about leaving her eyes open for too long drifted through her mind. "Listen, Punk, You don't have to worry about it. I'll take care of it, okay?"

"Okay."

Mazey's smile should have made CJ relax, except she knew her sister's trust was ill-placed. She couldn't afford to fail this time, because this was even bigger than her love for Mazey. CJ needed to know that somewhere, amid the muck and despair, there was a ray of unsullied innocence. She needed that.

The world needed that.

"Now let's go shopping, girlfriend." She put a lilt in her voice and held her palm up for a high-five.

Outside, she gave Mazey her helmet. They straddled the bike and headed for the outdoor store.

They dismounted at the huge boxy building where the doors opened with a whoosh, bathing them in cool air.

"Okay, we need—" Mazey pulled the list CJ had given her from her pocket. "A tent, sleeping bag, travel pillow…" She squinted at the writing. "And clothes and stuff."

"Yeah, let's ask somebody where the 'and stuff' aisle is."

Mazey pointed. "I see tents."

"Lead on, sista." She threw an arm across Mazey's shoulders. This was their day. She wasn't going to let it be spoiled by bad memories and perverts.

Mazey stopped by a four-man stand-up tent. "Oh, this one is cool. It's even got a little porch, see?"

"Yeah, except there's not much storage on the bike. Everything has to be as small and light as possible."

"Oh, right." She walked to a more traditional two-man pup tent.

CJ stepped across the floor to a one-man, mummy-style tent. "Like this one."

"That'd feel like a coffin, and there's not even room to keep your other stuff inside."

"Yeah, but it packs small."

"So does this one, see?" She pointed to the display for the two-man tent. It was made for backpackers and folded to the same size as the one-man.

"Good eye, Punk; you sold me."

"And you'd have room for someone else in there, if they were small…"

Her hopeful look ripped a hole in CJ's shrapnel-torn heart. "Aw, Mazey, you know—"

"I know, I know." She walked to the next display. "Sleeping bags are over here."

Two hours and seven hundred fifty-seven dollars later, CJ had everything she could imagine needing that would fit on the bike.

"Thanks for helping, Punk. Now, for the good part."

"What good part?" Mazey's exuberance had wound down as she crossed things off the list, probably imagining CJ riding off in a cloud of exhaust, leaving her behind.

CJ knew how long summers could be in that house. Maybe she'd research a space camp to send Mazey to. She'd be safe, having fun, and CJ couldn't think of a better use for her fat bank account. "We're going to the bookstore."

"*That's* what I'm talking about!" Mazey pumped a fist in the air.

They returned home, the bike loaded like a Sherpa's yak. When they got everything unpacked CJ suggested Mazey read for a while, then headed for the kitchen.

Patsy was poking something in the frying pan, squinting past the smoke from her cigarette. "'Bout time you got home. Burgers for dinner."

CJ glanced around. "Where's…" She couldn't bring herself to say the ridiculous nickname. "What is his real name, anyway?"

"Wayne."

"Where's Dwayne?"

"I said—"

"Wayne. I added the 'duh'."

"That's not nice. And he's out with his buds."

CJ took the spatula from Patsy's hand and turned off the burner. "Come sit." She led her to the table.

Patsy shot CJ a 'what now' look and mashed the cigarette out in the overflowing ashtray.

"About Dwayne—"

"Wayne. Show a little respect."

"Respect is earned, and he's not even working." She took a breath. "He's starting to mess with Mazey."

Patsy's eyebrows shot up, but from her jerky eye movements CJ knew it was for show. "You're just reading him wrong. He's friendly."

"He's the kind of friendly that has no place around a nine-year-old. And you know I know the difference. Or are you going to say I'm 'imagining things' again?" That had worked for Patsy until she came home to CJ's black eye, and bleeding furrows down her boyfriend's face. Then, she believed. Drama ensued, and by morning he was gone. That was the day CJ started calling her mother Patsy. "Did you ever hear what happened to old Bruno?"

Patsy flinched. "I don't know. Don't want to know."

"Well, you can't say you don't know this time." CJ crossed her arms over her chest and stared her mother down.

"You don't understand." Patsy shook out and lit another cigarette. "He's got connections. He got me that gig on Monday night."

"Oh, bullshit. It's just a drinking buddy of his, and if you don't pass muster you'll be asshole first out the screen door, and you know it."

"But this is my last chance. I'm losing my looks, and without those I don't—"

"So you're telling me that your non-existent singing career is more important than your daughter's safety?" CJ was on her feet, looming over her mother. "God, a barn cat is a better mother than you. Why did you even have kids?"

Patsy's eyes narrowed and her thin lips disappeared. "Who said I ever wanted them?"

CJ straightened as if she'd been slapped. "What?"

"It's not anything like I thought it would be. The whining, squalling, always needing something, ruining my body. The money... I wish I'da—"

"Don't!" When CJ shoved a finger in her mother's face, she jerked back. "Don't you dare say it." She took a breath to replace the one that had been knocked out of her. "You were always selfish and a bit narcissistic, but I never thought you were evil."

"I didn't do it, did I? I know you don't have any respect for me, but give me credit for having respect for a human life." Patsy's face twisted with malice. "Don't you get all high 'n mighty with me, sister. Why are you not going back to the Army? Hmmmm?"

Nope. She wasn't getting dragged into a firefight. Especially since she had little righteous ammo. She tightened her muscles to stop the shaking in her hands. "You're not going to do anything about him, are you?"

"Once I'm settled at the Honky Donk, I'll cozy up to the owner. Then I won't need Blade's help. I'll move up to a better place, and..." She trailed off under CJ's smoking glare. Her face crumpled. "You don't know what it's like. I was meant to be a country music star. Somehow it all went off the rails, and now it's almost too late..." She sniffed.

Maybe it's impossible to accept the woman who raised you as a monster. A small pocket of pity still wedged deep in CJ's chest, like a small balloon of pus. Who was she to judge? After all, she'd inherited her mother's talent for screwing up.

But not protecting an innocent, much less your own child, was beyond her understanding. Rage burst like a flare, hot and red. "Let me tell you how it's going to be." She pulled her wallet from a back pocket, stuffed with bills left over from the shopping trip. She pulled out three one hundred-dollar bills. "I'm taking Mazey with me for the summer. By the time I bring her home, your boyfriend is in the wind. If he's not, I'm going to Social Services, and I mean it." Fingering the bills, she studied the pathetic, aging woman in front of her. Any pity she may have had for Patsy smoked like a fried electrical connection. "Got that?"

"You can't..." But when she looked into her eldest's eyes, she knew CJ could. And would. Patsy eyed the cash like a runway model eyes a steak, weighing what she wanted against her flesh and blood. It took about five seconds. "Okay."

CJ threw the bills onto the table and stalked to the bathroom, feeling like she might hurl. She threw cold water on her face, leaned her palms on the edge of the counter. What the hell had she done? She was the last one who should be in responsible for Mazey. Patsy's sly look squirmed through her mind. Well, second to last.

And that's really what it came down to. There was no one else. She stared into the mirror, at her short, dishwater blonde hair. At her wiry boy's body. At her inadequacies. "Sorry, Mazey. You get the booby prize." She straightened.

She'd do her absolute best, but her sister deserved so much more. Ignoring the siren call of her razor she opened the door, took the few steps to Mazey's room and, after hauling in a deep breath, knocked.

The door opened. Mazey's face lit up. "Come see what I found!"

"What's up?"

Mazey sat on the bed and turned the laptop screen. Beau Brown's name was below a high school photo.

"Punk, you gotta stop—"

"No, listen. This is cool. He was a baseball player, first base, and their team went to state finals his senior year."

CJ sank onto the edge of the bed. "What state?"

"Nevada. He grew up in Sparks, not far from Reno, where he met Mom. How amazing is that?" She stared at the photo as if memorizing his features.

They shared the same bone-straight black hair and all-in smile. "You do kinda resemble him."

"Do you think so?" Pride sparkled in her eyes, hope in her tone.

Who could blame her? At least she had one side to feel proud of, even if it was only in her imagination. "Oh, definitely." She pushed the laptop closed and turned to face her sister. "I need to talk to you, and this is really important, so listen close before you answer, okay?"

Mazey's gaze flicked over CJ's face, searching for clues. "Okay."

CJ took a breath, knowing this decision would change her life as well as her sister's. "What would you say to going with me for the summer?"

Mazey's mouth dropped open. "On your motorcycle trip? Seriously?"

CJ nodded.

Mazey let out a loud whoop and launched herself into CJ's lap. "Do you mean it? For really-real?"

CJ hugged her, trying to ignore the creeping worry. "As really-real as it gets."

Mazey pulled back to study CJ's face. "What about Mom?"

"I cleared it with her. It's you and me, kid."

She squealed, hugging CJ's neck until she couldn't breathe.

"But wait, because I gotta tell you some things."

Mazey frowned and let go. "There's a catch, isn't there?"

"No. If you want to go, you're going. We'll make stops that me and my friends and I planned when we were in the desert. But..." She studied her torn cuticles. "There's no telling what will happen. If we get in a...a situation and I tell you to do something, and you know — I mean, you *know* — that it's the wrong thing to do..." She looked up. "You have to promise me you won't do it."

Mazey cocked her head like a curious sparrow. "You'd never tell me to do the wrong thing, CJ."

The trees outside danced in the desert wind. "Not on purpose. But my judgment isn't so good sometimes, so you have to promise me."

"What happened to you over there?"

Her head whipped back to her sister, thoughts whirling in a dust-devil dance in her mind. "N-nothing. You're just smarter'n me. That's all I'm saying."

"Okay then, I promise." She hopped off the bed. "Ohmygosh," she chirped. "I've gotta get packed. When do we leave? Where are we going first?"

"Whoa up there, Punk. You need to know, this won't be five-star. We'll camp out, and you might have to pee in the woods a time or two."

"Like I care." Her eye-roll was beyond her years. "What do I do to get ready?"

CJ thought a moment. "Tell you what. Let's go shopping first. We'll need to get you outfitted before the stores close, because we leave in the morning."

By the time she finished the sentence, Mazey had grabbed her Hello Kitty purse and was bouncing on the balls of her feet in the middle of the room. "I'm ready!"

CJ could only hope *she* was.

~~~

That evening CJ stood, hands on her hips, perusing the huge pile of clothes, rocks, and books on the floor. "Punk, you're out of control here."

"Hey, you told me to get out everything I wanted to take." She'd been a whirlwind of activity for hours.

"My mistake. I should have said 'need'. We're on a motorcycle, remember? A lot of the space is taken up by the tent, sleeping bags, and camping stuff. There's no way we have room for all this."

Her shoulders slumped like someone had let the air out of her. "Oh, right."

"Separate it into two piles: what you can live without, and what you can't. I'm gonna pop some popcorn, and I'll be back."

"Okay."

CJ walked to the kitchen. Patsy and the sleaze were out at some friend's party, which was good. Her mother had been giving CJ traitorous looks, and she didn't want Mazey catching on as to why. She looked around the shadowy room while the microwave did its thing. She'd fled this place after graduation, knowing that the big world outside her mother's orbit had to be better. Auto mechanic hadn't been her dream job, but she'd made friends and it had been fun... until she blew it all up. Eddie, Logan, and Mateo's smiling faces drifted across her vision in the familiar horror film clip. She slammed her eyes shut on it.

When the microwave beeped she pulled out the bag of popcorn she no longer had an appetite for, she grabbed the salt, and returned to Mazey's room. Her stuff was now in two piles: one third, and two thirds the size of the original.

"It was hard, but I got it down." Mazey pointed to the bigger pile.

CJ pointed to the smaller one. "We'll be lucky if this one fits."

Mazey fell onto the bed with a groan. "I can't do it! I need all this stuff!"

CJ tossed the bag and salt shaker next to her sister on the bed. "Okay, let's see what you've got." She squatted beside the essential pile. "Oh, I see the problem." She sorted, leaving clothes and stacking books and rocks to the side.

"Wait! How'm I going to live without books? And my rocks are—"

"Are you kidding? Are you telling me you're not going to collect rocks from everywhere we go? And guess what? There are libraries all across the country, and you can use my laptop to Google stuff." She added more clothes from the smaller pile. "We're gonna be riding in all kinds of weather. You're going to need warm clothes, too; trust me."

She moved the 'keep' pile in front of the closet. "We'll pack this stuff in the bags in the morning. You want to see our route?" She pulled the map of California from her back pocket.

"Oh, yeah."

When CJ spread the map on the small student desk in the corner, it wobbled just the way she remembered. "Okay, we'll leave here, and…"

~~~

CJ opened her eyes the next morning to Mazey leaning over the bed, staring at her. She jerked back. "What?"

"Jeez, I thought you'd never wake up." Her sister was fully dressed in blue jeans, a red 'Bad to the Bone' T-shirt, and motorcycle boots they'd bought that matched CJ's. "How are we going to get started if you sleep all day?"

CJ lifted herself onto an elbow. Outside, the horizon was one shade of charcoal above black. She rubbed her eyes and groaned. "We're not leaving before dawn, Punk."

"Yeah, but we've gotta pack my stuff, get breakfast, and say goodbye to Mom." She shook her sister's legs. "Come *on*, CJ!"

"Okay, okay, I'm moving." She threw her legs off the bed, ducking her head to hide her smile. A buzz of anticipation shot down her nerves. How long since she'd felt that? She realized that she'd been thinking of this trip as an obligation — fulfilling the promise she'd made with her friends. Mazey coming along may not be the smart thing but, now that she was committed, damned if she wasn't looking forward to it.

By the time she finished her shower and walked to the driveway, Mazey was frowning at her clothes lying in the dusty grass.

"This isn't going to fit."

"Hang on, it will." She pulled her clothes from the side bags, rolled them into small tubes, shoved them into a heavy-duty black trash bag, and then into one side bag. Then she did the same with Mazey's in the other bag. The butane stove, pans and dishes were in the trip trunk, the tent and sleeping bags on top, held on by bungee cords. "Good thing you're a skinny kid. Next year you wouldn't fit."

They trooped into the kitchen where Patsy and Blade were slouched at the table, smoking.

CJ told Mazey to sit, then grabbed the pancake mix and a bowl. "Must've been some party. You look like Patsy Cline this morning."

Her mother's eyes were a roadmap of self-abuse. "Patsy Cline is long dead."

"My point exactly." She grabbed the griddle and turned on the stove.

Concentrating on cooking, she tuned out the mumbling behind her. Ten minutes later, she set the plates in front of them and settled gingerly in the last wobbly chair.

"Mom, we're going to Reno first." Mazey's voice had a bounce. "After that, we're going wherever we want. I want to see the petrified forest, and—"

"Blade, you won't forget to pick up cigarettes when you're out today, right?" Patsy shook another cancer stick from the ever-present pack at her elbow.

Mazey's face fell. Patsy's casual disregard was something CJ had always felt she should get used to, but never had. She pointed to Mazey, then back at herself. *You and me, kid.*

Her sister's smile had melancholy tinges at the edges.

Damn you, Patsy.

Blade squirted a quarter bottle of syrup on the pancakes and dug in, taking bites between drags on his cigarette.

When they were done, Mazey and CJ piled their plates in the sink. Someone else was doing dishes this morning. "Well, we're hitting the road."

"Oh my gosh, that's today!" Patsy hopped up and followed her daughters out to the driveway, where the trike squatted like a pregnant pig. "Oh, my baby." Patsy enveloped Mazey in a bony hug and hung on. "I'm not sure this is such a good idea." She glared at CJ over Mazey's head. "A little girl needs her mother."

CJ glared back, unmoved. "No argument here."

Mazey squirmed out of the embrace. "I'll call you and tell you all the fun we're having."

"Oh, that reminds me." CJ pulled out her phone and unlocked it. "Will you put your number in my address book?"

While Patsy typed, CJ lifted her leather jacket from one handlebar and shrugged into it. Mazey did the same with her matching one — another of their purchases from yesterday. CJ strapped on her skullcap helmet. "Here, give me yours."

Mazey handed over her full-faced one. She'd lost the matching helmet argument — no way CJ was risking her sister's precious head. She pushed it on, opened the face shield, then threaded the chin strap and tugged it tight.

"You're choking me."

"You're fine. It needs to be snug."

When Patsy handed over the phone, CJ was shocked to see genuine sadness in her eyes.

"Keep her safe. Promise?" Her lip disappeared between her teeth, and a tear slipped off her eyelashes.

CJ was jaded, but it would take a meaner person not to feel a bit for Patsy. Her mother's emotions may be shallow, but they were all she was capable of. "I'll be careful, don't worry."

Patsy sniffed.

"Besides, you'll be busy what with working and singing. Maybe you'll get a couple more nights at different bars around here once the word spreads."

Patsy's chin came up and her bony shoulders went back, pushing her unharnessed boobs forward. Impossible not to see that they were starting to sag. "You're right. I'll be busy. I'm going to need a few more outfits…"

CJ sighed and pulled two more hundred-dollar bills from the inside pocket of her jacket and handed them over.

Patsy patted CJ's cheek. "You're a good daughter."

CJ threw her leg over the bike, trying not to feel like she just bought her sister for two hundred bucks. "Let's hit the road, Punk. Daylight's burnin'."

"'Bye, Mom." Mazey clambered on behind, and her arms went around CJ's waist.

She fired up the bike, backed out of the driveway, and after a wave to Patsy they blew out of Victorville on a cloud of adrenaline and exhaust.

Chapter 4

They cut south the few miles to Hwy 395 and took it north. Mazey yelled in CJ's ear, asking about the weathered adobe saltbox houses that stared out at the desert through broken window panes. CJ told her they were built when the government offered free land to homesteaders, but neglected to tell them that you can't grow anything on a half-inch of rain per year.

They stopped for gas and a bathroom at the one-light crossroad of Kramer Junction. CJ was careful not to drip gas on the bike's red and cream tank. "Sorry this part is ugly. In an hour or so, it's going to get knock-your-eyes-out pretty."

"No way, this is amazing." Mazey unzipped her jacket. "I looked it up; there are three almost-ghost towns ahead. Can we stop and see them?"

CJ wanted to make it to Bishop today, and her tight shoulder muscles were reminding her that riding a motorcycle was more tiring than driving a car. "I don't know—"

"I read that they're still digging up gold in Randsburg. It's a 'do not miss' on the *Rock the Rocks* site."

A website for rockhounds? Who knew? "Okay, okay." What the hell, this trip had always been about seeing new things and exploring. Maybe having Mazey along wasn't bad. It would force her to stay in the present rather than excavating the past. She hung up the gas nozzle. "Let's hit it, Punk."

A half-hour later, they pulled up to the Randsburg General Store. Without the wind, heat engulfed her, blasting up from the engine and the tarmac. Sweat that the wind had been drying itched its way under CJ's arms and down her back. She unzipped her jacket, now knowing what an oven-roasted chicken felt like. "Let's get inside before we're crispy."

Mazey slid off and headed for the door, unbuckling her helmet. After glancing up and down the deserted, heat-shimmery street, CJ followed. Pulling open the door, she was met by the dusty must of old building and the delightful brush of cool.

Mazey sat at the soda fountain (original since the 1800s, if the sign was to be believed), her jacket hung on the back of the barstool, her face flushed an alarming red.

CJ walked over. "Oh crap, I was in such a hurry to get out of there that I forgot sunscreen."

"I'm okay."

"You're not. You're sunburnt. And I'm sorry. I'm an idiot." She scanned walls lined with wood cabinets below a lapped wood ceiling, then strode to the sundries aisle and snagged a large tube of SPF 100. When she got back, a woman was setting out glasses of ice water.

CJ held up the sunscreen. "Could you add this to our tab?"

"Sure, hon. Do you want something to eat?"

"I'll have a BLT with fries." She screwed off the lid, squirted some onto her fingers, and touched it to her sister's hot cheek.

Mazey squirmed away, frowning. "I'm not a baby. I can do it." She took the tube. "I'll have the same. And maybe ice cream?"

The waitress smiled. "I'll take that order after you're done eating."

CJ hung her jacket on the barstool and set her helmet on the floor next to Mazey's, "Where is everybody?"

"Well, our population of sixty-five don't come out in the heat of the day. Neither do the tourists. Most of them, anyway."

Duh. Just because she was used to hell's hot breath didn't mean everyone was. Especially her little sister. Mazey may have grown up in the desert, but it had to be 112 degrees out there. CJ took the tube and spread cool lotion over her own burning cheeks. "I'm not used to looking out for anybody else, Mazey. You're going to have to pay attention and tell me what I'm missing. Okay?"

"I can be responsible for myself."

"Except you didn't think of sunscreen either. It's going to take both of us working together to stay safe, okay?"

"Okay. Isn't this place cool?" She picked up the placemat covered in facts about the general store.

"Yeah, thank God." She fanned her face.

"There's a museum! Can we go? I'll bet they'll even have pyrite and Aru."

"Aru?"

"Short for the Latin Arum. That's where the periodic chart came up with AU for gold."

CJ shook her head. The one thing Patsy got right was her youngest daughter's name. She *was* amazing.

They'd just gotten their lunch when the door opened, and a scruffy, sweat-stained, dust-covered guy about CJ's age walked in.

"Hey, Luke! The usual?" the waitress called.

"Yeah, Tina. Thanks."

He slid into the seat to the right of Mazey, despite the fact that every other seat was open.

"Hello."

"Hi," Mazey said.

"Where are you girls from?"

"Around," CJ said.

"Victorville," Mazey chirped. "But we're starting a cross-country trip today, and—" She frowned when CJ's boot connected with her shin.

"Oh, that's cool." He addressed Mazey. "Guess what I'm doing?"

"What?"

"Prospecting. For *gold*."

"Ohhhh," Mazey breathed. "Did you find any?"

The waitress brought him what looked like a ham sandwich on a plate. Mazey was held rapt and missed Tina's eye roll, but CJ didn't.

"I have. Not a lot yet, but enough to keep me in ham sandwiches." He took a huge bite.

"What strata did you find it in? Volcanic? Sedimentary? Around quartz, I'll bet." Mazey's eyes were lit with rock-hound fervor.

"Wow, are you an assayer?"

Mazey giggled. "No. I'm nine."

"Well, you could'a fooled me."

CJ ate, monitoring him and the conversation, planning to step in the second it turned weird. But it was mostly about the rigors of prospecting.

When they were done eating, Mazey asked for ice cream.

CJ left cash on the counter, stood and pulled her jacket off the back of the chair. "Sorry, Punk. We've got to get back on the road — lots of miles ahead of us this afternoon."

"Hang on just a second." Luke wiped his at least two-day beard with a napkin. "I have a proposal for you."

"Of course you do," she muttered, shrugging into her jacket.

"I'm good at what I do. But I need supplies. Dynamite, pickaxes, you know, prospecting equipment. What if you went in as partners with me? You front me some money, and when I hit it big we share in the profits. Fifty-fifty. I can make us a ton of money."

"Yeah, no thanks. Come on, Mazey, let's go."

"But CJ, we could be rich!"

She put a hand on her sister's shoulder and propelled her toward the door.

"You're gonna miss out on a stellar opportunity here!" Luke called before the door shut behind them.

Mazey shrugged out from under her hand. "He's legit. I can tell he knew what he was talking about."

"Have you ever heard the saying, 'If it sounds too good to be true, it is'?" Mazey's naivete was charming, but she was going to need to grow up on this trip or CJ couldn't leave her with Patsy at the end of the summer — Blade or no Blade. She was a sitting duck for headaches, heartaches, and worse.

CJ sighed. Her knee-jerk reaction back in Victorville had landed her in this. She was going to have to see it through, even if it was hard. The trip she and the guys had planned so carefully had morphed to a Memorial Ride. And now it was feeling more like a quest to save a princess. Well, she was no hero, and the end seemed as far away as looking down the wrong end of a telescope. A lament carried on the wind that she almost recognized. It sounded a bit like 'Taps'.

"CJ, you listening to me?"

"Put your jacket on." She lifted her helmet off the seat.

"Do I have to? It's so hot."

"You wouldn't say that if you ever saw road rash. It's like someone took a cheese grater to your skin."

Mazey sat in sullenness for ten miles, until the road took the curve at the foot of the Sierras. The tops were snow-capped despite the valley's heat.

"Those are for-real mountains!" Mazey yelled in her ear.

"Not for Afghanistan, but for California, yeah."

After a few miles, the shorter White Mountains rose on their right.

"This is awesome. We should move here."

CJ chuckled. "Do you see anywhere to work?"

Mazey pointed. "Mom could get a job there." Tucked up a gentle slope in emerald grass at foot of a mountain sat a farm, pretty as a postcard.

"Could you imagine Patsy milking cows, shoveling sh—manure?"

"Yeah, probably not. But I would."

For the peace of that place? "So would I, kid. So would I."

Three hours later, they rolled into Bishop. It felt cooler, but the sign on the bank flashed ninety-eight degrees. The highway was the main street through the busy, single-story, non-descript town. CJ pulled over at a gas station and mini-mart. Mazey slid off and worked the buckle of her helmet. "Are we there yet?"

"Within a mile of it. While I fill up, why don't you go in and find us something for dinner? I'll be in in a minute."

"Sure." She walked away.

After gassing up, CJ parked in an empty parking space and walked in. Mazey had her arms full: ice cream, microwave stew and milk, among other things.

CJ smiled. "Looks good, except we don't have a microwave. Or a fridge."

Mazey looked down and her cheeks got even redder. "Oh, duh."

"Hey, you've never been camping. No big deal. Let's go look."

They walked out ten minutes later with water, canned stew and chips for dinner, cookies for dessert, and instant oatmeal for breakfast. There was no room to store the purchases, so Mazey held the bag in her lap.

The Bishop Creek Camp was nestled in a grove of sycamores. Tent camping had the best spot, on the grass where it was cool, shady, and the creek happily babbled by. Most of the campers were in RVs, so she and Mazey had the area to themselves.

"Oh, I like it here," Mazey said, sliding off the back.

CJ shut down the bike and dismounted while Mazey dropped the plastic bag onto the picnic table and headed for the stream.

"Hey, we've gotta set up camp first." CJ unstrapped her helmet and set it on the picnic table, then shrugged out of her jacket.

"Oh, right." Mazey shed her jacket and helmet while CJ unhooked the bungees that held the tent and sleeping bags.

They laughed, trying to put the tent together. What looked simple when the clerk demonstrated it wasn't. They finally figured out how to secure the poles in the edge of the tent bottom and clipped the hooks to them, raising the thin material and pulling it taut.

While Mazey laid out the sleeping bags in the tent, CJ pulled the cooking supplies from the trip trunk.

She showed Mazey how to work the backpack camp stove and heated the stew right in the can. They sat on the picnic table and shared spoonfuls between handfuls of chips. "We're going to eat better tomorrow. You're a growing kid."

"Can't haul lettuce and fruit on the bike." Mazey shrugged. "No refrigeration, remember?"

Her deadpan expression didn't fool CJ. "Hard is not impossible."

The spoon clinked as Mazey nabbed the last potato. "We'll be going right through Reno, right?"

"Yeah."

"Can we stop?"

"What for? It's a gambling town. Nothing fun for a kid there."

"I thought maybe I could check out a car dealership."

CJ turned, but Mazey didn't meet her eye. "You're a little young to be car shopping."

"My dad used to work at a dealership there. Maybe I can find a clue that would tell me where he is now."

Her heart hurt for her little sister, so desperate to find connection that she wanted to chase rainbow unicorns all over the country. "Hon, people scatter nowadays. The odds of finding anything are tiny. I mean, if you were looking for me, would you find clues at my high school?" She put her arm around Mazey's bony shoulder and squeezed. "You've got me. We have this whole summer. Just enjoy it, okay?"

Looking at her boots Mazey nodded, her straight black hair curtaining her face.

"Tell you what." CJ dusted potato chip salt off her hands. "Why don't we get our tennis shoes on and go exploring?"

"Okay."

~~~

She woke to a hand over her mouth and her own scream echoing in her ears.

"CJ!" Mazey hissed.

The darkness revealed no clues, but when her breath slowed enough to hear the creek's burble she remembered where she was. Not in the desert, not that night. She went limp and took a deep breath that came out in a moan.

"CJ, you're scaring me."

The quiver in her sister's voice pulled her out of her personal hell. "I'm okay."

Mazey grabbed her hand and clung to it. Well, maybe CJ clung a bit, too.

"Who's Logan?"

"He was a friend." More than that. Logan was family. She took deep breaths, to help the nightmare fade. She might have more luck with that than avoiding the pain during the day. After all, dreams weren't real. Reality was more permanent. "It was just a bad dream, Punk." She hadn't had a nightmare since she hit the States — thought she'd left them in Afghanistan. But she shouldn't be surprised. Hell can always track you down.

"Was he a soldier?"

"Let's talk about something else. Something to put us back to sleep." She relaxed the grip on her sister's hand but didn't let go. "Know any bedtime stories?"

Her giggle came out of the dark. "No, but want to hear about my dad?"

The dad thing again. But CJ was too tired and heart-sore to crush anyone else's dreams tonight. After all, she *had* asked for a fairytale. "Okay."

"Well, he lives in a nice house in a decent neighbor-hood. He goes to work every day..."

Only half listening to her sister's litany, CJ pushed the door closed on the past. Crickets called and the creek gossiped in a language she could almost understand. Slowly, nature's lullaby and Mazey's voice eased her to a softer sleep.

The next morning, it took a while to get packed up. It seemed everything they'd taken out the night before had expanded, and they had to wrestle it onto the bike.

"Are you as hungry as I am, Punk?"

"I could eat a meteorite." Mazey pulled on her jacket.

"I'd have to check the ingredient label on that. We're getting a good breakfast in you, and none of that donut/pancake/waffle stuff, either. I'm talking eggs, bacon, pota-toes..."

"Quit talking about it and let's go."

She chuckled when Mazey's stomach growl was loud enough to hear through her helmet. One glance around to be sure they hadn't left anything, and they climbed on and she fired the engine. "Onward. Another adventure awaits."

She forced a lilt into her voice. Hiding whirlpools of depression was exhausting, but she was *not* dragging her sister into the undertow.

Mazey pointed out the library as they cruised back through town.

"Sorry, we've got to get some miles on today if we're going to get where we're going."

"Where are we going?"

"If I told you, it wouldn't be a surprise."

"I love surprises! Except Mom's."

CJ winced. Yeah, those were more forgotten rides home and missed parent-teacher conferences. "My surprises are epic. You'll see."

She pulled into the driveway of a diner in town and, noticing the office product store next door, got an idea. "Hey, you okay with getting us a table? I'll be right in."

"Ohhhkay." Mazey slid off and walked to the door, unbuckling her helmet as she went.

When the doors slid open, CJ strode to the electronics department to pick out an e-reader. This would be a win-win; Mazey would have something to read, and they wouldn't have to stop at every library they passed.

Ten minutes later, CJ walked into the restaurant and threaded her way through the crowd inside the door. The breakfast babble was loud, and waitresses cruised between tables like icebreakers in the arctic. Mazey waved from a table at the window. CJ walked over and presented the bag with a flourish. "Ta-da!"

Behind her glasses, Mazey's eyes got big. "For me? What is it?"

CJ hung her jacket on chair across the table and slid into it. "Well open it and find out, silly."

Mazey opened the bag and her mouth dropped open. Then she squealed and grabbed her sister's hand, squeezing hard. "How did you know? I've been dying for one of these!

I was going to buy one with my babysitting money at the end of the summer."

"Well, now you won't have to. They promised me it was all charged up, and I put money on an account so you can download what you want."

Mazey opened the bookish cover and swiped a finger. "Oh my gosh." She looked up, eyes full of tears. "This is the best present ever. Thank you."

"No big deal." Though CJ knew that, for her sister, it kinda was. Patsy only had money for rent, beer, and food (in that order), not presents. "Check to see if they have Wi-Fi. If they do, you can download something to read."

A waitress stopped by. "What can I get you two?"

Mazey didn't even look up from the e-reader. "I'm good."

CJ ordered for both of them. Seeing her sister happy made CJ smile. She'd almost forgotten what that felt like.

The temperature fell as the road rose before the bike's front tire. They traversed the long Owens Valley, each vista more beautiful than the one before. The sun shone soft on the land and breezes combed the meadows, bringing the scent of growing things and the faint tang of pine.

God, she wished the guys were here to see this. They'd spent stolen minutes that built to many hours, dreaming of this trip. Logan had wanted to lie on a California beach and bake until he couldn't remember what Wyoming winter felt like. Mateo wanted to replace the desktop image in his head of unending Nebraska corn with ocean rollers, hitting the beach. Eddie had wanted the freedom of the bike, and the warm wind running its fingers through his hair.

"Oh beautiful for spacious skies," Mazey sang in an off-tune warble.

"For amber waves of grain…" CJ sang back.

Soon they were singing at the top of their lungs. When they finished, CJ launched into "You're a Grand Old Flag".

They messed up the verses, so they ended up making up their own words and laughing like fools.

Her mind drifted to the land of what had been.

They'd quit for the day and headed for chow. For an Army FOB (forward operating base), this one was pretty safe. The massive concrete blast walls took most of the flak and stood strong. But even that had fallen off lately. If it weren't for the murderous heat and the turbans of the Afghan troop trainees, she could believe she was back in the States. The desert outside Vegas, maybe.

She stepped in the door behind the guys, taking the tepid air in deep. The Mess had swamp coolers going full blast, making eating bearable. Even barely cool felt delicious after the heat pressing unrelentingly against her skin.

Mateo, first in line, grabbed a tray. "You'd think after almost six years, I'd be used to the heat."

"Hey, I'm just happy to get away from ass-deep snow and subzero temps." Logan took the next tray. "You ever sat in a deer stand at seven am, in a twenty mile an hour wind?"

"No, but can't be worse than the deck of a trawler in a December storm, soaked from the spray," Eddie said. "That'll turn your balls to raisins, boys."

"Sounds pretty good to me right now." CJ took a tray. "Especially since I don't have any raisins. Sucks to be you."

Once her tray was filled, CJ headed for an empty table. "Did you bring the map, 'Teo?"

He settled on the metal bench and pulled a folded map from his pocket. "Right here."

Mateo was the one who'd come up with the idea that they take a cross-country motorcycle trip on their next leave. They'd signed up around the same time and had spent the last year requesting leave at the same time. The final approval came a week ago, so the trip this coming June was in full planning stage.

CJ studied the highlighter-spotted map. "Whoever's state we're in gets to pick what we see there. The other states, we'll decide together."

Eddie spoke up. "That makes Nebraska and Wyoming a quick trip. There ain't shit to do there."

Logan and Mateo jumped in and the good-natured trash-fest was on.

"Hey," Logan said, "let's head over to Eggers tonight and crash the poker tournament. They've got cheap beer night on Tuesday."

"You'd know." Eddie shook his head. "Somebody better call and be sure they're stocked up."

He had a point. Logan could inhale a startling amount of beer without effect, and CJ had a niggling feeling they'd be organizing an intervention sometime in the future.

"Hey, I'm a growing boy."

"Maybe," Mateo said, "but your brain cells sure aren't."

"Let's meet at the gate at eight. That'll give us time to shower."

CJ sighed. "I can't go."

"Why not?" they asked in unison.

"I'm putting in extra hours." She pulled a color photo of an Indian trike motorcycle from her back pocket and smoothed it out on the table. "I'm buying this baby for the trip."

"I'd give you shit about a girly bike, except that's epic," Eddie breathed.

"Yeah, but it's not cheap. I need the extra money."

Mateo's dark brown eyes oozed concern. "We can pool our funds and help you out—"

"Nope. I got this." She snatched the photo, careful to fold it along the creases and returned it to her pocket. "But thanks." Yup. Family.

"Crap. Won't be any fun tonight without you," Logan deadpanned. "I love taking your money. You've got the worst poker face I ever seen."

"Better'n having the worst face I've ever seen, like yours."

When Logan lunged she jumped up, grabbing her tray. "You guys have fun. And don't take all your money this time, y'hear? Last time, the Marines kicked your butts."

CJ came back to herself when a hawk flew low overhead, caught an updraft, and something in her chest lifted with it. *Guys, can you see this?* The lead weight of loss hit like a cudgel, and her spirit fell to earth with a splat. They were *supposed* to see this. They *would* have seen this. If only...

"Where are we going?"

Mazey pulled CJ from her rosary beads of regret. "We'll be there in a half-hour."

She turned off at the Mammoth Lakes exit, and the road rose to rocky hillsides covered in firs. CJ hadn't planned the entire trip, but when she researched the first leg and saw this she knew Mazey would be enchanted. When they turned again it was onto a barely-two-lane road, and after a few twisties she pulled into a dirt parking lot where a bus idled.

When they dismounted CJ told Mazey to wait, and she went to the tiny store to secure two bus tickets and a camping site for the night.

When she walked back, Mazey asked, "Devil's Postpile. What's that?"

"Hence surprise. Let's put up our jackets, but we'll just leave the helmets on the bike. I don't think anyone will mess with them."

The bus ride was short with switchbacks, but when it stopped Mazey whispered in an awed voice, "Columnar basalt."

Tubes of rock like a giant's pick-up-sticks lined the hundred-foot wall beside the bus.

"You want to see it up close?"

"You think?" Mazey scooted out of the seat and walked to the front, bending over so she could look out the windows. "I remember reading about this, but never thought I'd see it."

The bus driver told them that volcanic activity formed the area, and how cooling lava broke to form the 'tubes'. They wandered, Mazey explaining the geology. Most of it was above CJ's paygrade so she let it flow over her head, just enjoying watching her sister enjoying it.

Despite the signs prohibiting it, she looked the other way when Mazey slipped a couple chips of rock into her pocket. When she got home, maybe the rocks would spark good memories.

Back at the camp store they cruised the limited dining selection, paid for their choices along with a shower for each of them, and walked out.

"Let's get set up, then come back and get that shower," CJ said.

"You sure can use one." Mazey waved her hand in front of her face.

"You..." CJ chased her to the bike, tickling her to laughter.

Their site was a good one, away from others, on another small stream. "See the bear box?" CJ pointed to a metal container with a locking mechanism on their site.

"Bears?" Mazey gulped. "I didn't sign up for bears."

"Well, they lived here first so we deal. They're small black bears and aren't likely to hurt you unless you get between a mother and her cubs, or you have food they want. So all food goes in the box unless we're eating it. Not only that but gum, toothpaste, or anything else that smells like food to a bear."

"How would I know what that is?"

"If it goes in your mouth, it's bear food."

Eyes wide, Mazey glanced around. "Noted."

"Let's set up. I'm dying for that shower."

It took them less time to set up than the night before, and CJ imagined in a few days this would be almost automatic.

When they were done Mazey came out of the tent with a towel, her shower stuff, and a change of clothes. "The showers looked huge. Wanna go together?"

CJ's heart stuttered. The outside scars were only a preview of the ones on the inside, and no way she was letting Mazey see either one. "You go ahead. I'll get dinner started."

It was dark by the time they finished dinner and cleanup. CJ made hot chocolate and they carried their mugs to the meadow beside their campsite, spread one of the sleeping bags, and laid down.

Mazey asked, "Want to know the names of the stars?"

CJ crossed her arms behind her head. "I know the Big and Little Dipper, but that's about it. Enlighten me."

Mazey's upturned face was pale in the full moonlight. She pointed. "See the upside-down trapezoid there? That's Hercules."

"I failed geometry. I don't even remember what a trapezoid looks like."

"Hang on. This is why I brought my e-reader." She opened it and showed CJ an illustration.

"It looks like a stick man I drew in kindergarten."

She pointed again. "See it?"

"Yeah, but how the heck did they get that it looked like Hercules?"

"It's supposed to be him standing on Draco's head."

"The guy from Harry Potter?"

Even in the dark, she caught Mazey's 'are-you-an-idiot?' look.

"Hello, they named these in ancient times."

"Oh, right." CJ held in her smile.

She pointed again. "There's Bootes, the Herdsman."

"The one that looks like a kite? Were these people doing drugs?"

"See, it follows Ursa Major around the sky, and… never mind. It would take too long to explain."

The Milky Way stretched from the horizon, a cloud trailing diamond chip stars on a blanket of black velvet. CJ relaxed. "Whatever their names, they sure are beautiful."

"I knew you'd get it."

"All that space makes me feel insignificant. Antlike." But it wasn't a bad feeling, like maybe all the things she worried about didn't really matter in the big picture. Not that she believed that, but it was a nice wish.

"To me they're like friends. You can count on the stars. They never change. Think about all the centuries of people who looked up and saw the same ones we see now. It's like we're linked to those people, holding hands all through time."

Weird how they came from the same background yet saw things so differently. But then, Mazey was young and naïve. It hurt to think how she'd become jaded and hard once the world had a chance to do a number on her. "How did a punk kid get so wise?"

"I spend a lot of time thinking."

"You sure do."

They lay with their own thoughts for a time.

"I wonder how Mom's singing test is going?" Mazey's voice was small.

Patsy hadn't crossed CJ's mind since they pulled out of the driveway in Victorville. "Oh yeah, that's today."

"Can we call her tomorrow to find out?"

"Sure, if you want to."

"How come you call her Patsy?"

CJ felt her jaw go tight. "'Mom' is a title you earn."

Mazey rolled on her side and propped her head on her hand, so she could see CJ's face. "She tries really hard, you know."

CJ snorted.

"No, she does. She always has a job and brings home groceries…"

And child molesters. "I guess I just have higher standards for motherhood."

"She does the best she can. It's just that her picker is busted."

"Huh?"

"Seems like she always picks the wrong places, the wrong jobs, the wrong boyfriends. I help as much as I can, but I'm only nine."

CJ rolled onto her side and laid her hand on her sister's cheek. "You've got it backwards, Punk. She's the adult. You're the kid. She's supposed to help *you*."

"No, we have to help each other. Isn't that what families do?"

This kid understood in her heart what she'd never seen in reality. Where did she get that kind of trust? That kind of hope? "You're a better person than I am."

"No way. I wanna be like you. You're not afraid of anything."

"It's an act, trust me. Tell me what you're afraid of."

Mazey rolled onto her back and stared up at the stars. "Not living up to my potential."

Holy shit. CJ was three times Mazey's age, and that thought had never crossed her mind. "Are you sure you're not a grown-up in a kid suit?"

Mazey giggled.

They talked about everything and nothing for an hour, until she realized Mazey was dozing off.

CJ sat up with a sigh. "Come on, let's hit the sack. It's late, and we have a long day ahead of us tomorrow." They stood and she gathered the sleeping bag. "Grab the cups and rinse them out, and put them in the box, okay?"

Mazey yawned, grabbed the cups and wove her way back to the campsite, half asleep on her feet.

Chapter 5

CJ came awake with a start. Rustling. Bumping. Grunting.

"Wha—?" Mazey mumbled.

"Shhhh." Even over her freight train heartbeat, CJ knew the sounds weren't far away.

Shuffling coming closer. Heavy breathing and an unholy stink.

"W-w-what is it?"

"Shh." Flashlight in one hand, switchblade in the other, CJ knelt, leaning forward until she was an inch from the netting at the tent's entrance, straining her eyes to pierce the dark. She pressed the button on the flashlight. Light shone off fur. Wild eyes flashed in the light, a few inches from her face. She fell back, a scream caught in her throat.

"Bear!" Mazey whispered a screech.

"SHHH!" CJ shifted, putting Mazey behind her. "It's not much more than a baby. The mother will be close by."

When the large cub bawled, the stench of dead things rolled over them.

Mazey slapped a hand over her mouth and nose.

Bang! Then a rumbling roar came from the picnic table, and scratching and snuffing.

"I think I just peed a little." Mazey's shaky whisper came from over CJ's shoulder. "What are we gonna—"

CJ turned, put a finger to her lips, and whispered, "We're gonna sit here. They'll go away."

Sure enough, within ten minutes the bears moved on. Mazey fell asleep in CJ's arms, but it was a long time before CJ closed the knife or her eyes.

The morning dawned to bird song, but CJ took a ten-second look around before she crawled out, knife in hand.

Mazey was tucked right behind her. "Oh no," she moaned, running to where the Indian lay on its side covered in dirt and what looked like dried slobber.

CJ followed, glancing to the trees, the creek, the road.

Mazey fell to her knees, moaning, stroking the butter yellow leather saddlebag split down the middle like someone had taken a blade to it, the contents scattered over a six-foot area. "Your beautiful bike! This is all my fault!" she wailed.

CJ walked up behind her. "You are not responsible for bears, Punk."

Her sister's narrow shoulders heaved with sobs. "It is. I was half asleep, and I forgot what you said about putting the cups in the bear box. I just stuffed them in the saddlebag!"

"Hey. It's okay." CJ dropped to her knees and tried to take her sister's shoulders in a hug, but she sidled away. "A bike is just a hunk of metal. The bag can be replaced."

"No, it was the most beautiful thing ever, and I ruined it!" She turned to CJ. Her face beneath the tears and snot was a mask of despair. "You can take me home. I don't deserve this trip. I'm a loser." When she dropped her head her hair fell, hiding her face.

CJ sat on her heels, stunned. "Mazey, seriously." She lifted her sister's chin. "You matter. The motorcycle doesn't."

Mazey sniffed. "That doesn't make my mistake okay."

CJ tipped her head. "Are you always this hard on yourself?"

Mazey's lips firmed and her shoulders straightened. "I'm better than this. I don't make mistakes."

CJ had always admired Mazey's intelligence — and maybe secretly envied it a bit — but she hadn't realized it came with a price. Potential was a heavy burden for such small shoulders. She shook her head. "Everyone makes mistakes, Mazey. A friend once told me that you should be happy to make mistakes, because you can't learn anything by being perfect." Mateo's shock of black hair, long face, and laughing eyes floated up from the dark waters of her memory. She shoved it down before it could pull her under.

"I never thought of it that way." Mazey slammed a fist to her palm. "But I promise I'll pay closer attention."

"Lighten up on yourself, kid." CJ tucked a chunk of hair behind her sister's ear. "Now, let's get the bike upright and check it out. I'll bet except for the bag, it's just dirty."

"And it stinks." Mazey pinched her nose. "I'll get water from the creek, and we can give her a bath."

"Her?"

"Yeah. We should give her a name."

"Okay, while you think of a name I'll get breakfast out of the bear box."

But first they worked together to heave the bike back on three wheels. Mazey washed away the worst of the mud, revealing four deep scratches in the tank's paint.

Mazey's face crumpled. "Not the beautiful tank!"

CJ tipped her head. "Oh I don't know, I think it's kinda badass. How many bikes can say they survived a bear attack?"

Mazey sniffed and ran her fingers over the scratches. "I thought of a name."

"Yeah? Spill it."

"Lola."

"Is that a star? Near Draco, maybe?"

Mazey gave her first smile of the day, big and toothy. "Nope. She's the toughest wrestler on WOW."

CJ chuckled. This kid was something else. "Here I thought you only watched the science channel."

She giggled. "Mom and I watch every Thursday night."

Such a mix of little kid and brainiac. "That reminds me, you want to call Patsy?" CJ pulled her phone and checked the time. "You'll probably wake her up, but I'm kinda curious how she did, too." She hit speed dial and handed over the phone. "Here. I'll get breakfast ready." She walked to the picnic table to give her sister privacy.

But Mazey returned in no time, holding out the phone. "No signal."

"Oh, duh; sorry. We're in Sticks County, Nowhere. We'll try later. Now come eat."

They sat on the picnic table and ate instant oatmeal out of the mugs CJ had scrubbed clean of bear slobber, then scoured with boiling water.

"Where'd you get the pig sticker?"

"Huh?"

"The knife. That was line from a Western that Blade was watching one day. I always wanted to use that in a sentence."

"It's just in case."

"Glad you didn't have to take on a bear with it."

"Hey, I'da done some damage."

"You'da been dinner."

CJ snorted. "Probably."

"Did you have to kill anyone over there?"

Mazey's curious stare bored through the flimsy barrier of CJ's chest wall, into her war-torn heart. The vision of her friends laughing faces punched more holes. Oatmeal went down the wrong pipe, and she spent a minute or two wheezing and hacking while Mazey pounded on her back.

When she could breathe again, she said, "Why don't you wash the dishes. I'm going to sew the side bag together."

Mazey lifted the mugs. "How?"

"Use the pig sticker to make holes, then I'll use the leather shoelace from my boot for thread."

"Were you a Girl Scout or something?"

"Nah. You learn to make do with what you have in the desert. You should have seen my friend, Mateo. I swear he could have made a space shuttle with baling wire and duct tape."

"Well, I hope we don't have to. We're only two days in, and Lola's already got scars."

"Yeah, but it always looks bad for the wrestler in the beginning of the match, right?" She ruffled Mazey's hair. "Don't ever bet against underdogs."

~~~

An hour and twenty-five miles under the front tire later, Mazey pointed. "Hey, let's take that road."

What the hell, one road was the same as another once she threw out the planned itinerary. She slowed for the turn to what the sign said was the June Lake Loop.

Mazey pointed to a sign that read: *Oh! Ridge*. They didn't have long to wonder at the name because, when they topped the hill, down a rocky slope was a sapphire blue lake, the sun fracturing the water, diamonds dancing in the chop.

"Oh!" Mazey said.

CJ took a breath and held it. She blinked, as if she could burn a snapshot into her brain. "Wowzer." When she realized the bike had slowed she twisted the throttle and they cruised through a bustling tourist village, taking a curve to find a waterfall rushing down the mountain ahead.

"That is the prettiest thing I've ever seen," Mazey breathed.

"Me, too." Her desert-trained eyes soaked in the striated greens around every turn. A mile later a stream ran beside the road, emptying into a placid lake they passed a mile later. God, if only the guys could see this.

Eventually, they met up with the highway once more and turned north. They cruised up the pass and over. Mazey tried to get her to turn at Bodie, an old silver mine ghost town, but CJ shook her head. If she let her sister choose the stops, they'd never get out of California.

The crossed the border to Nevada and stopped for lunch in South Lake Tahoe. CJ splurged for a window seat in a decent restaurant overlooking the huge sapphire lake. Mazey snapped photos on CJ's phone like the tourist she was.

"Can we call Mom now?"

"Knock yourself out."

Mazey dialed, then shook her head.

"We'll try later."

"Hey, CJ?"

Mazey's fingers dug into her forearm. "What?"

"Can we stop in Reno?"

"Come on, Mazey. What do you expect to find? The odds of anyone still working at a car dealership over a decade later and remembering a guy who worked there for maybe a year? Gotta be close to zero."

"Maybe, but there's also a tiny chance he could still be working there. It won't take but a few minutes. Please?"

Why couldn't she just let it go? Finding her father would be a disaster, even if she could manage to locate him. He'd only be another Blade. Or worse. CJ looked up from her fries to tell her sister no.

Mazey's pound-puppy eyes dissolved CJ's resolve. She didn't want the responsibility of being a dream-killer. Especially to Mazey, who would learn soon enough that dreams were only bedtime stories you tell yourself in the dark.

"Come on, pleeease?"

Mazey had already heard that too much in her life. "Oh, all right. But just a few minutes, okay?"

"Thanks, CJ. It means a lot to me." She picked up her burger and took a huge bite.

"For a little punk, you sure can put away the groceries."

"Yeah, that's what Mom says."

While they ate, CJ looked up directions to the dealership, and an hour later they walked onto the showroom floor crowded with new cars, the smell of new rubber heavy in the refrigerated air.

A hopeful salesman approached, but hope died when CJ asked for the administration office. He pointed to a back hallway.

Only one glass-walled office was occupied, by an older lady in jeans and a too-tight red polo shirt, gray braids twisted around her head.

CJ knocked on the doorframe.

She looked up from a stack of papers. "Can I help you?"

"Yes." Mazey stepped just inside the door. "I'm looking for an employee of yours. Beau Brown?"

The two lines between her eyes deepened. "We don't have an employee by that name."

"He worked in the body shop."

"Not in the seven years I've worked here."

CJ put a hand on her sister's shoulder. "Come on—"

"Can you look it up in your records? It's really important."

The woman's eyes narrowed. "Why?"

Seconds stretched. CJ squirmed inside, biting her lip to keep words in. Mazey wanted this. She was going to have to take the hit.

"He's my dad."

The woman's brows shot up, but after a few seconds her fingers found her keyboard. "Let me check."

The keyboard clacked. "Ah, here. A Beauregard Brown worked in the body shop, back in '09."

Under her hand, CJ felt a jolt go through Mazey. "That's him!"

"He only worked here for six months."

"Do you have a forwarding address?"

"Hardly." She snorted. "He didn't show up for work one day, and we never heard from him again. Didn't even come back for his last paycheck." She looked up from the screen. "If you ever find him, tell him to contact me and I'll send his wages."

CJ had taken a step to leave when Mazey asked, "Could I have a copy of his driver's license?"

The woman gave her a hard look.

"Please. The only photo I have of him was from his high school yearbook."

"I'd be fired I did that."

"No one cares about an expired driver's license from ten years ago."

CJ didn't have to see her face to know she was giving the woman the orphan-eyes.

When the lines around her mouth softened, CJ knew the woman couldn't kill a kid's dreams any more than CJ could. "I'll do it. But if you ever get caught with this..."

"I'll tear it in pieces and swallow it." Mazey used her index finger to cross her heart.

The printer whirred, and the woman handed over a piece of paper.

Mazey folded it and stuffed it into her pocket. "Thank you. This means a lot."

CJ squeezed Mazey's shoulder and they turned and walked back to the bike. "I'm sorry, Punk, but I told you—"

"So don't tell me again! Just don't say anything, Okay?" She stomped away.

They geared up in silence, mounted Lola, and headed east.

Her heart went out to Mazey, but bedtime stories don't come true. And this only verified what CJ suspected — another of her mother's losers. Who doesn't pick up their last paycheck?

The speed limit jumped to eighty, and the empty road stretched ahead. Prairie grasses bent in the wind of their passing. The mountains rimmed the horizon like industrious anthills. At least the temperature had dropped a bit — she no longer felt like she was sweating in the sauna of her jacket. Aside from the occasional car, they were alone.

CJ's mind drifted, as it always did, to the guys. She had been the keeper of the list — things they wanted to see on this trip. Everyone pitched in one 'tourist moment' in each of the states they'd travel through, but if it was your home state you had full say. You could choose three places you wanted to stop — including, of course, your home town. She had scrapped the itinerary, but she was determined to go to each of her friends' homes and talk to their family. Much more was owed, but at least that.

Snippets of film clips drifted through her mind.

Mallet on metal was the music of her days, but that day it was giving her a headache. She stopped tracing wires, rolled the creeper from under the Humvee, and sat up. "Damn, Eddie, give it a rest, will ya?"

The banging ceased and his head of tousled black hair came up, revealing his pirate's smile. "Ah you're just pissed 'cuz Logan took your spanner."

"He took my..." She scanned the tools sprawled in the sand beside her charge. "Logan, dammit!" She pushed to a stand and swiped sweat out of her eyes. "I'm gonna kill him. Where is he?"

Mateo's arm appeared from under the troop carrier beside her, pointing down the open-ended Quonset hut.

She spied movement against the backdrop of white-hot Afghan sun. She walked over to an ATV that looked like it had gone through a shrapnel-storm, and probably had. "Logan, you take a tool one more time without asking, and—"

He rose on the other side of the vehicle, his broad shoulders blocking out the sun. "What you gonna do, beat me up?" He vaulted the hood, grabbed her, put her in a headlock, and gave her a noogie.

"Quit!" It took a while to break the hold but when she finally did, she backed away, breathing hard. "Show a little respect for your betters, you goober." But she couldn't help her smile. He was irritating, but he was also fun-loving, true blue, and the closest thing to a big brother she'd ever have.

"You got the wrong guy. Talk to Mateo. Hey dude, don't you guys grow peanuts in Nebraska?"

"Screw you, Davey Crockett. We grow corn, wheat, and potatoes."

"Davey Crockett?"

Mateo waved an arm, all they could see of him from under the Humvee. "Your family runs a hunting lodge in the middle of nowhere, right?"

"Hey, that's funny, right there." Eddie jumped in.

Logan wrinkled his nose like he smelled something bad. "Whatever you say, Ahab."

"Nah. My dad's Ahab. I joined the Army to get away from the smell of fish."

CJ chuckled. "That, and because boats make you barf."

"Yeah, that too."

She came back to the present and realized she was smiling when a bug flew into her mouth. Logan's home was first, in Wyoming, then Mateo's in Nebraska, and finally, Eddie's, in Boston. They'd have to haul butt if they were going to fit them all in. "Hey," she yelled over her shoulder, "you okay with a long day? I'd like to make Utah by tonight, but it's like three hundred miles."

"Whatever." Mazey pulled her e-reader from her jacket and propped it on CJ's back.

Wyoming would be after Utah. She imagined stopping in Medicine Bow, to pull up in front of the big log home Logan had showed her photos of, climbing the steps and knocking. Her guts slicked with ice. What would she say to his mom? His dad? His younger brother, who Logan had bragged had won the wide receiver slot on the football team this fall? She'd thought that what happened in the desert was the hardest thing she'd ever faced. She'd been wrong. Living with it was worse. Every day, a new layer of lead piled onto the weight, until she bowed under it.

She shook her head, sending the thought into the wind. She'd worry about that when she got there, and she had a state and a half to figure it out. Who was she kidding? She'd worry the whole way there. The cuts on her thighs itched, and she tried to convince herself it was because they were healing.

The centerline flashed by in a metronome's beat. Until a flash of white in the brushy sameness of the landscape caught her eye. "Antelope!" She pointed.

"Oh, how sweet." Mazey tucked the book back in her jacket. "There's another!"

Pretty soon, they were singing an offkey rendition of "Home on the Range", their disappointments left behind. For now.

~~~

They were still three hours out of Salt Lake City when the black boiling clouds rolled with thunder. CJ pulled off at an underpass. "You'll need to put the e-reader somewhere dry and get into your rain gear."

"Oh, this is gonna be fun." Mazey sounded like she meant it.

They donned their matching, lightweight, yellow two-piece rain suits. CJ could only hope they'd stand up to what looked to be what Mateo had called, a 'toad strangler'. "Don't forget your feet." She pulled out two plastic shopping bags and handed them to Maizie.

"Do I have to? It'll a hassle to lace my boots back up."

CJ'd read tips on the internet, and this looked like a great one; pull the bags onto your stocking feet, tie the handles around your ankles, and put your shoes back on. "Your choice, but I imagine you'd be pretty miserable with cold, wet feet."

Mazey bent to loosen her laces. "Why don't we just wait it out under here?"

CJ eyed the dystopian horizon. "This isn't just a shower. I'll bet we're gonna be storming all the way to Salt Lake. This is part of the gig, Punk."

"Is it dangerous, riding in the rain?"

"Lola's three wheels will make our traction better, and that's why I chose yellow for the rain suits. Easier to see us." But she was nervous being responsible for Mazey's safety.

The smell of ozone and hot, wet asphalt filled her head. Silver-dollar-sized drops splatted the concrete, and lightning flashed. CJ counted... She felt the thunder clap in her chest, but the storm was still miles away. A spark of worry zipped along her nerves, an ancient warning from her primordial brain. She'd stay hyper-alert.

Was this another mistake in her long line of screw-ups? But they couldn't very well hunker down in this underpass — it'd be dark before this storm let up. Staring out into the rocky landscape, she balanced, poised on the knife-blade of decision.

Damned if you do...

Hell, she was already damned.

In ten minutes they were ready, and while Mazey mounted the bike CJ noticed the exposed gear on the trunk: tent, sleeping bags, and travel pillows. It was all going to get soaked. Well, nothing to be done about it now. She got on and fired the engine. "Hang on, Punk—just think of it as another adventure."

As if the storm knew they'd left shelter the rain let loose, a curtain that lowered visibility and bounced off the pavement so hard it created a mist. The only good thing was that there was little wind, and between her helmet and the windshield only stray drops splattered her face.

"Holy poop!" Mazey yelled.

CJ was too busy trying to see to respond. When her forearms cramped, she made herself loosen up on the handgrips. Thankfully there wasn't a lot of traffic on the three lanes on their side, and everyone had slowed. The road rose, and CJ remembered from the map that they were heading up the Silver Zone Pass.

The temperature dropped, and rain dripped from her helmet down her neck. Crap. She should have put the hood up first, then put her helmet on. Well, she'd know for next time.

A jackrabbit made a jolting run in front of them. "Shit!" She jerked, then held fast — a swerve would take more traction than they had. The front wheel missed the confused hare by a hair.

"Did you hit him?" Mazey yelled over the thunder.

"No. Shhhh. Gotta concentrate." At the taillights flash ahead, she cut the throttle and feathered the brakes. They slowed to twenty, then ten. She squinted through the rain. "I think there's a wreck up there."

Mazey stood on the running boards to see over CJ's head. "There is. Eighteen-wheeler, about a mile up." The suspension dipped when she sat. "Man, rain hurts at this speed."

"Don't stand again. It's dangerous."

In a few minutes they eased on the shoulder to squeeze around a jackknifed truck, and she kept to the slow lane all the way down the pass. Thank God for three wheels; she couldn't imagine how dangerous this would be on two. By the time they hit level road the thunder and lightning was behind them, but the storm settled into a soaking, day-long drizzle.

CJ was cold, wet, and tense. She'd hoped to shield Mazey from the worst of the rain, but her sister shivered against her back. With the increased speed came more wind, and cold.

She'd have stopped at the first exit and given up for the day, but it looked like the road to nowhere—no buildings, no gas stations, no hotels.

An hour later, the Great Salt Lake came up on their left — gray, still, and pockmarked with rain. She pulled off at the first exit at West Valley City. Shy of Salt Lake, but she had to get Mazey warm and dry. "We're hoteling it tonight, Punk."

"G-g-g-good." Her teeth chattered on the words.

At the first intersection she turned in at the Great Lake Hotel, one of those motor inns where the rooms on three sides faced the parking lot in the middle.

They got the last room, with a queen bed. She rode the bike to it and Mazey took the sidewalk, which was sheltered by an overhang. By the time CJ cut the engine, Mazey had the door open with the metal key on the faded plastic key fob. CJ undid the bungees and took the sleeping bags in first; they'd need all night to dry out.

She stepped into the smell of harsh antiseptic cleaners and the ghosts of smokers past. The carpet was indoor/outdoor, the pattern failing to hide stains of dubious origin. "Home sweet home."

Mazey looked around, fists on hips. "Beats camping out tonight."

"Can't argue with that." CJ stepped into the tiny bathroom. Both the toilet and shower showed rust stains, with grime buildup in every corner. "Well, maybe I could."

They took trips to the bike, bringing everything in not only due to the rain, but to keep it safe; this place was pretty sketchy. They peeled out of their raingear to find what wasn't damp was downright wet. "You get in the shower first, Punk."

"Not arguing. I'm permafrost."

CJ took one last trip to the bike to put the plastic covers over the seats. This rain had the look of an overnighter. When Mazey stepped out of the shower, CJ pointed to her flip flops. "No walking barefoot on the carpet. There's probably germs here that antibiotics won't kill."

The water-saver showerhead was miserly, but the water was blissfully hot. She stayed under the spray until the shivers left her and her muscles unknotted. When she came out, Mazey was standing at the window.

"Do we have to go out to dinner? I just got warm."

"Well, I'm sure the FDA would not approve, but I saw a vending machine in the breezeway. Want to see what they've got?"

"Absolutely."

CJ opted for chips, crème filled cupcakes and a soda, and Mazey got peanuts, gummy-bears, and a chocolate bar. They sat on the bed, eating them. "Tomorrow, we'll get a good breakfast before we head out." She ruffled her sister's still-damp hair. "You did really well today, Punk. Any other kid would have whined."

Mazey shrugged. "I did some thinking, and it took my mind off being cold."

"What did you think about?"

Her guilty look told CJ she'd be sorry she asked. "Facebook."

"Huh?"

"Old people are on Facebook, so I thought... do you have an account?"

Oh no, not the dad thing again. She sighed. "Yeah. But there are a ton of people there, and I doubt—"

"I know, I know, but can I just check?"

That reminded her. Why hadn't Patsy called? "After we call your mother."

"Oh, yeah." Mazey held her hand out. "She's your mother, too, you know."

Like she needed to be reminded. CJ lifted the phone from the nightstand and handed it over.

She hit speed dial. "Hi, Mom. Where have you been? I was getting worried."

CJ couldn't hear the words, just chirping babble.

"Uh-huh. That's good. Wait, what?"

Lines formed between her brows. When CJ caught a slight quiver in Mazey's lower lip, she snatched the phone away. "What's going on, Patsy?"

"Oh, Cora Jean. The tryout went so well. Seriously, they just loved me."

"Great. Why is Mazey upset?"

"Well, Phil, the owner, doesn't have any openings here in Victorville, but he owns a bar in Bodfish and he says I can go on permanent there, two nights a week. Do you believe it? This is the start I've been waiting for all these years."

Patsy squawked on like a Blue Jay on caffeine, but CJ tuned it out. She'd been through Bodfish (no one had reason to go *to* Bodfish), a blue-collar agricultural area about thirty miles outside Bakersfield. A dive bar in Victorville was Nashville compared to any bar in Bodfish. When Patsy paused for a breath, CJ jumped in. "But that's got to be two hours from the house."

"Two and a half, actually. But I checked. They have a market, and I should be able to get a job there."

"Wait. You're talking about *moving*?" Her voice rose in timbre and pitch. "For a two-night gig in a dump bar, in the middle of nowhere? Are you on drugs ?"

"Dial it back, Cora Jean. I don't need the negativity. Dolly Parton started in a—"

"What about Mazey?" Her sister stood looking out the window. Even her back looked forlorn. "Did you stop for one second to think about her? And when were you going to call and let her in on this development? After you moved?"

"I thought you'd be happy. Blade can't come because of his parole, and she'd'a known if she were *here*."

CJ ground her teeth. She wasn't going rounds with Patsy with Mazey listening. "We'll call you back. Sometime." She mashed 'end' almost hard enough to crack the screen.

How could she leave Mazey with that woman at the end of the summer? One problem at a time. She stood and put her hand on her sister's shoulder. "Come on. I'll fire up the laptop and sign you onto Facebook."

The sheen of hope in her sister's eyes was both her reward and her punishment.

Chapter 6

Mazey's voice came out of the dark as they lay on the lumpy mattress that night. "Why are you always so sad?"

CJ started. "You think I'm sad? Aren't we having fun?"

"Yes and yes. What happened over there? Did soldiers get killed?"

Not appropriate conversation with a nine-year-old, especially not right before bed. Time to deflect. "I've seen you mad, but never sad. How come?"

"Because there's always something better than being sad."

"Um, yeah, but..."

"No, really. I figured this out when I was a kid. It's about what you focus on. There's so many things around to be happy about. You just have to notice them."

God, she was so sweet. If only life was that simple. "Good for you."

"No, not just me. It works for everyone. You can do it, too."

"Things are different when you get older, Punk."

"I don't think so. I think you always have a choice. Try it when you're sad. Look around. The world is amazing, and just waiting for you to notice. Everyday things, like a sunrise, or a bird singing, or even a dandelion growing in a crack in the sidewalk. If you look for good things, it'll keep you from being worried or sad."

CJ chuckled. "A grown-up in a kid suit, I'm telling you."

"Tell me about your friends over there. They're important to you, and I hardly know anything about them."

She lay there a moment, trying to see past the tragedy to the good times. "Mateo was a farm kid. He didn't say much, but when he did it was worth listening to. A 'still waters run deep' kinda guy." She chuckled. "Eddie teased him about it once, and Mateo told him, 'Wise men speak because they have something to say; fools because they have to say something.' Said it was from Plato, but Eddie thought he was dissing him. They almost got in a fight over it. But that was Eddie; he was a hothead. But funny? One of the funniest guys I know — knew. A little wiry guy, but his swagger was huge."

"What about Logan?"

"Ah, Logan." She smiled into the dark.

"Sounds like you were in love with him."

"What? No. He was the brother I never had. A big guy — six-five, with shoulders that barely fit through a doorframe. A football and wrestling star in high school. But inside he was a teddy bear, with an iron sense of right and wrong."

"I think I'd have liked him."

"Ah, Punk, you would have loved him." She reached to squeeze her sister's hand. "Sleep now. We'll have more adventures tomorrow."

"Okay." She rolled away to face the window. "CJ? Thanks for bringing me. This is the best thing that's ever happened."

Which said more about her sister's life than the trip. "You're welcome. 'Night, Punk."

CJ lay awake for the longest time, hands under her head, staring at the water-stained ceiling, for once allowing herself to remember. They'd been the unlikeliest of friends:

Logan, from Medicine Bow, Wyoming, who missed the woods.

Eddie, from Boston, Massachusetts, who missed the salt air.

Mateo, from Scottsbluff, Nebraska, who missed the farm.

And her, from everywhere, California, who didn't miss a damned thing.

Friends — hell, they'd been family. Turned out she'd had to go halfway around the world to find where she fit.

Logan had been first. When she'd been sent to Bagram Airfield as the only woman mechanic, she caught crap. She'd kept her head down and worked hard, figuring the hazing would die when they saw she could do the job. And it did, mostly. But there was always one asshole in the bunch — and hers was Steve McLellan.

It was jokes at first. Mean ones, with her as the punchline. Then it degenerated to filthy talk and innuendoes, to the point where she worried about being out alone. It seemed everywhere she turned he was in her face. She considered complaining to the brass, but she wasn't naïve. A guy like that would always make you pay — somehow.

Logan was just another guy in the crew then. But one day he came around a corner to see Steve had her cornered when no one else was around, heaping abuse on her bowed head.

Two days later, Steve had an accident that blew out his knee: ACL, MCL, and cartilage. The details were fuzzy, and Steve wasn't talking. When he got out of the hospital, he was transferred Stateside.

When she asked Logan about it, he just winked and clicked out of the side of his mouth. "Shame, that. Guy should be more careful." He made sure she was included in the group from then on. He became more like a big brother to her.

Until he died, along with the rest of the brothers she adopted as her own, leaving her to try to figure how to go on without them. And it felt she was getting farther away from that every day.

~~~

When a laser strip of sunlight cut through the crack in the blackout curtains to fall on the bed, CJ eased from under the covers, slipped into her flip flops, and padded to the window. She'd laid out the sleeping bags to dry under the heating unit the night before. The insides were dry, so she flipped them over as quietly as she could and walked to the shower to ease tense muscles. Three more short razor cuts on her left thigh released the rest. For now.

Maybe Mazey was right. It was all in what she focused on. She dressed, and emerged, determined to leave the sadness behind — trapped in the walls of this ragged room.

Mazey was up, dressed, and stuffing her now-dry-but-dirty-clothes in her heavy-duty trash bag. "Why didn't you wake me up?"

"You looked so cute sleeping. I didn't want to disturb you." She ruffled her sister's hair. "I'm starving. How about you?"

"It's a good thing that bear isn't around today. I'd eat him."

CJ stepped to the window and snapped open the curtains to a cloudless azure sky. "At least it looks like a pretty day." But under her skin, the jitters were already building. She'd looked it up: they were only five hours from Logan's hometown of Medicine Bow.

They packed up and ate breakfast in Salt Lake City. It felt right to get to Logan's family home after the sun went down. Probably had something to do with hiding in the dark but, hey, as long as she kept that promise...

That meant they had some time to kill. Mazey was such a trooper in the rain yesterday and, given Patsy's move, CJ wanted to do something with the day that her sister would enjoy. She pulled her phone, did a search, and hit paydirt. "Hey, Punk. Do you know what a Trilobite is?"

Mazey looked up from her waffles. "Who doesn't?"

"I thought they were those cute little fluffballs from that Star Trek episode, but apparently not." When you don't have cable, you watch a lot of old reruns.

Mazey rolled her eyes. "They're extinct marine arthropods. And they're way cool."

"How'd you like to go find some?"

"What? Where?"

CJ consulted her phone. "We go south on 1-5 about fifty miles, then there's some dirt road, and then it's going to involve hiking. You up for that?"

"Heck yes. Let's go."

CJ laughed when her sister tried to shove a huge bite into her mouth. "Punk, they've been there millions of years. I think we can finish our breakfast." She handed over her phone so Mazey could look up the site.

It turned out to be more like ninety miles, and the last seven were dirt — hot and dusty, and full of ruts. CJ rode at walking speed, dodging holes. If they broke down out here... She was about to give up and turn around, when Mazey pointed to a quarry on their left. CJ gladly shut the bike down. They left their riding gear on the bike, changed shoes, slathered on another layer of sunscreen, and grabbed the water jug they'd bought at the last gas stop. "You ready?" CJ asked. "Where should we start?"

Mazey scanned the huge area below. "Since this is a public site, the darker shale areas have been pretty picked over. But there should be a bunch buried in the dried mud that washed down." She pointed to where the quarry petered out, about a quarter-mile away. "Let's start there."

It was in the nineties on the ridge — it'd be a furnace down there. But the excitement on her sister's face was worth a bucket of sweat. Besides, you probably couldn't stop a rockhound on the scent anyway. She followed, picking her way around rocks and down a scree of shale.

By the time they reached the bottom and set off for the end, runnels of sweat slithered down CJ's spine. The quarry was a huge bowl of loose rocks, and shade was as scarce as the breeze they'd left at the top. The sun seared everywhere it touched, as if they were bugs under a magnifying glass. The baseball cap helped but sweat still slipped into CJ's eyes, burning and blurring her vision.

Mazey finally called a halt and squatted beside what looked like a dried creek bed. She pulled a long tube sock from her pocket.

CJ squatted beside her. "What are you going to do with that?"

"It's my rock sock." She pried a small stone out of the dried mud. "Here's one! See?"

It looked like a small beetle-like creature about the size of a penny. "That is ugly."

"Maybe, but the trilobites were the most successful of all the first animals. They were around for two hundred seventy million years." She dropped the rock into her sock and moved down a step.

"Then I guess I shouldn't diss them. They did way better than we're doing." CJ searched the dirt and pried up a rock the size of a quarter that had several small trilobites in it. She dropped it into her shirt pocket, stood, and moved up the gully a yard or two.

"Found another!" Mazey called.

Within ten minutes CJ lost what little interest she had, and sat on a flat rock. Heat burned through her jeans. It felt like sitting on a griddle. Damn, if there was only some shade. She hadn't been this hot since Afghanistan. She pulled her hat low, closed her eyes, and drifted.

Even with Logan's support the mechanics had held her at arm's length, watching her when they thought she didn't notice. She made a few feeble attempts to contribute to the jokes that flew around the Quonset but they usually fell flat, making her feel more the outsider. The building was made of metal, the interior hot despite being open at both ends. The guys bitched about the heat incessantly.

One day, she got an idea. She came back after dark to rig up a 'break area' at one end by commandeering a few camp chairs. Then she connected some new fuel hoses together, punched tiny holes every two inches or so, and strung them above. An old water pump supplied the power.

The next day, when the guys asked about it, she flipped the switch. A cooling mist rained down. She was an outsider no more.

Sure wished she had that mister now. She swatted a fly off her elbow. Without Mazey's distraction from the heat's misery, memories made inroads into CJ's head, making her feel like she was back there — the morning she'd woken in the hospital, alone with her pain, and the details that now haunted her nights and bled into her days, staining everything with red-tinged regret.

Her lungs tightened, laboring to pull in the molten air. Panic shot down her nerves, sending her heart into overdrive. Her eyes snapped open.

I can't breathe. I've got to get out of here.

"Mazey!" She leapt to her feet. "Mazey!"

"You don't have to yell, I'm right here." Her sister knelt about fifty yards away, head down, digging in the dirt.

"We have to go. Now!"

Mazey looked up. "What? What's the matter?" She must have seen her sister's panic because she stood, lifted the rock-stuffed sock, and hurried over. "What's wrong?"

"It's too damned hot. I can't breathe. I've gotta get out of here." CJ hated the screech in her voice, but she was as incapable of controlling it as she was her feet. She sprinted away.

"CJ, wait!" Mazey scrambled after her. "Slow down!"

But CJ couldn't.

When she hit the fall of shale, she charged up. When her feet slid in the loose rocks she used her hands, too, but there was nothing solid to hold on to. She backslid. Legs pumping, she gained a few feet only to slide again. Her lungs worked like forge bellows, pulling in hot air and pushing it out just as fast. If only she could get to cooler air... or shade. When she lost purchase the third time, her legs gave out and she slid on her butt almost to the bottom, where Mazey waited with wild eyes.

"What can I do?"

CJ couldn't get enough air to speak. A detached part of her whispered, *Hyperventilating. Panic attack. Possible heat-stroke.*

"Crap. I forgot the water." Mazey touched her arm. "Do not move. Just breathe. I'll be right back."

CJ closed her eyes and watched sparks dance in the dark.

"Here. Drink this." Mazey held out the jug.

CJ took small sips of hot water between breaths that had begun to slow.

"Open your eyes." Mazey held out a flat piece of beige rock about four inches across with several dark markings on it.

"What is it?" When her eyes focused she saw delicate wings and bodies.

"Insects. They died and left their shadows on the rock. Cool, huh?"

"That is."

"Told you. Cool things are all around us. You just need to focus on them. Are you better?" Her voice trembled.

"Oh Punk, I'm sorry to scare you. The heat got to me. I just had to get out of there."

"It reminded you of Afghanistan, didn't it?"

"What makes you think that?" Time to pull the pieces of herself together again. For her sister.

"I've never seen anyone look so scared. Since there was no reason for it..."

CJ handed the rock back and wiped her hands. "Is it okay with you if we leave?"

"Sure." She held out her hand and pulled CJ to a stand.

The slope wasn't as hard when she picked her way, choosing her steps carefully.

At the top she pulled in lungfuls of the hot breeze. "What do you say we go find some A/C?"

~~~

They stopped for dinner at a roadside diner about twenty miles from Medicine Bow. It was cool enough that they took their meals out to a picnic table under a tree.

Mazey played with her chicken nuggets after eating only two. "I found a ton of 'Browns' on Facebook, but only two Beaus. One was in high school, the other was seventy."

CJ hadn't eaten any of her salad. Panic bubbled the closer they got to Logan's home. Food wouldn't sit well with the jumping-bean party going on down there.

Mazey heaved a sigh. "There are a lot more women than guys on there. I'm thinking about where to look next. I know from Mom where he was born, and his middle name and his birthdate from his driver's license." She swirled a french fry in ketchup but didn't eat it. "There are sites on the internet where you can put in facts like that, and they'll give you information about them, but it costs."

CJ pulled herself from her worry to catch the end. "What? No. I'm not paying money so you can get your heart broken. Not happening."

Mazey's lower lip came out. "I'll earn money and pay you back."

"Isn't about the money, Punk. Look, have you ever met a boyfriend of Patsy's that wasn't a loser?"

"N-no." It came out a mouse's squeak.

"Me neither, and I've met a lot more of them than you have. Look, I'm not being mean, just realistic. The odds are miniscule that he's a decent human."

"What about your dad? What was he like?"

She threw her hands in the air. "Hell if I know. He was in the wind before I could remember him. And you know what? I haven't lost a second's sleep over it." The sleep she lost was over much more important things.

When Mazey dropped her head her hair fell, hiding her face.

CJ lifted her sister's chin with a finger. "Look at me, because I'm gonna tell you something really important."

The pain in Mazey's eyes was too old for her years. CJ couldn't help much, but if exposing her own pain would help her sister... "You're not stuck forever with the family you were born into. You can pick your family, Punk. I know, because that's what I did."

"You mean Logan and the other soldiers?"

This kid listened well and remembered even better. "Yup. They were family. You can do the same."

"Except for you and Mom, I don't know anybody I'd want to be family with."

And someday when life broke Mazey's rose-colored glasses, Patsy would fall off the shortlist. "You will. When you get a bit older, and the kids mature to your level." She put an arm around her sister's shoulders and squeezed. "You just have to trust me on this one. It *will* happen. In the meantime, you've got me." She leaned in close. "Forever and always. Okay?"

"Okay." Her lips thinned. "But I'm not giving up on my dad. You can't make me."

CJ sighed. "I know." She checked her phone. They had an hour before full dark. "Now, tell me more about all these wonderful things I should notice." Maybe it would help get her mind off the visit.

~~~

Riding after dark was very different than in daylight. The air was rich with the scents of the night, when the plants released the oxygen-rich breaths they held all day. The cool delicious wind brushed her face and reached a finger down the back of her jacket to stroke her spine, drawing a shiver. The road was dark and empty but CJ scanned the sides, watching for the twin-beam flash of animals' eyes. This was Wyoming — there could be everything from squirrels to moose in the brush, seeking food, water, or a mate. Crickets cranked up a squeaky night song, with the occasional frog's bass note.

There was probably more, but CJ was too jumpy to notice. She'd told Mazey they were stopping at an old friend's house just to say hi. CJ had the 'Hi' part down, but what came after, she had no clue.

The road twisted before the bike's headlight, then hit a long straight. The mountains were invisible in the dark, but she could sense their looming presence just the same. When lights came up on her left, she slowed.

"Is that it?" Mazey asked over her shoulder.

"I think so." She slowed further as a huge log home materialized out of the dark, sitting a at least fifty yards back from the road. Ignoring the driveway, she pulled off in the gravel on the right side of the road and turned off the engine and headlight.

Logan had told her so much about this place, she'd have known it anywhere. Warm yellow light spilled from the front windows onto the covered front porch. She sat listening to the tick of the cooling engine and the snatches of conversation starters that she'd considered and discarded all the way here. She'd decided she'd try to keep it light.

But she was fatigued: mentally, physically, emotionally. She had no business doing this today. She had a vision of her sitting on their overstuffed couch, melting to a pathetic puddle of hysteria in these good people's home. They didn't need that. And she didn't deserve their sympathy. They were dealing with their own grief.

The lungful of air she took in straightened her spine. *Get it done, soldier.*

"Why didn't you pull in the drive?" Mazey whispered, as if somehow she knew not to disturb the night.

"I don't know." It seemed more committed than she felt. "Will you be upset if I go alone, Punk? There's something I have to do."

"But—"

"I won't be long, I promise." CJ threw a leg over the tank, slid off the bike, pulled off her helmet and waited, hoping Mazey wouldn't start an interrogation.

It was dark, but she must have seen something in CJ's face. "I'll be fine. Go do what you have to do."

CJ put a hand on her sister's thigh and squeezed. "Thanks. Come get me if you're scared."

"I won't be."

CJ's feet dragged her across the street, down the stone inlaid sidewalk, and up the steps to the deep porch. Her heart lurched. The dried-flower wreath on the door had a dusty black ribbon draped across the center.

The front door was mostly beveled glass, allowing a glimpse into the great room. Logan's dad and mom sat in recliners, his mother held knitting in her lap. His younger brother lay on the floor in a football jersey and jeans, and they were watching a football game on the TV that hung over a large river rock fireplace.

Three ghosts walked past her, crowding in the door, Logan yelling, 'You can start the party, we're here!', like he always had.

Something in her chest collapsed, making it hard to breathe around it. Tremors palsied her hands and the long muscles of her legs.

What was she thinking? No way she was walking into that Norman Rockwell scene and remind them of the gaping hole in their lives, much less telling them it was her fault. To what purpose? It wouldn't help them. She took a few wobbly steps back until her butt hit the porch railing. She'd hoped this trip would bring her a bit of closure. Or if not that, at least a lessening of her burden. Instead the weight got heavier every day, and it was getting harder to go on. She might not have made it this far if her sister hadn't come.

She took a deep breath and forced her shoulders to relax as she blew it out. A few more, and the panic eased. A few more, and her brain stopped racing. Without the white noise, she realized why she'd come. It wasn't for his family. It wasn't for her.

She was here for Logan.

Remembering a Jewish custom to honor the dead she patted herself down, found the trilobite stone from the quarry in her breast pocket. She pulled it out, kissed it, and set it gently on the porch railing. "They're okay, bud. They're okay. You rest easy now," she whispered, flicking tears from her lashes. "Love you, man." She turned and retraced her steps to the bike.

"You okay?" Mazey asked.

Oddly enough she felt not okay, but a tiny bit better. "Yeah, thanks." She swung her helmet onto her head and buckled it.

"You're not going to tell me what that was about?"

"Not tonight."

"I'm not a kid, you know."

"You are the most not-kid nine-year-old on the planet, Punk. I just need some time to process, okay?"

"Okay. But sometime, we *are* going to talk about what's going on with you. Now, we going to find somewhere to camp?"

CJ threw her leg over. "On our way."

Chapter 7

The next morning they packed up, left the small private campground, and rode to find some breakfast. CJ made it a point to pull in at diners where all the well-worn, mud-splattered trucks were parked. Farmers knew good eating. This one was in the middle of the small-town main street.

They sat on swivel stools at the bar and watched through the order window as the cook flipped eggs and poured pancakes onto a sizzling griddle. They ordered from a young waitress who hustled back and forth, delivering dishes, taking orders, and refilling coffee mugs.

CJ stirred cream into her coffee. "Well, what do you want to do today, Mazey?"

"What do you mean? We've gotta get down the road."

"Actually, we don't. I scrapped the itinerary. We can go wherever you want." She felt her sister's sharp focus on the side of her face.

"Does this have something to do with what happened last night?"

CJ sighed. She owed Mazey some explanation, but it sure couldn't be the truth—at least, not all of it. "Maybe partly. But mostly, I realized that I don't need to stop at the places my friends and I had planned. We're free go anywhere we want." She turned to her sister. "Anywhere *you* want."

Mazey's brows came down and a furrow appeared between them. "Sometime you'll tell me about them, right?"

Probably not. "Sometime, Punk."

Mazey held out a hand to shake. "Okay, except we'll decide together. We each get a fifty-fifty say."

CJ smiled for the first time, it seemed, in forever. "Works for me."

The waitress picked up their plates at the window and slid them across the worn Formica, then poured CJ more coffee. "If you're looking for something to do we have a parade through town in an hour, and the Sweetwater Fair is happening down at the fairgrounds."

Mazey's expression flipped to delight. "Oh, cool. What parade?"

"It's our Founder's Day celebration."

CJ chuckled at Mazey's hopeful look. "Sounds like fun."

When they finished eating, CJ left a huge tip for the waitress and they walked out to Lola to put up their riding gear, then cruised the sidewalk to find a place to watch the parade. People were packed three-deep. Families mostly, from grandmas in folding chairs to toddlers, faces smeared with goo, anchored in mom's firm grip. "Everyone must have the day off — it's not even the weekend."

"I guess. Isn't this cool?" Mazey dodged a boy about her age chasing another through the crowd.

"Hey!" A man stepped out and grabbed the slower kid by the upper arm. "Settle down. You're gonna hurt somebody."

"Yessir." The kid ducked his head and, when released, walked fast after his friend.

People looked out for each other here. Amazing.

"Over here!" Mazey waved from a clot of people ten feet ahead.

CJ hurried to where she stood, snugged against the curb. "Good job, Punk."

Up the street a deep bass drum-beat started up, and others joined into a rolling cadence. People quieted, then clapped out the rhythm.

A current of excitement rolled through the close-packed crowd, sweeping CJ and Mazey up with it.

"Here they come!" a little girl yelled, pointing up the street.

A drum major in a gold uniform and tall white-feathered hat high-stepped at the front, blowing his whistle to the beat. Behind him the woodwinds started up, followed by the brass section. It was a rousing score — from the cheers, it had to be the high school's fight song. They were a bit out of step, hit a flat key every once in a while, and several uniforms were ill-fitted, but CJ loved it. She hooted and threw her fist in the air.

The sound swelled as they came abreast, CJ feeling the throbbing beat in the walls of her chest. They were young — tall, squat, fat and pimply, but red-faced and serious. They played their guts out.

Next came a cadre of teen girls on beautiful palominos in silver trimmed saddles and bridles. The riders wore red western shirts with white fringe that swayed with their horses' steps. They waved to the crowd and yelled, "Go Bobcats!"

Behind them, a tractor pulled a wagon stacked with hay bales. The banner read: 'Sweetwater County Queen & Her Court.' Three girls sat on the lower tier in full-length gowns of sapphire, crimson, and emerald. Sequins flashed in the sun as they waved to the crowd. The beautiful girl on the top tier wore a glittery gold gown and a sash declaring her queen.

No high school girl in California, especially the pretty ones, would be caught dead in a gown on a hay wagon. But things were different here — the crowd wolf-whistled and cheered.

Mazey tugged CJ's elbow. "This is amazing."

"That is so sweet!" CJ pointed to the next group — a trio of baton twirlers in tights and tutus, the oldest no more than eight. They hurled their batons into the air, and maybe one out of the three actually caught it while the others scrambled to retrieve theirs.

Mazey laughed. The crowd cheered.

A fire truck and ambulance came by, lights and sirens going. At the end was the county sheriff's car. The big man leaned out, waving to the crowd who cheered him.

When nothing but glitter and litter remained of the parade, bystanders drifted away in clumps.

"Can we go to the fair now?" Mazey asked.

"Race you to the bike." CJ took off, dodging people, but made sure Mazey beat her.

She stopped by an ATM then rode the three miles out of town. She slowed at the fairgrounds where a man in a neon vest waved vehicles into a grassy field and parked between two massive pickups.

"Do you think anyone will mess with Lola?" Mazey folded her jacket and tucked it under the bungee cords that held the sleeping bags on the back.

"Hope not. I can lock the bike, there's but no way to lock the bags." She glanced down at the shoelace-repaired one and decided not to replace it. Lola looked kinda badass this way.

CJ lay her helmet beside Mazey's on the seat and tucked the bike key into her pocket. "You ready?"

"Past ready." She set off for where a Ferris wheel rose from the edge of the field.

It wasn't as big as a county fair but it had several rides, including a merry-go-round, Ferris wheel, and an Octopus. The warming air was ripe with the smell of popcorn, suntan lotion, and cut grass. People were everywhere: in line at the 'guess your weight' stand, the duck shoot, the hot dog stand. The biggest line was to buy tickets for the rides.

"Well, what first, Punk?"

"I wanna ride the Octopus until I hurl."

"Wow. Not a goal of mine but lead on."

Ten minutes later, CJ had a fistful of tickets. Mazey led the way to the ride with a bucket at the end of each of its eight arms. Calliope music competed with the babble of the crowd, and above it all the diesel chug of the ride.

A little girl stood tiptoe, tugging on her mother's shorts. "Can I have a candy apple?"

"Mom, I want cotton candy!" Her older sister tugged on the other leg.

The frazzled young woman looked like she just wanted some quiet. Not likely today. And it'd be worse if she gave in to her kids' sugar pleadings.

"This is going to be epic!" Mazy chirped.

They were next in line. "Have you been on one of these before?"

"Nope. But I'm gonna love it."

CJ smiled. It was so easy to make her sister happy. And making Mazey happy made *her* happy. Maybe they'd just jump from fair to fair, across the country — she could think of worse ways to spend the summer.

The carnie let a pair of teens out of one seat and waved her and Mazey over. They scrambled in, CJ making sure she took the outside seat. He locked the bar across their laps, leaving their feet dangling free.

Their cage lifted, and the man released the people in the bucket behind. "I can't believe we're doing this!" Mazey squealed.

The diesel chug raised to a roar. "Hang on!" CJ yelled as their cage flew up.

"Eiiiiiieeeee!" Mazey let out a little girl screech that hit CJ's eardrums like an ice pick.

The arm reached the top of its trajectory then dropped, so fast and smooth that CJ's stomach didn't have time to get the memo; it stayed weightless until they bottomed out and started up again. Every time, Mazey squealed like a piglet with a megaphone.

The fair blurred as they sped up, colors whirling together to an impressionist painting. CJ held herself from falling into Mazey at the top, but Mazey was laughing too hard to hold on so she slid, slamming into CJ, which made them laugh more.

By the time they came to a stop and the man let them out, they staggered off, dizzy and giggling like drunken coeds leaving a bar.

"Again!" Mazey stepped to back of the line, but CJ caught her by the neck of her t-shirt.

"Nope. I want lunch, and if I do that ride again I won't."

"Oh yeah, food. Okay."

They bought corn dogs at the Lions Club booth then walked the midway, trying not to dribble mustard on themselves. They passed a booth where you tossed quarters into fishbowls to win the goldfish it contained. "I'd love to do that one," Mazey said. "But a goldfish might not like riding a motorcycle."

"I'd guess not."

They stopped to watch people shooting ducks with Daisy rifles at one booth. At the next, they were using a squirt gun to shoot into the mouth of a clown. CJ dropped her trash into a can. "You want to try any of these?"

"Nah, those things are rigged; it'd be a waste of money. Besides, even if I won something there's no room on Lola to carry it home."

"Well, no rides for at least an hour. You don't need to get sick—"

"Over there!" Mazey pointed to a tent with a black sign. *Madam Futura's Fortunes* was spelled on it with silver glitter. "I want to do that."

CJ smiled. It would be money wasted, but... "Okay, but hang on, Punk." She grabbed Mazey's shoulder and turned her so she could see her face. "You know this isn't real, right? That whole, 'tall dark stranger thing'?"

"Yeah, I'm not a baby, you know." But her smile didn't dim. "Let's go."

There wasn't a line, which said something about the wisdom of the townsfolk. A girl about Mazey's age took her money and waved them in with a flourish. "Madam Futura will see you now."

CJ stepped in, hand on Mazey's shoulder, and waited for her eyes to adjust to the darkness. A fan in the corner blew desultory air, and in the center of the small tent stood a black cloth-draped card table, with a cheap desk lamp. The woman behind it was beautiful. Her skin glowed in the dim light, her long black hair threaded with silver, though her face was unlined.

"Welcome. Come, sit."

Mazey sat. CJ stood behind her.

"What do you wish to know from Madam Futura?"

Mazey leaned in. "I'm looking for my father."

CJ held back a groan.

The woman pulled a large card deck from under the table and flipped over five cards. They had dark pictures on them, with odd symbols in gold. "You will find him. A tall man, with hair like yours."

"Is he nice? Does he know about me? Is he looking for me?" Mazey's voice spiraled up, and CJ laid a calming hand on her shoulder.

"The cards do not say. But you must go south to find him."

"South where? What state?"

"The cards—"

"That's enough, Punk. Let's go." She squeezed Mazey's shoulder. This woman was not sending her sister off on a wild gander chase.

The woman looked up, as if seeing CJ for the first time. "You. You are in pain." Her brows came together. "I see lines on skin. You believe something to be true which is not." She beckoned. "Come, I will read your cards for free."

"Yeah, thanks, but no thanks." Heart slamming, CJ snatched Mazey up by the shirt and rushed her through the tent flap, then stood outside, waiting for her eyes to adjust.

"CJ, you should—"

She tried to control her breathing so Mazey wouldn't notice.

"But Madam Futura might be able to help you."

"All that woman can help with is lifting money from people's pockets."

"But she said—"

"Remember the gold prospector? This is like that. Come on." She took Mazey's hand. "You want to ride the Octopus again?" Hurling would be preferable to this conversation.

"No." Mazey pulled her hand away. "I'm not going anywhere until you tell me what's going on with you." She crossed her arms over her chest. "I'm serious."

CJ sighed. "We're having so much fun, let's not ruin the day, okay? I promise, we'll talk tonight."

Mazey gave her a side-eye. "On your honor? As a soldier?"

No longer a soldier, she didn't have honor, but it was the promise that counted. "Yes."

Mazey's smile told CJ she'd dodged a bullet. For now. "Race you to the Octopus!"

~~~

By the time the sun dipped toward the horizon, the heat and the fun had worn them out. They ate dinner at picnic tables set up behind the food truck to benefit the high school band and asked a local where they could find a campground for the night. They were directed to a nice one, five miles down the road at the edge of a field where horses grazed. They set up camp, then wandered over to the fence. Several of the horses ambled up, and CJ and Mazey gave them neck and butt scratches.

A soft golden dusk fell on the meadow. A cool breeze combed the grasses and the horses' tails, bringing the scent of rich dirt and growing things. When crickets started up their evening concert the night's peace stole into CJ, loosening her muscles and her tongue. "Logan, Eddie, and Mateo are the guys I worked with over there. We got to be really close friends. We'd planned this trip for over a year." She took a deep breath of the tranquility surrounding them. "They were killed two months before we got leave."

"Oh my gosh, CJ. That's horrible." Mazey's hand found hers and clasped it. She waited quietly, as the last of the light drained from the world.

"It was stupid. We shouldn't have been there."

"You were there? Why didn't you tell me?" Mazey grabbed both her arms. "Were you hurt?"

"No. Nothing important. No one needs a spleen."

"What? Where? Show me."

CJ lifted her T-shirt to show the two small scars to the left of her belly button. "No big deal."

"Why didn't you tell me this?" Mazey exclaimed. "You *are* a hero."

"Don't you *ever* say that." She lowered her tone and her pitch. "I'm not."

"That's horrible. I'm so sorry." Mazey's arms came around CJ, her head tucked into her armpit. "You still have me. You'll always have me. Forever and always."

"I know, Punk." She held her sister, the breeze tracing the cool tracks down her face.

Chapter 8

With no itinerary to drive them they slept in, then had breakfast at the picnic table in front of their tent.

Mazey lingered over her cereal. "It's so pretty here. Could we stay for the day?"

The sun was warm on CJ's shoulders, and cicadas rattled in the trees. "Why not? A day off would be nice. Anything special you want to do?"

"Nah. Just read, pet the horses, and be lazy."

"Sounds like a plan. I'll take our clothes down to the laundry room. Almost everything we own is filthy."

"Could we call Mom? We haven't checked on her all week."

CJ handed over her phone.

Mazey dialed. "Hi, Mom." A pause. "We're having a great time. We saw a parade and went to a fair yesterday. I rode the Octopus, and I about squished CJ. We're at a—"

Her sister's frown put CJ on high alert.

"Already? Where is this place? Is there a school close? What's it like?"

Long pause.

"Oh. That's good."

Palm up, CJ waggled her fingers.

"Hang on, Mom. CJ wants to talk to you." She handed over the phone.

"So you're in the bustling town of Bodfish now, huh?" Sarcasm dripped from her words.

"And I have a job already. There's a small family-owned grocery, and they hired me as a stocker. Next opening, I'll move up to checker."

Upwardly mobile, that was Patsy. "Where are you staying?"

"A long-stay motel. They have some duplexes around here somewhere. I just have to check them out. Oh Cora Jean, the best part is I'm singing at the bar three nights a week, and they love me!"

Given the clientele, she could imagine they'd be happy for road-kill if it could warble a tune. "That's good. What is the school like? Do they have a gifted program?"

"I haven't looked into it yet."

Her sister's face was hidden by hair, and CJ was suddenly livid for her. "Jeez, you didn't think Mazey would ask? Could you move it up on your priority list?"

Her exasperated sigh blew in CJ's ear. "Cora Jean. I got here two days ago, and I already have two jobs. Do you think you could cut me some slack? You two won't be here for weeks."

"Whatever." CJ handed the phone back to Mazey then crawled into the tent to unzip the windows before it transformed to an oven. She gathered their dirty clothes in a garbage bag and carried it to the picnic table.

Mazey has her e-reader open, the phone beside her.

"You done?"

"Yeah." She looked up. "Why are you so down on Mom? She has a dream, and she's doing some pretty scary stuff to make it come true. You know she did this all alone— no more Blade."

"I know. But Mazey, you've heard her sing. Do you think she's going to end up with a recording contract?"

"That doesn't matter."

"Sure does to her." And it would affect Mazey when she failed. Again.

"Except, she's happy now. Even if she never gets farther, at least she's not going to wonder what would have happened if she had tried. That's something, isn't it?"

"Not really. When the dream pops like a soap bubble she'll be stuck in that dusty little dirt road town, feeling like a failure." She picked up her phone and tucked it into the back pocket of her jeans. "I wouldn't wish that on anyone."

Mazey cocked her head. "Don't you have a dream, CJ?"

A flush began on her chest, rising up her neck to burst on her face. "I gave those up a while ago." Not the nightmares, though. Her gut churned in that same early-morning-wake-up stew of guilt, regret, and desperation. "Now, go check to see if you have any dirty clothes I missed. I want to get this done before it gets hot."

Mazey stood. "Okay, but I think it must be kinda sad, not having a dream"

She walked to the outbuilding, wishing she could dream, but it'd be silly to waste time on things she'd never have.

There was a 'leave a book, take a book' shelf in the two-washer laundry room, and CJ grabbed a spy novel to read while waiting. It was interesting, so when the clothes were done she carried it back to the campsite. She and Mazey read all afternoon on a sleeping bag they spread under a tree.

That evening CJ picked up burgers in town for dinner and took them back to camp for a treat.

They sat at the picnic table. "This was a good day," Mazey said around a mouthful of fries.

"It was." Funny how dumping the itinerary had unloaded a trunkful of stress. "So, where to next?"

"Can I have your phone?"

"Sure." CJ pulled it out and handed it over.

"I was looking at a map today..." She scrolled. "What if we go through Colorado? I would love to see the old silver mining areas. Then New Mexico has amazing rock formations... What?"

"You want to go south because of what that five-dollar fortune teller said."

Red bloomed on Mazey's cheeks. "Hey, you said you didn't care."

She sighed. "I don't. Just don't insult what little intelligence I have. I may not be as smart as you, but I'm not stupid, either."

"Sorry." She pushed the phone across the table.

"That's okay, Punk. We can go south. But let's be honest with each other."

She studied the wood grain of the table. "Okay."

CJ stood, walked around to sit next to her sister, and set the phone between them. "Now, show me the route you were thinking about."

It was full dark when Mazey yawned. "I'm going to go to bed."

CJ looked up from her book and clicked off the flashlight. "I want to finish this. I'm going to the laundry where there's light. I can keep an eye on the tent from the window there. Are you okay with that?"

"Sure." She yawned again.

"Okay, sleep well. I'll only be gone an hour or so."

"'K." She shuffled to the tent.

The laundry room was empty. CJ dropped the paperback on the bookshelf and slid a stool to the end of the folding table by the window where she could see the tent by campground's security light. She plugged in her phone and opened the browser to the internet.

Mazey was not going to stop searching for her father, and CJ had to know what they were in for if Mazey *did* find him. Her conscience pinched a bit, paying for a people-search website when she told Mazey no. But it was her job to keep her sister safe.

She entered her credit card info, then unfolded the copy of Beau Brown's driver's license that she'd lifted from Mazey's dirty jeans and entered all the information.

Then waited, glancing up every minute or so to be sure the tent was undisturbed.

Fifteen minutes later, she had the report. She sped through the details, until words stopped her like hitting a wall. *Arrest and conviction, Assault & Battery, Reno, Nevada.* It gave the year. "Oh my God." No wonder he never picked up his last paycheck — he'd been in jail!

There was also a conviction in a civil fraud suit listed.

Well, that was the end of that. She closed out of the site and pocketed her phone. Mazey could have her dreams, but CJ had no intention of allowing this one to become reality.

~~~

They stayed on the interstate the next morning because it was shortest; only three hours east to Cheyenne, then south, putting them in Boulder by lunchtime. Mazey had chosen the Fiske Planetarium as their next stop. Since she wanted to see the sky through their telescope at night, they had time to burn.

She parked the bike and they walked the Pearl Street mall. CJ loved the Bohemian feel of the college town. She avoided the head shops, but they wandered in boutiques featuring tie-dye, hemp, organic cotton, and even yak fibers from Nepal. Jewelry stores had toe rings, ankle bracelets, and studs for piercings in places CJ didn't want to think about. It was fun and funky.

She found a souvenir shop, where she bought Mazey an eye-smacking neon tie-dye T-shirt with a peace sign in the middle, and for herself, a red one with the cartoon Woodstock logo — a dove perched on a guitar.

They tried a vegetarian diner, which was good, but decided they'd stick to being carnivores. They rode out to the planetarium at dusk.

Mazey scrambled off the back as soon as CJ braked to a stop. "Hurry. I want to see everything before we do the telescope." She fumbled with the strap to her helmet, awkward with rushing.

CJ smiled. "Punk, you told me the stars have been there way before our planet was formed. I think they'll be there in ten minutes."

"I know, but hurry, will ya?" She danced in place.

"Okay, okay, I'm coming." CJ finished tucking her jacket in the bungee cords. The parking lot was only a quarter full, a good sign.

A single-story brick building was topped by a white half bubble of plastic, made up of cells that made it look like a honeycomb. CJ followed her sister's skipping steps across the tarmac. Had she ever been this excited about things? She cast back to the dim corners of her mind, but the only memories that came were tinged in dirt and melancholy. She'd hadn't been a sad kid, or a depressed teen, so it must be the way she felt now that melted the good memories.

Mazey held the door open. "Come on, slowpoke. The show starts in two minutes."

CJ paid for their tickets, then followed her sister down a broad hallway. She wanted to stop to read the plaques beneath the artwork that lined the hall, but Mazey grabbed her hand and tugged. CJ had to run to keep up.

Mazey stopped at the open double doors. A college-age kid took their tickets and waved them in. It was a huge theatre, and she now understood the honeycomb that topped the building; it was for this room. Theatre seating for must have been two hundred people, though less than half that were seated. Mazey pulled her to two seats beside each other, and CJ settled in.

The deep rumble of timpani rolled over the crowd, rising to a crescendo, leading into a classical piece CJ almost recognized.

Mazey lay her head against the back of the seat, took CJ's hand, and squeezed. "I'm gonna remember this my whole life."

At her sister's touch, a spark of excitement hit CJ like a shock of static electricity and danced along her nerves. The dome lit, becoming a three-sixty screen showing a fish-eye view of the launching of the space shuttle. That faded to a three-dimensional view of the Milky Way, and the crowd let out a collective sigh. It was as if you were floating among the stars.

Mazey's face was a pale half-moon of rapt awe, her mouth open slightly, the light sparkling in her eyes.

CJ's heart skipped with happiness. Is this how a parent felt, watching their kid see a hummingbird or a butterfly for the first time? She never knew that wonder could be contagious. No wonder adults went nuts over their grandchildren. Hundreds of opportunities for experiencing those "first times". She laid her head back in the seat and was transported.

Thirty minutes later they stepped into the hallway, blinking their way back to the real world.

"Did you see the meteorite against New York's skyline? It was three times as big! Can you imagine if it hit? No wonder the dinosaurs went extinct. The dust storm would cause nuclear winter."

Mazey chittered on, and CJ took the time to peruse the artwork. Who knew that astronomy was so fascinating? In that theatre she'd felt her mind expand to its limits, then push past them. No wonder Mazey was a committed fan.

"Next comes the best." Mazey practically skipped to the elevators, and CJ was glad she'd splurged for the tickets to the telescope.

"We came at the perfect time — we're going to see the Perseids!"

CJ tugged the end of her hair. "Is that like going to see the wizard?"

Mazey rolled her eyes. "The meteor shower. Through a real observatory telescope."

This kid was so cute. How could her mother and the other people who touched her life not see how incredibly special she was? They stepped into the crowded elevator and turned to face the door. CJ put her arms around Mazey's shoulders and whispered in her ear, "I love you, you know."

Mazey turned her head and kissed CJ's cheek. "Love you right back."

~~~

Light hit CJ's eyelids, waking her. Inches from her nose, the tent's nylon bulged in a huff of wind. She rolled over. Mazey lay on her back, scrolling on the phone. "What're you doing?"

"Checking Instagram for my dad."

CJ's stomach jumped, remembering the truth she'd discovered. "Stop, Mazey." She held out her hand for the phone.

"Why?" She frowned and scrolled faster.

"Because you're obsessed with this. It's not healthy."

"I'm just trying... do you think he could be in a different country? I didn't even think about that, but there's a Beau Brown in Mexico—"

CJ snatched the phone away.

"Why are you doing this?" Mazey glared at her, her voice as hard as one of her fossils.

CJ tucked the phone under her pillow. "It's my job to keep you safe, and—"

"It's *not*. You're not my mother."

"Never claimed to be. But I took on the responsibility for you when we left Victorville."

Mazey sat up, grabbed a T-shirt, and dragged it over her head. "There's nothing wrong with me looking for my dad. You think I'm some little kid who can't handle things. You think you know me, but you don't. You left when I was four!"

"And you're throwing a fit like you still are four."

"You're mean." She snatched a pair of shorts and wriggled into them, then pulled on her shower shoes. "This is my dream. If it doesn't work out, fine. At least I know I tried. Like Mom." She ripped open the zipper to the tent. "Not like you. You just sit in your sadness and never even try to make anything better. You're all broken inside." She crawled out of the tent but turned back, her accusatory glare a laser, burning through CJ's skin. "I think *you're* the one who can't handle things."

The words hit CJ like a grenade. Instead of admitting the truth in them, a white-hot anger flared. She jerked on her sweats, threw on a T-shirt and crawled out of the tent, breathing hard. She stalked for the bathroom. The door banged open at her shove and slammed against the wall, echoing loud in the cinder-block room. Mazey looked up from washing her hands. "Look." Hands on hips, CJ tried to catch her breath. And her temper. "I don't know much, but I know this. Tracking down your dad is not a good idea. I know you have all these pictures in your head about what he's like, but what if he's not? He could be dangerous, Mazey."

Her sister rubbed her hands on her shorts to dry them, then closed the few steps to her sister. "If you don't have any dreams, I feel sorry for you — but you're not killing mine." Her words had sharp points and her closed face was as firm as a rock wall. "I know my father is a good man."

"How do you know that, Mazey?"

"I just *know*." She pushed the door open and was gone.

Chapter 9

Packing up was now routine. No words were needed or spoken by either party. CJ worked around the pinch in her heart where Mazey's dart had hit home. Her sister didn't know CJ *had* tried. Over and over. But it always came out the same. She'd once dreamt of being an EMT, helping people who were sick, hurt, and scared. That was before she found out she couldn't be trusted with auto maintenance, much less people's lives.

And yet here she was, her sister's life in her hands. A weasel of panic was loose inside, ripping and tearing, trying to get out. She never should have brought Mazey with her. If Patsy was even a marginal parent, she wouldn't have allowed it. But she'd done it to save her sister from Blade, and now even that was pointless since Patsy left the sleaze behind anyway.

What had she been thinking, wandering around out here, no purpose, no itinerary? She'd scrapped the reason for coming, and she wasn't about to take up Mazey's hunt for her ex-con father. Maybe it would be best to head for Patsy's new place, drop Mazey off, and leave. CJ had to figure out how to live the rest of her life.

Mazey was mounted by the time CJ pulled on her helmet. They'd talk tonight. Mazey wouldn't like it, but hell, she might as well get used to disappointment — she was destined to a life full of it.

She stayed off the interstate. The back roads were safer for a woman and kid alone. She told herself she wanted to see the mountains of Colorado — that's why she headed south. Each curve brought a new vista: evergreens marching down the hillside to an emerald valley, distant peaks wearing snow beards, the winding ribbon of blacktop ahead. The sun was warm on her shoulders and the breeze carried a hint of honey. Her awareness expanded with the view, and she reminded herself to look for good things. Daisies at the side of the road, bowing their pretty heads to the passing cars. Wispy clouds trailing to mares' tails in the winds aloft. She imagined bears sleeping in the impenetrable deadfall beneath the mighty pines.

Her mood lifted as they climbed and climbed, humming 'Rocky Mountain High' to herself. Mazey must have heard, because she started singing along. By the time they rolled into the historic mining town of Leadville, her dark thoughts had burnt off like morning mist. She found an open spot and parallel parked in front of the brick-fronted buildings of Main Street. Mazey dismounted first, unbuckled her helmet, and stood waiting when CJ threw her leg over.

"I'm sorry, CJ. I was mad, and I said the first thing that came to my head."

"I know, Punk." She pulled off her helmet and unzipped her jacket.

"I had no right to judge you. I don't know what you went through." She touched CJ's shoulder. "But I'd like to hear more about your friends. Not hard things or sad things. Would you tell me happy stories about them sometime?"

This kid. Just when she'd decided Mazey was a brat, she said something sweet and way beyond her years. "Yeah, sometime." She clipped the strap of her helmet to the bungee cords. "We can carry our jackets."

"Where are we going?" Mazey shrugged out of her leathers.

"I saw the National Mining Museum up the street a block or two. Want to see it?"

Her answer was Mazey's hug, squeezing her so tight it pulled some of her pieces a bit closer together.

"You're the best. Seriously."

"I'll remind you of that later."

~~~

Two hours had passed when they walked out of the museum's dim interior to bright sunshine.

"That geode was as big as my head! Can you believe it's possible to mine asteroids in space? And the fluorescent rocks? I've read about them but, dang, they're beautiful, aren't they?"

The museum was okay, but the best part was watching Mazey enjoy it. CJ was beginning to realize it might not be as easy to leave her sister at the end of the trip as she'd thought. She ruffled Mazey's hair. "Let's go. I want to make Salida tonight. Supposed to be a great campground outside town."

An hour of mountain twisties later, they had dinner in the old mining town. When they got there the campground by the river was almost full, but they managed to snag a site between the fence and an old camper and set up the tent.

"Hey, neighbor." A young blonde woman in short shorts and a midriff t-shirt with a toddler on her hip stepped down from the camper trailer and walked over. "Wow, great bike!"

"Thanks," CJ said.

Mazey patted the seat. "Her name is Lola, after—"

"Not the WOW star?" She bounced the towheaded boy on her hip. He looked at them with huge eyes.

Mazey's face lit. "Yes! How did you guess?"

"I'm a huge fan of Women of Wrestling. Wouldn't miss it for anything." She extended a hand to CJ. "I'm Crystal."

CJ shook. "I'm CJ and this is Mazey."

"Great to meet you two. Where are you heading?"

Mazey cut her eyes to her sister. "South."

"Cool. I'm on my way to Hollister."

"California?" CJ smiled at the little guy, and he ducked his head into his mother's armpit.

"Yup. It's legendary, and I've never been."

"That's nice." CJ looked around. The campground seemed safe, and except for the belly shirt their neighbor seemed pretty normal, the little boy clean and appeared well-cared for. "Hey Mazey, would you mind if I go for a run? I haven't been out since we left home, and my legs are losing tone, sitting on the bike all day."

"I'm not a baby, CJ. Go."

Crystal jumped in. "Hey, I have the WOW Championship from last weekend taped. You want to watch it, Mazey?" She turned to CJ. "If it's okay with you, of course."

Mazey bounced on her toes. "Oh, can I? I'm dying to know who was crowned champion." She held a hand up to Crystal. "Don't tell me!"

She smiled. "You couldn't pry it out of me with a crowbar."

CJ scanned the trailer. It was old, with a few rust spots, but seemed well kept. "I'll only be an hour or so. I'll be back by full dark."

"Oh, yay!" Mazey and Crystal talked wrestling while CJ ducked into the tent to change.

Before she took off, she called Mazey over. "You okay with this?" She bent to tie her tennis shoes.

"Of course, why?"

"If you get uncomfortable for any reason head to the office, okay?"

"Jeez, you worry too much. I'm fine. You go have fun, and notice some amazing things, okay?"

"I'm looking at something amazing right here." She chucked her sister under the chin. "I'll be back soon."

"Go already." Mazey shooed her away.

She took off. The pain under the scar in her side faded as her muscles warmed. Outside the campground, a dirt path on the left skirted a drop-off to the river. She took that, happy to hear the familiar slap of tennis shoes on dirt. There were a few houses, but there were long solitary gaps between them. She came around a curve and found a fly fisherman below her, hip-deep in the river, casting — back and forth, back and forth. She waved as she went by, and he raised his chin to her.

This area was high desert. She recognized the dusty scruffy plants from her childhood and familiarity slipped under her skin, making her smile. How many miles had she run in terrain like this? Except the mountains rimming the horizon, of course. Straight ahead the sun sank low, forcing a squint, the heat only a faint shadow of the day's intensity.

Maybe Mazey was right. If she stayed anchored in the present, noticing the good things, the dark clouds that stalked her receded. If she could find a way to sustain this — to live inside this bubble of the present — could she someday run out from under her past? Could she somehow find the energy to trust herself again?

Seemed impossible to her now. But what if it wasn't?

When the sun was only a fingernail sliver at the edge of the world, she turned back, feeling loose inside her skin. She'd sleep good tonight, that's for sure.

It was full dark by the time she slowed to a walk at the entrance to the campground. A boom box blared a rock anthem somewhere to her right. The drive curved and a huge bonfire flickered through the trees, the light dancing on the canopy over her head. Great. That's just what they needed, rowdy neighbors.

The bonfire, boombox, and about ten bikers were clustered around the travel trailer next to their tent, their Harleys parked wherever they'd fit.

Her heart slammed her ribs. Mazey! She sprinted, her legs weak from lactic acid and adrenaline.

Mazey sat between two beefy guys in leather vests at the picnic table beside the trailer. She laid down her hand of cards, her smile bright in the reflected light. "Full house. That means I win, right?" She looked up. "Hey, CJ."

"What the *hell* do you think you're doing?" she yelled over the rock anthem and drumbeat riff of her heart. Another mistake. Another one she loved, put in jeopardy because of her.

The men looked up. "What? We're teaching her to play poker."

CJ walked around the table, clamped a hand on Mazey's shoulder, and lifted her.

"Ow, CJ." But she stood.

"Come on. We're out of here."

The guy on the left with a full sleeve tattoo growled, "Hey, if anyone should be upset, it's us. This kid is a shark."

"This *kid* is nine years old." She pointed to the table littered with cards and beer bottles. "Do you really think poker is an appropriate pastime?"

Mazey lifted the bills from the center of the table and handed a ten to the guy on her right. "Thanks for spotting me." She folded the rest and put them in her pocket.

"See ya, kid."

Crystal stepped out of the trailer, four bottles of beer clamped between her fingers. "What's wrong?"

CJ marched up to her. "I trusted you to watch my sister. I come back to a poker party? And drinking? What is wrong with you?"

"Well, jeez. Pull your panties out of your crack. The guys weren't hurting anything."

CJ loosened her fists. It wasn't like she could take them all on. "Come on, Mazey. Get packed. We're leaving."

"But CJ—" A glance at her sister stopped whatever argument she had. She followed meekly back to their campsite.

CJ burnt off her anger by heaving their crap into the bags on the bike. Mazey took down the tent. In fifteen minutes they were ready to go. Mazey climbed onto the back, avoiding her sister's eye.

CJ fired the engine and hit the gas, ignoring the heavy weight of the stares from the campsite next door. She turned onto the road and followed it out of town.

This was her fault. She knew Mazey was naïve. What was she thinking, leaving her sister with someone she'd known for all of five minutes? Now she remembered about Hollister — Harley heaven. Damn, damn, damn. Hadn't the desert taught her anything?

The road curved, leaving the lights of town behind. Ahead, the night was black as the inside of a bear. She had no idea where she was going, she was just going, flogging herself the whole way. Mazey sat back there, full of faith in her sister. *That's* how innocent she was. CJ slowed, then pulled off at a scenic overlook.

"Um…" Mazey's voice was small. "I don't think we can see the view."

CJ dismounted and paced, thoughts too jumbled to speak.

"I'm sorry, CJ."

"No, Mazey, I should be apologizing to *you.*" She kept pacing. "I left you with some woman I didn't know, because she *looked* okay. You shouldn't trust me. I don't make good decisions. I should never have brought you. This was a huge mistake, and I'm sorry… I'm so damned sorry, Punk—"

Mazey grabbed her arm, halting her steps and her words. "Jeez, overreact much? I'm fine. I was having fun."

CJ threw her hands in the air. "See? You didn't even know when you were in trouble. What if one of those guys took you into the trailer?" She sprinted for the bushes and hurled what was left of her dinner into them.

She was standing, hands on knees, trying to breathe, when Mazey's arm came around her. "It's okay. I'm okay. You're okay. We're okay. Okay?" She made small circles on CJ's back.

Nightmare scenarios shot through CJ's brain like gunfire: Mazey, struggling against those big men in the firelight, fire flickering over bloody faces, small arms fire. She wrapped her arms around her head to protect it, her Harley helmet morphing to a combat one. "Nooooo!" The word stretched out, one long moan. "I'm sorry. I'm so, so sorry." She wasn't sure if she was telling Mazey, or the ghosts clustered around her.

"CJ. CJ!" Mazey shook her shoulders, and the past broke away to slink back into the dark where it belonged.

"You're scaring me again, CJ."

She grabbed her sister in her shaky arms and held on. "It's okay, Punk. I'm okay."

Mazey's disbelief shone in the headlight. "But—"

"Come on. We're got to find somewhere to spend the night." Arms around each other's waists, they walked back to the bike. CJ wasn't sure who was holding up whom.

~~~

CJ awoke to bright breathless heat in the tent and an empty sleeping bag beside her. She checked her phone. Nine. She hadn't slept this late in forever. But understandable since they were up late, getting lost. No cell signal in the mountains reminded her she forgot to grab a state map yesterday. CJ had finally found a dirt fire road and drove down it a mile or so, far enough to know they were alone. They set up the tent and fell into it, exhausted.

She unzipped and stuck her head out of the flap. "Mazey?"

"I'm here." Her voice came from by the bike.

CJ pulled on her tennis shoes, tied them, and crawled out.

Mazey sat in the driver's seat, elbows on the tank, her e-reader propped against the windshield, reading.

"You okay?"

"Sure. Hungry, though. You?"

"Yup. Let me pee, and we can get packed up. If we go back to the main road and turn right, we've got to hit a town eventually."

And a half-hour down the road, they did. A sleepy little burg. They stopped at a food truck beside the only gas station and ordered breakfast tacos. They sat at a picnic table to eat, watching the sporadic cars pass. When they were done, CJ broached the explosive subject she had meant to take on yesterday. If she had, last night wouldn't have happened. "Mazey, I think it's time to head for home."

"What?" Her face came up with a wild-eyed-horse look. "We have weeks yet."

"Yeah, but last night made me realize how vulnerable we are. Two chicks, riding to places we've never been. Things can go bad, fast. I'd just feel better if—"

"No!" Mazey's face flushed from pink to cherry red and kept going. "I'll be more careful. We're fine. Besides, you've got the pig sticker and—"

"It's just not a good idea, Punk, I'm sorry. Besides, don't you want to see where you'll be living? Find out where the school is and all?"

"No. I want to finish the trip. I want to stay with *you*, CJ."

She shook her head. "I want to stay with you, too, but I've got things to do. I've been putting them off, but—"

"Oh, fine. You give up on what were supposed to do with your friends, and now you're making me give up on the only thing *I* want to do." She slapped her hand on the table. "You're really good at giving up, you know that?"

CJ held the stare-down. It wouldn't do for Mazey to know she could hurt her. "And you never give up. Shake the two of us in a bag, and you'd have a perfect person. But that's not real life, Mazey."

"I thought you were so brave, being a soldier. But you're just a scardey-cat. Go then. I'll be fine." She crossed her arms and hugged herself. "I don't need you. I don't need anybody."

The words hit a balloon of bitterness in CJ's gut. It broke open, spilling acid that melted the filter between her brain and her mouth. "Except your loser dad." The second the words were out, she wished she could snatch them back.

Mazey's face edged toward purple. "You take that back! He's not a loser!"

She leaned in to touch her sister's shoulder, but she jerked away. "Look, I know you need him to be a good guy. But that's just not real life, Punk."

"Whatever. I'm not talking to you."

Oh great, now the four-year-old shows up. Trying to slow her breathing, she glanced around and spied a 'Just-a-Buck' store across the street. "We both need a time out. I'm going to go across the street and buy some razor blades. Anything you need?"

"Do you think they sell *good* sisters over there?"

"I doubt you'd get better'n me for under a buck, but I'll look. Stay with the bike, okay? I can see you from the window." She dug through her pocket, found a couple of bills, checked both ways on the street, then crossed. Damned kid. Who did she think she was? Did she think her sister was too stupid to recognize manipulation? CJ wasn't sure if the pain in her stomach was from the hot sauce or the jab about her being a quitter. She pulled open the glass door and was smacked by cold air that held a hint of cheap cologne.

She stalked the aisles, grabbing blades, tampons, and antacids. How had this ever seemed like a good idea? It had disaster written in neon glitter. She made herself slow down, not wanting to go back across the street until she had herself under control. Mazey may act like a grown-up sometimes, but CJ *was* the adult.

She chatted with the check-out girl, watching her sister through the window. Mazey had her head down, thumbs flying over CJ's phone. Maybe she was texting her mother. That reminded her—she was going to have to call and tell Patsy the change of plans. She got her change, thanked the cashier, and headed across the street.

Her credit card lay beside Mazey on the picnic table.

"What are you doing?"

"I'm just..." She scrolled faster.

CJ walked around the table and read over her sister's shoulder. Her brain went into free fall, and her thoughts tried to catch up. "You used my credit card to look up your father on one of those sites?" She snatched the phone away. "After I told you no?"

"You told me before we left home that if you ever told me something that I knew wasn't right, to do what I thought I should. Remember?" There was no remorse on Mazey's face. Determination and mulish stubbornness, but not remorse. "He lives in Laredo, Texas."

"I know. What I want to know is why you thought it was okay—"

"Wait, you *knew*? All this time you knew, and didn't tell me? Why?"

"Because I was trying to protect you. Notice he wasn't only arrested, he was *convicted*."

Mazey's expression hardened. "Let me see." She held out her hand.

CJ only hesitated a moment. "You started this. Don't blame me when your dream goes up in smoke." She handed the phone over. "Look at the date. It was when we lived in Reno. That's why he left his job without picking up his check. He was in *jail*."

Mazey read on, her brows pulling to a frown. "But there has to be a logical explanation. Shouldn't we at least call Mom, and find out what happened?"

CJ rolled her eyes. God, the kid was persistent. "If we do, will you stop this obsession?"

"Yes."

"How can I believe the promise of someone who just stole from me?"

Guilt flashed in Mazey's eyes before she dropped her head, stuffed her fist into her pocket, and pulled out bills she'd won at poker. "I'm sorry. I was desperate."

CJ ignored the bills and hit speed dial, then speaker-phone.

It rang three times before Patsy's cigarette-rough voice said, "Yeah."

"It's CJ and Mazey. You're on speakerphone. We have a question for you."

"Shoot."

"Beau Brown. He was arrested the summer I went to track camp." What kind of person has an affair and gets pregnant in the two weeks her kid is at camp? "What happened?"

A heavy sigh. "What difference does that make now?"

"Mazey has a right to know."

"It was a bar fight. He beat up a friend of mine. Listen, I can't talk. I'm at work. I only answered because I was worried that something had happened to you two."

Not from her tone when she answered the phone, she wasn't. And she was deflecting. CJ had a long education in Patsy Newsome. She was hiding something. "It'll take two minutes. Tell her."

"I don't like your tone, Cora Jean, and I don't owe anyone an explanation for my life, much less to the children I brought into it. Now, I have to go if I don't want to get fired. Goodbye."

CJ and Mazey looked at each other.

"It wasn't his fault," Mazey said.

"I'll admit she's hiding something. But that doesn't mean he's a good guy." Puzzle pieces littered the floor in her mind, but they weren't coming together. She didn't have enough information. "Pull up that report again. I want to know what else it says."

Chapter 10

"Here are articles about my dad from the Laredo Star Daily," Mazey told her as she scrolled. "He volunteers with the local YMCA, coaches soccer, and owns a body shop that's won local awards with the Chamber of Commerce."

"No doubt he's a saint. Except for those two convictions, of course."

"But only one was criminal, and you admitted yourself, Mom is hiding something."

CJ held up a hand. "I know, I know. Let me think a minute." She walked to the bike, put up her purchases, and checked to be sure everything was secure. She always thought better when her hands were busy.

She considered the twists and turns in her own life. How they always ended in either blank walls, or swamps of despair full of fast-moving things with sharp teeth. The odds of this working out were about as good as CJ winning the lottery — when she'd never in her life bought a ticket.

But what if Mazey was right, and this Beau Brown *was* a good guy? If he was, and they went home now, CJ would be depriving her sister of a father. Mazey would have one decent parent. God, how did people have the guts to have children? The responsibility for another human on your shoulders, knowing you're only one bad decision from ruining their lives?

On the other hand, on this trip she'd gotten to know Mazey better, and she had to accept that her sister wasn't as much naïve as... unfailingly optimistic. She saw the best in people — in the world. If she were honest, CJ envied that a bit.

And if Patsy hadn't yet killed that, Mazey was tougher than she looked. She deserved the truth, no matter what it was.

She walked to where her sister stood waiting, hoping this wasn't another mistake. "Okay, here's the deal. We'll head that way."

Mazey clasped her hands to white-knuckled fists and bounced on her toes.

"When we get there, you will not approach him until I have a chance to check him out." She held up a finger. "But here's the catch, and it's non-negotiable. If I decide he's a loser or worse, I take you home. You don't get to meet him. I'm serious about this. After today, I'm not sure I can trust you. You have to swear that you'll abide by my decision."

Mazey lifted three fingers from her fist.

"I'll take that as a swear, even if you aren't a Girl Scout."

Mazey threw herself into CJ's arms, wrapping her legs around her sister's waist. "You are the best sister there ever was."

CJ chuckled. "Yeah, you should'a seen the ones at the Just-a-Buck."

She bought a map of Colorado and New Mexico at the gas station and they sat at the picnic table, mapping out the new route.

~~~

They rode Highway 25 straight south. Now that they had a destination, neither wanted to waste time sightseeing. The rest of Colorado and most of New Mexico went by in a blur of desert landscape and open vistas.

They were south of Albuquerque when they stopped for a gas-restroom-soda break at a huge gas station that served truckers with a restaurant, showers, and overnight parking. Mazey pumped gas while CJ went in to grab sodas and a snack. Wandering the aisles, she noticed two teenage girls — one blonde, one with black hair — standing by the small liquor display, whispering. The pale makeup and black eye shadow made their pimples stand out in bold relief. She could tell by their furtive glances that they were working up the nerve to steal a bottle of booze.

As she walked by, CJ whispered, "Don't do it," and kept walking.

She took her selections to the counter where the older lady there rang up her purchases.

"Hey!" She looked past CJ's shoulder. "I saw you. Give me the bottle. I'm calling the cops."

CJ turned to the two teens standing frozen like spotlighted deer.

"We didn't do anything." The blonde was all teenage bluster, but the dark haired one's face had gone even paler. But it was the dread in her eyes that stopped CJ. She knew that feeling down to her soul. Before she could think, she stepped forward. "There you are."

They both turned to stare at her.

"You know this lady isn't going to let you buy my..." She glanced at the bottle that appeared in the Elvira wannabe's hand. "Schnapps."

The cashier narrowed her eyes. "Right. The booze is for you." She wasn't even pretending to buy CJ's lame excuse.

"Jeez, why didn't you just hand it to me?" She added the bottle to her purchases on the counter and flashed her ID.

The cashier side-eyed her, decided she didn't want to call CJ a liar, and bagged the Schnapps without a word.

She snatched the bag and walked out, the two on her heels. She kept walking until she was beside the building, stopped, and pulled the bottle from the bag.

"Hey, thanks." The blonde reached for the bottle. "That was really cool of you—"

"Don't thank me yet." CJ broke the seal on the bottle, unscrewed the top, and upended it. Red stained the dirt.

"What the hell are you doing?" the dark-haired one screeched.

"You didn't ask for my advice, but since I just saved your asses you're getting it and you're going to listen."

They stood, their faces covered in teenage ennui.

"Look, everybody has shit in their lives. You do the best you can. But at least use what brains God gave you."

"You don't know anything about me, or my life," the pale one said.

"You're right. I don't, and I don't give a shit. I'll never see you again, and I'm as happy as you are about that. But I can't stand to see someone throwing their life away, and not even realize they're doing it. So shut up and listen."

They didn't move.

"Grow the hell up, little girls. Someday you may decide you actually have a goal beyond partying and driving your parents crazy. A prison record will close that door. Yeah, it may be a sealed juvie record now, but you'd better start looking ahead or your life is going to suck, whether you can imagine that or not." She put the cap on the empty bottle and tossed it into the filthy trash can and dusted her hands. "Wise up. You even drink stupid booze."

"It's the only bottle that would fit down my pants," the blonde said.

CJ snorted a laugh and took a step, but Elvira's hand on her arm stopped her.

"Why step in to save my ass? You don't even know me."

"Because I know what it's like to make a mistake so bad it changes you, and your future. And no matter how bad you want to, it's too late to fix it." She pulled her arm free and walked back to the bike.

Mazey squinted at her. "You don't want me to believe you're a good person but you proved it, right there."

She hadn't realized Mazey was close enough to overhear. "It cost me practically nothing, and it probably won't make any difference. They'll probably try it again."

"Or they might not. But either way, you did something good — for someone who didn't even deserve it."

CJ just shrugged.

"I don't care what you say. You're the best person I know."

"You need to broaden your influencers, kid." Her face burned, but a coal of warmth fired in CJ's chest just the same.

CJ was not going to tell her what happened in Bagram, for selfish reasons as much as not wanting to burden her young soul. The deeper truth was, she liked Mazey looking up to her. She liked being seen a hero, even if it had zero basis in truth.

That's just how cowardly she was.

Chapter 11

Back on the bike, CJ tried to focus the amazing things everywhere that Mazey talked about. She'd love to believe the beautiful things in this world could sustain her. To believe that those, along with her sister's belief in her, would be enough.

But it wasn't. Because when she got down to the unemotional, irrefutable, diamond-hard *facts,* she had to admit to her biggest fear—

That maybe she didn't deserve to live.

Stop it. Live in the moment. Amazing things, remember?

Five hours later she pulled into parking lot of a blocky glass and concrete building, a rocky mountain behind it rising like a moonscape. "We're here."

"Cool. Where's here?"

"I just thought to myself, 'It's a good day to see a moon rock'."

"Whaaaat?" she squealed.

She pointed to the building. "New Mexico Museum of Space History."

"Oh. My. Gosh. This is the coolest thing *ever.*"

"You've said that, like, five times on this trip."

"Because it keeps getting cooler!" She scrambled off the back.

They were lucky. An expert was on hand today, giving a talk on lunar geology. When CJ asked if they could sit in, the receptionist told her it was only for college students.

When Mazey threw out enough facts proving her knowledge on the subject, the woman gave in.

Five minutes into the hour-long talk, it exceeded CJ's pay grade. But Mazey was rapt, watching the presentation on the newly completed geologic map of the entire moon. After, Mazey insisted on walking down to the line of students to talk to the presenter. She had questions. When it was her turn, she asked him what she'd have to do to become a lunar geologist.

The gray-haired professor looked at her over his glasses. "How old are you, young lady?"

"Nine. You just showed me the career I want. But I need to know what classes to take in high school, so I'm ready for college."

He glanced at CJ, who just shrugged. "Trust me, if she says that's what she's going to be, you can believe it."

"Well, you have to focus on science and math. The higher level the courses, the better."

"Okay, then in college, what do I major in?"

"A double major. Astronomy and geology."

She turned to CJ. "My two favorite things!"

"You hit the motherlode, Punk."

Mazey and the professor were soon deep in conversation. Kids her age may not appreciate her sister, but sure adults did. CJ'd seen it over and over on this trip; people seemed drawn to Mazey and, watching these two interact, she understood why. Her sister had a strong... the only term that came to mind was *life force*. Mazey's curiosity and wonder at the world around her shone from her eyes, drawing people, as if they wanted a piece of that. As if being near, some of her vibrancy would rub off on them.

And it did. CJ was proof. Even *she* felt better around her sister. Watching the animated curiosity and delight on her sister's face, a better description popped into her mind.

Luminous.

~~~

Alamogordo had a nice campground, and the weather was cloud-free and temperate. They'd just set up camp when CJ's phone rang. She pulled it from the pocket of her jacket, trying to think who she'd given the number to. All became clear when her mother's name showed up on the screen. "What could Patsy want?"

"Put it on speaker." Mazey came up beside her. "I want to hear."

Having Patsy on speaker within earshot of Mazey wasn't wise, but she couldn't think of an excuse on the fly so CJ hit the button.

"Cora Jean? It's time to bring Mazey home."

Her voice wasn't high or fast, which ruled out panic. "What?"

Mazey waved her hands, shaking her head and mouthing, *No.*

"Why? We've only been gone two weeks. We've got plenty of time before school starts."

"I know. But...oh, CJ, the most amazing thing has happened. You won't believe it."

Red flags popping in her brain like whack-a-moles, she put the phone on the picnic table and sat. "Try me."

Mazey sat across from her.

"I've met a man. His name is Arlo, and he's sweet and kind and, get this—he's a western *songwriter*." Patsy's squeal made CJ glad she didn't have the phone up to her ear.

"Would I know anything he's written?"

"Well, he hasn't sold to Nashville. Yet. But he will. He's amazing," she gushed on. "He came into the bar one night when I was singing and came up to me after my set. And guess what? He's writing a song about me!" She sang, "I didn't set out to be a barstool angel. Back when we wore lower necklines and higher skirts, chasing the good times. I

135

was a dancing queen, dressed in neon lights… Hmmmm… Oh what fun we had watching the men watching us — something, something then — I loved me some bad boys. They didn't stay long, but Lord they put on the miles… that's it so far. What do you think?"

"That's the song he wrote for you?"

"Yes. Well, it's not done yet, and he won't show me the rest until it is, but, oh my God, how cool would it be if I was a hit on my *own song*?"

'Barstool angel' sure described Patsy, but it seemed the meaning had yet to rise through the glitter in her mind. She hoped for Patsy's sake, it never would. "Great. I'm happy for you. But what does this have to do with bringing Mazey home?"

"Well, he's a bit younger than me, and he can't have kids. He's dying to be a dad and can't wait to meet my Amazing Grace."

"Whoa, whoa." Heart slamming in her ears CJ stood, held a hand up to keep her sister in her seat, and walked away far enough not to be overheard. "You'd use Mazey as bait to trap a man?"

"Of course not, Cora Jean, and just once I'd love it if you'd give me the benefit of the doubt. He just wants to meet her, that's all. And besides, it's been two weeks, and the apartment seems empty without her. I miss my Gracie."

"So you'd ruin her summer because," better not to provoke, "you miss her?"

"I do," she whined. "I'm her mother. You have no right to keep me from my baby."

"Hang on a minute." Her arm lost a fight with gravity and fell to her leg. CJ knew Patsy. Threats would come next, and though CJ had the Blade argument it wouldn't carry weight with the law, since Patsy had left him. Red streaks shot across her vision like ammo tracers at night.

Not that she was crazy about the idea of finding Mazey's father, but CJ had promised, and she had no intention of breaking neither her promise nor her sister's heart. She jogged back to the table, held her hand over the receiver, and whispered, "Grab the Texas map."

Mazey ran to the bike, brought it back, and spread it on the table. She mouthed, *What's going on?*

CJ lifted the phone to her ear. "Give me just a minute, Patsy." She traced a finger over the quickest route to Laredo and consulted the legend. "I'll make you a deal. I'll get her home, but I need two weeks before we leave for California."

"I don't understand why you can't—"

"It's that, or I bring her home a week before school starts. Those are your only two options."

Pain in her eyes, Mazey put her hand over her mouth.

CJ winked to let her sister know she had this. "You know, they say possession is nine-tenths of the law."

"Who do you think you are, giving me ultimatums? I'm your mother, too, don't forget."

"Are you afraid this guy won't wait? Seriously, Patsy, do you have that little faith in your wiles?"

Mazey gestured to put the call back on speaker, so CJ did.

"No. No, he truly cares for me. And he loves my voice. He says he knows I'll make it."

"Mom, what's going on?" The tremble in Mazey's words ripped a hole in CJ.

"Oh Gracie, I just miss you so bad. My life is too empty without you."

"I miss you, too, Mom, but *please*, we're having so much fun. Today, I found out what I want to be when I grow up. I'm going to—"

"That's nice, dear." Her sigh hissed through the connection. "Oh all right, CJ. But at the end of two weeks, you'll come straight back. You listening to me?"

"Oh, I'm not only listening, I'm hearing." CJ hit 'end'. God, you should need to pass some kind of motherhood test before you got pregnant. Patsy would have failed.

But hell, if that were true, neither she nor Mazey would be here. And whereas that would be no loss on her part, but the world needed more Mazeys.

"What're we going to do, CJ?" Mazey looked across the table with that trusting, hero-sister look in her eyes.

CJ leaned over the map, tracing the most direct route south, through the Lone Star State. "We're gonna haul some buns, that's what, Punk."

Chapter 12

Laredo would have to be the southernmost part of Texas. The rest of the trip was a blur of day after day, mile after unending mile — six hundred and fifty of them. They pulled into Laredo with sore butts, chapped lips, and high hopes. Well, Mazey had hope, anyway.

The only thing CJ knew of Laredo was an old '45 her mom had played when she was little, so she'd expected a dusty little border town. Instead, they found a bustling city of commerce and a quarter-million people.

She skirted the downtown skyline and rode to a campground outside the edge of town that they'd researched the night before. It was a part of a national chain, with a small café attached to the office, a pool, and 'Kampin' Kabins'. CJ didn't want Mazey with her on her detective forays, so she rented one of the tiny cabins for a week, wanting a deadbolt between her sister and the rest of the campground.

The woman checked them in and told them there would be an ice cream social that evening before sundown.

Walking back to the bike, Mazey stopped to watch some raucous kids splashing in the pool. "I like this place. It's friendly."

CJ swiped sweat from the back of her neck. "I'm just glad we don't have to put in another long day tomorrow."

"Yeah, that too." Mazey rubbed her backside. "Can I walk to the cabin? My butt hurts."

"Mine too, Punk. Hey, after we get settled, you want to go swimming?"

"I'm in. Race you to the cabin!" Mazey took off on a foot path, dust puffing from her tennis shoes with every stride.

"No fair!" CJ jumped onto the bike and fired it up but had to stick to a sedate pace thanks to pedestrians on the paved drive that circled the grounds. There were very few tents in the trees by the road, but the campground was almost full of behemoth RVs in every shape and color. The cabins were on the back row, facing a golden pasture. The last slot before the cabins drew her eye because it didn't hold an RV. A rusted-out ranchero with a camper top and a blue plastic tarp draped across the back took up less than half the space. A bent old man sat in a nylon web chair, poking charcoal in the grill with a stick. On top was a cheap can of beans. He looked up at her passing and waved his stick. She waved back and pulled up to the row of red tiny houses with white trim where Mazey stood on the porch of #3. "Isn't this cute?"

CJ shut down the engine and threw a leg over. "Let's see." Inside was all pine, lit to a warm glow by a long window set high in the wall. There was a tiny table and two chairs, a small TV on the wall above it. A sink and a counter with a coffeemaker and a microwave took up the right wall. Ahead to the left was an alcove with a bunk bed, and to the right, an opening that led to a tiny bathroom. "It's small, but it looks like it's got everything we need."

Mazey twirled in the middle of the floor. "It's adorable. Like a 'Barbie goes glamping' house!"

CJ smiled. "Well, I'm glad you like it, because it's home for a while. Now, let's get Lola unpacked so you can get in the pool."

"You're not swimming?"

She thought about the scars on her thighs and shook her head. "I'll just sit on a lounge chair and see what else I can find online about Beau Brown."

~~~

That night began with the good dream. The one that almost made the others worth it. They'd taken a break under her rigged-up misters, drinking ice water and telling lies.

"You can't be Mafia, you're Irish," Mateo said.

"What, you never heard of the Irish Mob?" Eddie leaned back in his camp chair and put his feet up on a carton of air filters. "We make those dudes look like priests. Nobody messes with the North End."

"Nah, you're gonna go home and net mackerel with your old man. Admit it." Logan took off his camo cap and ran his hand over his glistening, bristly scalp.

Eddie shook his head. "Nayuh. Not me."

"Why not?" she asked.

Eddie's chest expanded on his inhale. He shook his head.

Mateo cocked his head like an inquisitive parrot. "You don't get seasick, do ya?"

"Not me." Red spread up from Eddie's T-shirt, staining his cheeks and the tips of his ears.

"Oh hell yeah, you do." Logan laughed. "Man, you got some bad karma, bein' born the son of a fisherman."

"I don't!" Eddie played with a ragged cuticle. "Just don't like it, that's all. All that dark water. No tellin' what's down there, lookin' up."

"I don't like dark water either," CJ said. "I live two hours from the ocean, and I never go."

"Wimps," Mateo said in a faraway voice. "When we hit the Cali coast on our trip, I'm running in, clothes and all."

"Just don't ride the bike in. Salt'll eat up that mutha'," Logan said.

"I can't wait," CJ said. "This trip'll be epic."

"Band of brothers, for sure," Mateo said.

"Well, brothers and one sister." Logan winked at her.

"Family, anyway," Eddie said.

"Family for sure," Mateo said. "Well, time to get our asses back to work 'fore the sarge comes and chews 'em."

CJ sat a few moments longer, basking in the glow of belonging.

Night. The winter wind whipped sand across the desert, stinging her eyes. The Humvee's engine vibrated beneath her, and the guys' laughter barely reached her ears from the back seat. A feeling of foreboding slithered over her skin, and the fear in her rose to let it in. *No, no, no, not here, not now!*

CJ woke when her head smacked the ceiling above her bunk. "GodDAMMit!" Her fingers found the beginning of a goose egg, but no stickiness.

"Bad dream again?" Mazey's small voice came from the lower bunk.

"It's okay, Punk. Go back to sleep." The sliver of sky through the long window showed purple with a tinge of pink at the bottom.

Bedclothes rustled. "Almost time to get up anyway."

CJ crawled to the edge of her narrow bunk and dropped to the floor. "They could'a given six more inches of clearance."

"I told you I'd take the top bunk. I'm littler."

Mazey's rumpled hair and sleepy eyes made CJ smile. "I may take you up on that tonight." She sat on the edge of the bed.

Mazey lifted the covers. "Come on in."

What the hell. She crawled in and let her sister's closeness banish the last wisps of the nightmare. She relaxed into the pillow. She was so tired. Like that song about running against the wind, all she wanted to do was find shelter, lay down her burden, and rest. But it seemed a long way from where she was now. Until then, she'd have to make do with moments like these, minutes of closeness stolen from someone who didn't know better than to let a sinner in.

Mazey's arm snaked around her neck. "What would happen if you let them go?"

The words hit harder than the ceiling. She tensed. "No can do, Punk."

"They're *gone*, CJ. And holding on hurts you."

"They were my brothers. I owe them."

"Wouldn't they want you to be hap—"

"How does fruit and waffles sound?" She threw the covers back and abandoned her shelter. "Gotta love having a fridge, huh?" She headed for the bathroom, and the blade that would bleed off a bit anguish.

An hour later, dressed and at the table with pancakes and milk in front of her, Mazey asked, "Since you won't let me come with you, can you drop me at a library on your way?"

"You've got your e-reader." She tipped her chin at the ever-present device beside Mazey's plate.

"Yeah, but for astronomy you need pictures."

The thought of leaving Mazey alone in a public place sent a shiver of skittishness down her spine. "I don't know. I could be gone a couple of hours."

Mazey clicked her tongue and rolled her eyes. "Yeah, like that would be horrible."

"Okay, we'll check it out."

"Jeez, you act like I'm a baby. How did I survive all those years when you weren't around?"

"Got me. It's a miracle." She ruffled Mazey's hair.

Mazey looked up directions to the downtown branch of the Laredo library on the phone and navigated from the back seat. They walked into the old building smelling of books and floor wax and stepped to the checkout desk. A thin woman with pearls and gray hair looked up.

"Hi," Mazey said, clutching a notebook in front of her. "I know Astronomy is in the 520s, and Geology is in the 550s, but where would I find Physics?"

The woman's brows went up. "540." She pointed down a towering book-lined aisle.

"Thanks." Mazey half-skipped away.

The librarian watched her go, then turned to CJ. "How can I help you?"

"I was wondering…if you could just keep an eye on her? I'll be back in an hour or so."

The woman's nose flared on her exhale. "Babysitting is not in my job description. If you want—"

"Look, have you ever had a nine-year-old ask you where the physics section was? She does not need a babysitter." CJ squirmed inside. She hated leaving Mazey, especially after the disaster at the campground, but she needed this woman's help. "We're from out of town, and I'm just asking you to keep an eye out if someone tries to kidnap her from your building. Okay?"

The librarian looked down the aisle where Mazey disappeared. "All right. I can do that much."

"Thank you." God, this was hard. "Very much." She forced her feet to the door.

She'd decided to start where Beau Brown lived; a home could tell you a lot about a person. Though, when she thought about it, she and Mazey had come from the same house and couldn't be more different. But she had to start somewhere.

CJ drove, noticing the neighborhoods. Seemed to her they had colors. Downtown was charcoal: old streets with cracked-window corner marts, graffiti, blown litter, and a few abandoned cinderblock buildings. Anyone who lived there, it was because they couldn't get out. The outskirts of town were the gray of a cloud-covered day: small stuccoed houses like the places she'd grown up in, with dusty yards and dusty, old car-lined streets. A few houses were dressed in pink, turquoise, or lime green, but rather than cheerful they looked like tired streetwalkers in garish makeup.

Beau's neighborhood was dove gray with a sprinkle of glitter. The lots were larger, sprouting neat, one-story brick ranch homes. Yards were neatly mowed, with the occasional late model car in the drive.

She supposed there were sterling silver neighborhoods somewhere, but they'd be gated—beyond reach of the likes of her.

She turned onto Los Feliz Drive, wishing she was driving something more easily forgettable. A Camry maybe, or a Jetta. Nothing to be done about Lola, though. She cruised slowly, watching the mailbox numbers. Number 112 was typical for the neighborhood, a blond brick ranch, the driveway terminating at a garage with a picture-windowed second story. The deep green yard looked as though a weed wouldn't dare venture over the property line. The hanging planters out front dripped colorful annuals. Her heart jolted. A slim woman in a straw sunhat knelt by one of the beds, digging with a small spade, a flat of plants beside her. She looked up and gave a little wave. Bright white teeth, blonde hair in a braid, sleeveless white blouse, and capris, she looked like a model in a magazine ad. He'd sure traded up from Patsy. CJ waved and kept to her sedate pace until she turned the corner.

Beau's wife didn't work? His business must be making good money.

She checked the time and decided to ride by Beau's shop before picking up Mazey. She followed the directions she'd written on a small piece of paper this morning and taped to the inside of the windscreen. The boulevard was broad and lined with car dealerships. The body shop was tucked between, a one-story brick with a window revealing a waiting room, and lots of bays busy with cars. The sign out front proclaimed it, 'Brown's Body & Paint'.

CJ knew Lola stood out like a zebra in a horse herd — she wouldn't be able to come by often without attracting attention, so she had to make this count. She pulled into an empty parking space, turned off the ignition and dismounted, rehearsing her lie as she walked to the door.

The air inside smelled of engine oil and rubber, and for a few sobbing heartbeats she took in the perfume of home. Well, it had been home until she slunk back from the Army. A thin man in a ponytail and tats on the backs of his hands looked up from a computer screen. "Can I help you, miss?"

Waxed floors, the clean windows, the stack of shiny wheels set up in a pyramid display against the wall. Neat, welcoming, and profitable from the look of it. She stepped to the counter. "Um, yes. I'm here to talk to someone about painting my bike."

The guy looked past her to Lola. "Oh, nice. Don't see a lot of Indians on the road nowadays."

"Yeah, old school, that's me."

He smiled. "You'll want to talk to the owner. He wouldn't let anyone else touch bike paint."

Oh shit. She'd planned to get the lay of the land first. But what could she say? She didn't want the best for her bike?

"Hold tight. I'll get him." He lifted the receiver on the desk phone, and his voice came over the loudspeaker: "Beau to the front desk, customer waiting."

CJ paced to the wheel display, changing her plan on the fly while chewing her lower lip.

Before she was ready, a deep voice came from behind her. "Can I help you?"

She turned. Beau Brown was tall, and broad through the shoulders. He wore a denim shirt tucked into jeans and work boots. Straight black hair just like Mazey's was combed back, but there was gray at the temples and his neatly trimmed goatee was salt and pepper. But what held her was his eyes. Soft, brown and...kind. She didn't trust that, of course, but it was the first word that popped to mind.

"Miss?"

"Oh, yes, sorry." She shook her head.

"Scott said you have a bike you want painted?"

"Yes, come outside, I'll show you." She led him to where Lola sat, dirty and road-weary. Now that they'd stopped for a bit, she'd need to get the oil changed and give her a good bath.

Beau circled the bike and squatted by the scratches in the tank. "Oh wow." He ran his fingers over them. "Almost looks like a bear did this."

CJ stuffed her hands in her back pockets. "It did."

His head snapped up. "Seriously?"

She nodded, brain working furiously on plan B. Or C. Anything that would extract information without seeming odd.

"Well what doesn't kill you makes for a good story, right?" He stood in one fluid motion. "You don't want to change the colors, do you? They're classic."

"No." She didn't even want to paint over the scratches, but she'd needed a cover story. "Nice business you have. Been here long?"

"In this location for five years. We were in a building downtown before that." He ran his hand over the seat like you'd pet a pretty horse. "Are you in a hurry to get this done?"

"No! I mean, um, not really." *Come on, Maxwell, get it together.* "Can I see some of your work? No offense, but—"

He held up his hands. "Hey, I get it. Bikes are personal."

"Do you ride?"

"Used to. My wife threatened me with death by nagging if I didn't quit after we married."

"Really?" She didn't even try to keep the scoff out of her voice. If he was a wimp, she could see why he didn't last around Patsy — she liked her men telling her what to do, not the other way around.

He shrugged. "Momma ain't happy, ain't nobody happy, right?"

"I'll take your word for it."

He led the way around the back to a metal sided building. Inside was a paint shop, and the reception walls were hung with several motorcycle tanks, painted with flames, skulls, howling wolves, dice, and an American Flag. He opened a binder on the desk. "Here are photos of the work we've done."

She leafed through it. Page after page of gorgeous bikes. This guy was really good.

"You live nearby?"

"No. I'm just visiting." She closed the book.

"How long are you here for?" His gaze roamed her face.

She looked up, wary. "Why?"

"Well, if I can't get to the bike for…" He walked behind the counter and clicked a keyboard. "Three weeks. Will you still be here?"

"Um, I guess I could do that." Didn't really matter. She didn't intend to paint Lola anyway.

"Okay, do you just want the tank restored to original? Though if I were you, I'd do something different."

"What do you mean?"

I think this would be cool." He grabbed a small pad of paper and a pencil and sketched for a few moments, then pushed the pad across the desk to her. Above the scratches, he'd drawn a bear paw print, and lettering in a circle around it that read, 'Bear tested. Bear tough.'

"Oh I love that!" It burst out of her on a laugh. Very clever, this man.

"So, can I book you?"

"Um. I'll have to check. Do you have a card so I can call you?"

"Sure." He pulled out his wallet and handed over his business card.

"Okay, thanks. Talk to you later." She strode for the door. She didn't trust his clean-cut nice-guy routine for a minute (he had been Patsy's boyfriend, after all), but she had to admit he was talented. Not hard to see why he was doing so well.

But that didn't make him good enough to meet Mazey.

Even speeding, it took fifteen minutes to get back to the library. She spent the whole time picturing awful scenarios: Mazey harassed by homeless men, accosted in the bathroom... She jogged up the steps and into the reception area.

The librarian crooked a finger at CJ, a stern look on her long face.

Heart racing, CJ hurried over. "Is Mazey okay? Have you seen her recently? Where—"

"She's fine, embroiled in thermodynamics at the moment." She raised an eyebrow. "Your sister is an intelligent, polite, and precocious young woman. Very rare these days. Any time you bring her in, I'll be happy to help her."

CJ had been so tied up in doomsday scenarios, it took a moment for that to sink in. "Th-Thank you. Though no one but Mazey gets credit for that. She's an amazing kid."

"CJ!" Mazey ran up, arms full of books. "What did you find out?"

"We'll talk about that in a bit, Punk." She ruffled her sister's hair.

"I'm sorry, Mazey, but we don't allow reference books to be checked out. But would you like to apply for a library card?"

Mazey reached up and set the stack of books on the desk. "We don't live here." Her gaze lingered on the books like she was leaving her friends. "But can we come back sometime, CJ?"

"Of course we can. Now, you ready for some lunch? I'm starving."

"Me too." She waved to the librarian, then put her arm around her sister. "Let's go."

Chapter 13

Mazey sat across the plastic fast food table, hands clasped to fists, a yearning in her eyes that tugged at CJ's ragged heart. "I've thought hard about this. But you've proved to be mature for the most part on this trip, so I'm not going to hold anything back. Whatever I find out about your dad, I'm going to tell you."

The smile that broke was so bright it made CJ blink.

"But." She held up a finger. "Don't forget, you agreed to abide by my decision at the end of this."

"I will, promise. Now tell me what you found out."

She did, giving not only facts but her impressions as well.

Mazey was so rapt, CJ had to remind her several times to eat her burger.

"I knew it, I told you he was a good guy!"

"Not so fast, Punk. I was with him all of fifteen minutes. It's gonna take a lot more than that—"

"I know, but I'm just saying. I *know*."

Mazey was so naïve, she hadn't known Blade was a slime. How the heck could she know anything about a guy she'd never met? Wishing on one of her stars would be about as likely to make that dream come true. But seeing her sister happy made CJ glad of it. Let her believe as long as she could — innocence was way too rare in this world to be anything but precious.

"What comes next?" Mazey asked.

"Once you've digested a bit, how about a swim?" CJ wadded up the paper her burger came in.

"No, I mean, what's the plan? How are you going to find out more?"

"That's what I'm going to work on while you're swimming."

Mazey's smile lowered. "You're never going to swim with me? You're not afraid of water, are you?"

"What? No."

"Then why not?"

She'd always liked to swim but couldn't remember the last time she'd been in a pool — before the Army, for sure. She could buy spandex bike shorts to cover her shame. "Maybe I will. I'll need to stop at a sporting goods store on the way back, though."

Mazey hopped up. "Waiting on you, slowpoke."

The afternoon was a blast. They messed around in the pool, CJ launching Mazey off her thighs, splashing each other and having fun. *Fun.* When had she let herself go to just have fun? When she remembered, her mood went into freefall. The softball games on the base.

Mazey teased CJ back from the sadness by imitating the preening of the teen girl lifeguard. When someone set up a water volleyball net, they joined in the spirited competition.

The sun was nearing the horizon when they got out — cold, pruney, and happy. CJ wrapped Mazey in a towel and rubbed to warm her. They toed into their shower shoes and walked home, chatting about the day, CJ taking deep lungfuls of the smell of chlorine and summer sunshine, not even begrudging the sting of sunburn on her shoulders.

~~~

The next morning after breakfast, Mazey asked if she could wait at the library again. CJ thought she'd probably be safer there. She couldn't expect Mazey to sit in the tiny cabin all day, and she knew the lure of the pool would be strong. She didn't want Mazey there without her supervision — that lifeguard was more concerned about her tan line than watching the kids.

Now CJ just had to figure out how to get more intel. She'd love to talk to some of Beau's employees, but she couldn't just walk in there and start asking questions.

She left Mazey at the library, deep in a discussion with Ms. Carter, the librarian, about microfiche.

CJ couldn't scout the house again so soon, so she headed for Brown's Autobody. Across the street from the auto mall she spied a coffeeshop. She decided to stop, since she was out of brilliant ideas. Maybe his employees would stop in for a caffeine hit, or a sandwich at lunch. She parked behind the building. Lola was anything but forgettable.

Three hours, five cups of coffee, and many internet pages scrolled later she got lucky. The guy behind Beau's counter yesterday walked in. Adrenaline dumped into the caffeine in her veins—she popped up and scooted into line behind him. "Hey, how you doing?"

He turned. "Hey."

"I came into Beau's yesterday, remember?"

"Oh yeah. The lady with the Indian."

"Yep. How do you like working there?"

"It's all good."

Great. A man of few words.

"Is Beau a good boss?"

"The best."

"How so?"

Scott lifted a 'what's it to you?' eyebrow.

"Hey, my bike is my baby. I want to be sure he's a good guy." Jeez, that was lame.

He hesitated long enough that she thought he wouldn't answer. Then he took a deep breath and shot a look around. "He hired me right out of prison."

Alarm shot down her spine.

He must have noticed her flinch. "Nothing violent. I just got behind on my child support payments."

"Oh." She relaxed.

A gap opened and they stepped up. Scott was now second in line.

"Beau took me down to the courthouse and paid my back payments. I got a side hustle but it's probably going to take a couple years to pay him back, and he says he's okay with that. *That's* the kinda guy he is." He turned away, but then turned back. "Oh, and he coaches my son's soccer team."

She tucked her hands into her back pockets. "Wow, sounds like a saint."

"In my book, he is."

The last woman ahead of them walked away, and he stepped to the register and ordered. When he had his food he turned, nodded to her, and walked out.

She ordered to-go sandwiches for her and Mazey.

For all her digging for dirt, she had to admit that Beau Brown did look like a saint. But saints don't have records, and lawsuits, and God knows what else — everyone had a side that wouldn't show up on the internet.

Over lunch in their cozy kitchen, CJ brought Mazey up to date on what she'd learned from Scott today.

Mazey's smile was smug.

"Nobody's perfect, Punk."

"I'm not looking for perfect. I'm looking for a good dad who'll love me." She put her nose in her e-reader.

Would Beau love Mazey, or see her as an unfortunate mistake? That was the big question, one that couldn't be answered until she met him. But CJ wasn't anywhere close to allowing that, and the clock in her head was ticking the hours until they had to leave for Mazey's other parent. The one whose idea of love was flat messed up.

And CJ didn't have a clue how to get from where they were to allowing Mazey and Beau to meet. All she knew was, she didn't want Mazey's innocent belief getting crushed by a loser rejecting her. That bore thinking about. "We can't swim for an hour. You okay if I go for a run?"

"I'll just stay and read."

CJ changed to knee-length, cut-off sweat shorts and a T-shirt in the bathroom, then walked to the door. "Be sure you lock this behind me now."

Mazey didn't look up. "Yes, mother."

CJ stepped outside, took a deep breath and a couple of stretches, then took off. She followed the paved drive around the campground until a path appeared on her right. She veered onto it and sped up. The land was flat and dressed in brushy chaparral. She flew across the landscape, fine dust puffing with every step, breath coming harder than usual. She needed to find a way to run more often. It cleared her mind and her body, the only way she knew to release the tension that built like the simmering of an unquiet volcano. Besides cutting. She needed to stop that. Allow her thighs to heal. She ran out two miles and when she turned back, sweat ran down her face and arms, making tracks in the gritty dust. A swim was going to feel good.

When her feet hit the road around the campground, she slowed to a walk.

"You active?"

She looked up. The old man with the rusty Ranchero sat in the same chair, with hopefully a different can of beans on the grill. "Pardon?"

"Military. You active?"

Her heart, which had settled into a trot, surged to a gallop. "Not any more. How did you know?"

He grinned. Well, the top half of his mouth did. The bottom half was caved in, as if missing a denture plate.

"Takes one to know one. Once you learn to march, it never really leaves you." He pointed his stick. "Your hands."

She looked down. Her fingers were curled tight, her thumb over the index finger. She'd never noticed she still did that.

"What branch?"

She was anything but comfortable with the subject but didn't want to be rude. "Army."

"Hooah. Come on over."

She stepped to the edge of the tarmac, but her feet would carry her no farther.

"Name's Murph."

"I'm CJ. Where did you serve?" She itched to leave, but the brotherhood of military etiquette was ingrained.

He pointed to his hat. It read *Korean Veteran*, and on the bill: 'Sergeant, 9th Infantry'.

"Damn tough station."

"It was. I see you had it bad, too."

She jerked back so hard her spine clicked.

"It's in the eyes." He took a spoon and stirred the beans. "Told you, takes one to know one."

"Yes, sir. If you'll excuse me, I have to get back to my sister."

"Stop by if you want to chew the fat sometime."

"Will do, sir." She double-timed it back to the cabin, feeling like she ran naked.

~~~

The next day was a bust. After CJ dropped Mazey at the library she rode downtown, stopping at the Chamber of Commerce. The lady there could only tell her that Beau was a member in good standing. She stopped by the courthouse and looked up his property tax records, and the recording of the deed on his home. She walked back to the bike, shaking her head. Dry as dust old records. What the heck had she expected to uncover, a Washington-sized scandal? This was a dead-end. What next? She had wracked her brain, but short of marching Mazey in and introducing them she'd used up her options. Then, remembering, she stopped at a motorcycle shop and had Lola's oil changed.

She was sitting in the sun in a metal chair while she waited. Her phone rang, but it wasn't a number she recognized. "Hello?"

"CJ, it's Beau Brown. The paint guy? I just wanted to let you know I had a cancellation, so I can get to your bike today if you can bring it in."

She glanced up at the sky. *If* someone was up there, he was messing with her. "Um… hang on." Her brain smoked through options, but finally decided. She liked his design, and it would make a neat reminder of the trip. "Sure. I can drop it by this afternoon. But I'll have to arrange a rental. Do you know where—"

"Don't worry about it. I've got a loaner here. Not pretty to look at, but it's reliable."

"Wow, that'd be great."

"Okay, I'll be expecting you."

She clicked 'end'. The missing step had just fallen into her lap. If she took Mazey with her, it would be a chance to see how he was around kids anyway. It might work — as long as Mazey kept her promise, and her mouth shut.

She walked into the library to find Mazey scanning a bulletin board by the front door.

"CJ, come look." She pointed to what looked like a wanted poster but turned out to be about a missing person. "Isn't that the old guy at the campground?"

CJ leaned in. "It looks like him, but he said his name was Murph. Probably short for Murphy. This guy's name is Peter Stanislavsky."

"But maybe he changed his name. Or gave you a fake one. Look at the photo. It's him."

It was, right down to the missing teeth and the Korean War Veteran cap.

"It says he's been gone over a month. Wonder why they didn't put out a Silver Alert for him?"

"There might have been, Punk. We're not exactly plugged into the local news." She put her arm around Mazey's neck. "I'll ask him. Now, how'd you like to meet your dad?"

"Whaaat?" she screeched.

"SHH!" the librarian hissed from the circulation desk.

"Sorry, Ms. Carter," Mazey stage-whispered, grabbed her sister's arm, and dragged her outside.

Mazey bounced on the seat all the way to the shop. CJ pulled in, dismounted, and grabbed her sister's arm when she would have run ahead. "Hang on, bullet train." She waited until Mazey's gaze fell on her. "Remember your promise. You're not going to say anything to give away who you are. You're going to speak only when spoken to. Got it?"

"Got it." But she was already looking beyond CJ to the shop.

"Punk." She shook her sister's arm to get her attention. "I'm serious. This is really important, and rushing could screw everything up."

"I *know,* CJ."

CJ hesitated, searching the depths of Mazey's eyes, looking for subterfuge. She didn't see anything but joy.

"Can we go before they close for the day? Please?"

"Okay. But stay with me."

"Yes sir." She saluted, and executed a perfect about-face.

They walked to the paint shop hand-in-hand, CJ's heart slamming, Mazey's breath coming hard. CJ paused, hand on the door. "You ready?"

Mazey swallowed. "I've been ready for nine years."

CJ pulled the door and walked into paint fumes and cool air.

"Wow." Mazey's eyes went big, seeing the bike tanks on the wall.

"Yeah, he's good."

Beau walked around the corner, wiping paint spattered hands on a rag. "There you are." He glanced to Mazey. "Who's this?"

"This is—"

"Your daughter," Mazey said.

He froze, head cocked.

CJ spun. "Seriously?"

Mazey just shrugged and walked the few steps to her father. "I'm Mazey. I'm nine. My mom is Patsy Newsome."

It was like someone had cut Beau's facial nerves — his slack mouth fell open a bit. But his eyes... they changed from milk to dark chocolate, like Mazey's did when emotion swirled in. His gaze took her in, from tennis shoes to cowlick. Then his eyes narrowed, and his lips thinned to a ruthless line. "The hell you say."

CJ snapped to attention and took a step that put her sister behind her. "It's true. Do the math."

"You waltz in here off the street and...did *she* send you?"

Alarms went off in CJ's head. "You mean Patsy? She doesn't even know we're here."

"What do you want? Money? Is that why you came?" He raked his hand through his hair, loosening a chunk to fall to his forehead.

She took a step back onto Mazey's tennis shoe and stumbled a bit. It gave shock time to turn to anger. "No. Your daughter just wanted to meet her father. She's been telling me for weeks what a great guy he would be. I warned her what to expect from yet another of Patsy's losers, but hey, she's nine." She shrugged. "I guess she had to grow up and live in the real world sometime. Thanks for the lesson,

Dad." She turned to her sister. The quiver in her lower lip and anguish in her eyes was like gasoline on the fire in CJ's chest, and she turned back. "Fuck you. Thanks for nothing." She put her arm around Mazey. "Let's go, Punk. You don't need him."

They were almost gone, when the voice came from behind. "Hey, wait a min—" The door closed on the rest.

At the bike, Mazey stood head down. "I'm sorry, CJ. I didn't mean to say it." Her hands twisted at her side. "I know, that's two lies I've told. But it just was there, inside me, and it busted out. I couldn't hold it back, CJ, I promise. Please don't hate me."

She understood well how hard things inside fought to get out. Who was she to judge Mazey, when she couldn't keep her own demons inside? "I could never hate you, Punk. I love you more than anyone on the planet."

Back at the cabin CJ asked if Mazey wanted to go to the pool, hoping to distract her from the disaster.

She walked to her rumpled bed. "No, thanks. I think I'm just going to take a nap."

CJ followed her. She didn't like that lifeless expression. Her sister was never unexpressive. It scared her. "Me too." She pulled off her tennis shoes. "Scoot over."

Mazey lifted the covers. CJ slid in and put her arm under her sister's head, trying to telegraph empathy and support. There was nothing to say that the sperm donor hadn't already said; nothing could make it better.

Yet another mistake chalked up on CJ's list for the afterlife (if there was one). Sure Mazey pushed and bugged, but CJ was the grown up. She never should have—

"Tell me a bedtime story." Mazey settled her head on CJ's chest, her voice much younger than a nine-year-old's.

"Well, let me think." She scrambled through her memories for one with a happy ending. "Okay, here's one. We had softball teams on base over there. Helped us stay in shape and relieved the boredom. Me and the guys wrangled our way onto the same team — the Brew Crew." She smiled at the wistful memory. "We made up rules, and the whole league adopted them. We had our priorities — everyone was drinking beer, and if a fly ball knocked over a can it was an automatic out. Eddie was our shortstop, I was catcher, Logan pitched, and Mateo was in the outfield.

"One day, we were playing the Cereal Killers. Or maybe it was the Hit for Brains, I don't remember."

Mazey's snort of laugher was her reward.

"The score was tied, bottom of the ninth, two out. Their heavy hitter was up, and after two balls cracked one into deep center field. Mateo lost it in the sun, and it bounced off the tip of his glove. He runs for it, while their guy is ripping around the bases. Luckily, the guy wasn't fast. Mateo lined it to Eddie, Logan ducked on the mound, and Eddie smoked it to me, standing over home plate. He was just a heartbeat too late. The guy slid home, took my legs out from under me, and we fell in a heap, dust billowed. Their team is going crazy, jumping around, yelling that they won. And they had. Until…"

"What?"

"His right foot hit my beer on the way by. He was out. But the other team swore it was my foot that trashed the beer, not their guy's. The benches cleared, guys were in each other's faces, and it was about to get rough. Until the ump yelled, 'Heeee's *out!*'"

"Your team won?"

I chuckle. "Big time."

"That was a good story."

She was not about to tell Mazey about the celebrating that night or working with a massive hangover the next day. "So now, go to sleep."

When her breathing evened out to tiny snores, CJ gently shifted her and got out of bed. Poor punk. The fact that CJ'd been right all along did not help. She ached for yet more innocence lost. She lifted her phone from the kitchen table and turned it on, after checking to be sure it was on silent. She'd turned it off when they left the body shop.

Several missed calls and one voice mail, all from a Laredo area code. She glanced to the lump in the covers of the bottom bunk. She could ignore it. Delete the voice mail without ever listening; Mazey would never know what Brown had to say. They'd pack up in the morning and head for California, and Patsy's next adventure, in missteps.

Or CJ could listen, then decide if she'd tell Mazey or not. Yeah, that sounded right. She tiptoed to the door, slipped out, and closed the door softly behind her.

The late afternoon sun fell hard onto the tiny porch, making CJ squint to see the screen. When she found it, she hit the button to retrieve the message.

"CJ. This is Beau Brown. Listen, I was poleaxed today, okay? You gotta admit, you just kinda dropped a bomb and walked away. I've had time to absorb the news and do the math, but really, after seeing Mazey, I hardly need a DNA test to know she's mine.

After how I reacted, you probably don't want to hear from me again. I can explain, but it's gonna take some time and I don't really want to do it over the phone. Could we meet somewhere? If you don't want Mazey there I understand, but please, will you call me back? It'll all make sense when you hear the history, promise.

There's a lot at stake here for me, too, so please call me?

Okay, hope to hear from you.

Bye."

Chapter 14

CJ spent the next hour while Mazey napped, trying to decide. If she followed her instinct, it was a hard no. But her instincts sucked, and this was Mazey's future. When the door opened and Mazey's bedhead peeked out, she was no closer to a decision. "Hey, sleepyhead. Burgers for dinner. Then want to go swimming after?"

"Yeah, I guess." The life had gone out of her voice.

"Cheer up, Punk. You've got a whole new adventure waiting for you back in Bodfish."

Mazey shot her a look that said she feared for her sister's sanity, then closed the door.

"Guess I can't blame you there, kid." She sighed and followed her sister inside.

After dinner, they decided to do laundry while waiting for dinner to settle. CJ left Mazey in the laundry room with her e-reader and money for the dryer, then stopped at the cabin. She put the two leftover hamburger patties, buns, and small container of potato salad in a sack and walked to Murph's campsite. She wanted to be sure he had something besides beans to eat, but also wanted to find out if he really was AWOL.

He didn't appear to be there, though his truck was. "Murph? You around?" She walked to the picnic table and set down the bag. "Sarge?"

With a crinkle of plastic the blue tarp moved, and a pair of worn tennis shoes emerged, followed by the rest of

Murph. "CJ. Good to see you." He sat on the tailgate, blinking into the sunset for a few moments, then stood and, with an unsteady gait, walked over.

"I'm sorry, did I wake you?" She reached to help, but then dropped her hands. He seemed a proud old guy.

"Eh, anymore if I sit quiet for more than ten minutes, I fall asleep."

She raised the paper bag. "We had hamburgers for dinner and had leftovers. Didn't want it to go to waste..."

His grumbling stomach answered for him. He smiled. "Well, I can't very well argue with that, now can I? Will you eat with me?"

"Just ate, but I'll keep you company."

"You sit right there." He pointed to the picnic table. He emptied the bag and puttered around, getting a plastic fork and paper towel for a napkin.

"Do you mind if I ask you a personal question, sir?"

"Don't you sir me; I'm enlisted, same's you. And you can ask. Whether you get an answer's up to me." He sat and picked up the burger.

"I saw a notice today in the library about a missing person. The name was different, but it was you in the photo. Are you all right, sir — Murph?"

"Right as rain, child." He took a bite of hamburger.

That's when she noticed he was missing the index finger and half of the next on his right hand. "I just wanted to be sure, because it sounds like someone's missing you pretty bad."

He heaved a sigh that had a lot of weight in it. "My kids wanted me to go to one of those old folks' homes. I agreed. The only other option was getting passed from one of them to another like an old family Bible no one wants, but you can't throw out. And it's fine. Food is bland and the company blander, but that's okay. I'm not picky."

He turned to her. "But sometimes I need to keep my own company. To get out and remind myself I'm not completely used up yet, even if the kids think I am." He took a deep breath of summer air. "Get out in nature. See the Lord's work, up close. I'll go back, eventually." His bushy eyebrows came down, and he cut his eyes to her. "You're not going to turn me over to the enemy, are you?"

When he winked, she realized he was kidding. "No way, Sarge." He seemed mentally sharp, and except for living rough, he seemed capable. In the meantime, she'd keep an eye out.

"Murph is what my buds in Korea called me, 'cuz they couldn't pronounce Stanislavsky."

"Ah, I see."

"Now. I've trusted you with high-level intel. Your turn."

Alarm shot down her nerves.

"What happened over there to give you those mournful eyes?"

"I-I'm sorry. I promised my sister we'd go swimming." She stood and extricated herself from the picnic table bench. "I-I've got to go."

"Then you go, girl. Come back when you have time."

She felt his stare between her shoulder blades as she walked away. She wasn't ready to face talking about the desert. Not on top of Mazey's daddy issues. But she wasn't running from everything. She pulled her phone from her back pocket and dialed Beau Brown's number.

"CJ, thank you for calling. I wanted to—"

"Meet me. Tomorrow morning at..." She wanted a neutral, public place. "The St. Augustin Plaza, in front of the church."

"I'll be there. What time?"

"Ten."

"Okay. Will Mazey be with you?"

"Not if I can keep her away." She clicked 'end'.

The plaza was an old-time square surrounding a church from the founding of the town in 1755. They'd seen it on the way to the library but hadn't had time to explore it yet.

Mazey was back at the cabin, folding clothes, when CJ opened the door. She tightened her resolve and grabbed the bull by the horns. "I talked to Beau Brown."

"What?" Pink rose from her bathing suit top to mottle her neck.

"Yeah, he called."

"Well, what did he say?" Her jaw was tight, but CJ hated the hope in her eyes.

"He said we blindsided him with the news, and he wanted to talk."

"Well, we kinda did."

CJ stepped over and took the T-shirt from her sister's hand. "No, *you* did. Sit."

"And?" Her hands were fisted on the table.

"I'm meeting him tomorrow at ten."

"I'm going."

"No, you're not."

She threw her hands in the air. "I can't blurt this time — he knows everything."

"I'm not worried about what you'll say."

"Then why can't I go?"

"Look, Punk, we don't know what will happen. I'm not letting him hurt you again."

"Haven't you figured it out by now?" She didn't sound mad, or wheedling—she sounded sure. "You see me as too young just because I see the good things. But I handle bad stuff, too. The bullies at school, the nights all alone when Mom is out, the disappointments."

And here CJ had thought Mazey didn't notice those things. She noticed; she just didn't focus on them. A super-power coping skill CJ envied.

Mazey grabbed her sister's hand. "If Beau is a sleaze, I can handle it. If he doesn't ever want to see me again, I can handle it. What I can't handle is coming all this way and then leaving without knowing."

"You already know. You were there today."

"But he called back, CJ. Why would he do that if everything wasn't said yet?"

"I don't know. We'll find out tomorrow."

"Right. We." It wasn't a question.

She sighed. "Yeah, I guess you deserve that much. I just hope I don't have to pick up the pieces after."

Mazey hugged her neck. "Thank you, thank you, CJ. You'll see, it'll be fine."

It could be a lot of things, but fine wasn't one of the outcomes she'd bet on. "Yeah, yeah. Now, are we going swimming or what?"

~~~

Mazey was up with the dawn the next morning. Around eight, CJ finally got tired of being stared at and got up. She managed to avoid her razor when she took her shower — which made it a good day already. She pulled on jeans and a T-shirt, and when she stepped out of the coffin-sized bathroom Mazey had breakfast of cereal already on the table, and a hot cup of coffee for CJ. "You trying to soften me up or what?"

Mazey held a chair out for her sister. "No. Just a thank-you."

"You're welcome. Now, sit and eat."

By the time they cleaned up the meal and straightened the cabin, it was time to leave. Early, but CJ wanted to arrive first. She helped Mazey with the chin strap of her helmet. "I need to tell you some things. Important things, so listen up."

"Okay."

"You are going to be a silent observer. I agreed that you can be there, but you will say nothing until and unless I tell you it's okay to talk. Is that clear?"

Mazey nodded.

"I need to hear you say it. You've ignored me twice before, and this is too important for you to do it again." She held up a hand when Mazey would have said something. "Not only that. No squeals, sighs, or anything else that lets him know what you think or feel. I mean it, Amazing Grace Newsome. No 'mistakes' this time."

"Okay, CJ."

"If you do," She raised a finger. "We are coming right back here, packing, and hitting the road for California. Today. Do you understand me?"

Mazey met her gaze. "Yes, ma'am."

Short of forcing her to take a blood oath, there was nothing else CJ could do. "Then let's go."

The weather was hot, but it was cooler on a bench under a tree facing the old church. Mazey fidgeted, and CJ tried not to. "Hey, Punk."

"Can I talk now?"

"Only until you see the whites of his eyes. Know what this old church reminds me?"

"What?"

"All the stuff it's seen since it was built. War, fire, shifting borders, and yet it's still standing."

"Yeah? So?"

"Well, that's one of your amazing things, right?"

"Gotta admit, it is. Thanks, CJ." She gave a lopsided smile.

"Just remember that. You'll still be standing at the end of today, no matter what happens."

Beau stepped out of a car that was parallel parked on the street. "Uh-oh, incoming."

Mazey's shoulders jerked and her spine snapped straight.

CJ stood. "Remember, not a word."

Mazey's lips pressed to a thin line and she slid her hands under her thighs.

Beau walked over and stopped in front of them. "CJ. Mazey." He waited. "Hello, Mazey."

"She's under a gag order," CJ said.

"Wow, that's cold."

"I think the fact that we're here makes that a lie. You wanted to say something?"

"I've spent hours thinking of what I want to say. But I imagine first, you're going to want to know about my record."

"Good place to start." CJ folded her hands across her chest.

He gestured to the bench. "Would you sit?"

She didn't want to give up the height advantage but didn't want to seem petty. Besides, Mazey could probably use the company. She sat.

"First, the assault conviction." He squatted and settled his butt on his heels. "It was a bar fight."

"That figures," CJ said.

"Hold judgement till the end, will ya?" He looked to Mazey. "Let me start at the beginning. I met Patsy at a bar, I'm pretty sure it was the day you left for camp, CJ. We talked for hours, and she took me home after last call." He held up a finger. "To talk. We sat at the kitchen table and talked all night. She was…so interesting. So free." He looked to the street, but CJ was sure he didn't see the traffic. "I admired her ambition, her can-do spirit, her…sparkle." He glanced to Mazey. "I think you inherited that sparkle."

What? Patsy had Mazey's love of life? CJ remembered no sparkle in Patsy, but she had a different perspective. A selective one. "And?"

"Days later, I realized that some of that sparkle was from drugs."

Mazey pulled one hand from under her leg and tugged CJ's T-shirt, her distress palpable.

But CJ remembered that summer. Patsy's moods had vacillated between lethargy and frenzy. CJ hadn't understood then but, looking back, she knew Beau was telling the truth. She patted her sister's knee. "She did that summer, Punk."

"It was Friday night. She wanted to go to the bar. I didn't. When she got frantic about it, I agreed to go. She was antsy and distracted, until she saw a sketchy dude at the pool table. She said she'd be right back and went to him. They talked for a minute until he went back to playing pool. She grabbed his arm, and he swung around. The pool cue hit her in the side." He ran his hand through his hair, in what CJ was coming to realize was a reaction to stress. "I was there in a heartbeat, quick enough to overhear that she was trying to score drugs...with no money. The guy didn't appreciate my interruption. He punched me, and it was game on.

"When he threw a wild punch that hit Patsy, the whole bar joined the fight. When the cops showed and broke it up, several bystanders told him it started with me and that dude. They put the cuffs on me, but the dealer was long gone. Probably didn't want to get caught with stuff on him.

"Because Patsy wasn't talking and the guy was in the wind, the battery charge was dropped but the assault charge stuck. I got ten months, and a three thousand dollar fine — I was out in six."

"Why did you leave town without picking up your last paycheck?"

"If you've ever been in jail, you wouldn't have to ask that. I wanted to as get far away as fast as I could. I never looked back." His gaze strayed to Mazey. "Until now."

Birds argued in the tree overhead, and the church bells chimed the hour.

CJ vowed to worm verification of his story from Patsy, even if she had to nag her to death to get it. "And the fraud charge?"

He pushed to his feet and paced a few steps, turned, and paced back. "That was me being young and naïve. I learned auto body work from my dad as a kid. I kept traveling for a few years after Reno, working here and there, moving on when it suited me. I landed a good job in Albuquerque, working for a guy with a string of body shops. He liked my work, and after only a few months he offered me a partnership. Said the business was getting too big for him to handle alone. I'd manage the guys in the shop and he'd handle the customer service and the books. I told him I had no money to invest, but he said he didn't need money — he needed someone he trusted, and he'd take a chance on me.

"I figured this was my chance to move up, a stepping stone to having a shop of my own one day." He shook his head. "I worked my a — butt off. I got the shop humming, and the employees were happy and doing good work."

CJ could guess what was coming.

"Everything was great until the sheriff showed up one day, serving papers for the partners to appear in court for a case of fraud. I asked my 'partner' to explain, and he said he would the next day — he had a pressing appointment." Beau chuckled. "It must have been pressing, because he hopped the river to Mexico that afternoon with everything in the bank account. No one has seen him since."

"Oh, that's awful," CJ said, then wished she could bite back her words. He could be whitewashing the whole story.

"He'd been estimating low, then inflating bills and charging for parts that weren't even used. The word got out, because the next week there were three more fraud cases. I testified but they didn't believe I knew nothing of what was going on, and since my partner had vanished it all came down on me. He set me up, then left me holding the bag of snakes." He held up his hands. "I'm not whining. I *was* legally a partner, and since I was too dumb to look in a gift horse's mouth I guess I deserved it. I was just lucky that it only took the total assets left in the company and every penny I'd saved to settle the cases." He stopped in front of CJ. "Scoot over. I gotta sit down."

CJ moved so he had space beside her, not between them. "If that's all true, I'm sorry."

He frowned at her. "What made you such a skeptic?"

"Twenty-some-years' worth of Patsy's boyfriends."

"Is she still doing drugs?"

"No. Her addiction is sleazy men."

"Thanks."

"No, I didn't mean…" She realized her words make it sound like she'd already made up her mind. "So tell the rest. How did you wind up in Laredo?"

"I headed south after Albuquerque, just drifting, looking for somewhere warm to settle. I hit town and stopped in to eat at The Pit Boss, a barbeque place. I knew I'd found my new home when the manager stopped by to see how my meal was. I fell in love right there, but it took a year to convince Linda to marry me." He smiled. "I worked two jobs and saved every penny until I could open my own shop, four years ago. I'm not rich but we're comfortable, business is good, and I'm happy." He leaned forward, rested his elbows on his knees. Eyes downcast, his smile melted. "Shortly after we married, we discovered that Linda couldn't have children. We'd planned to single-handedly raise a football team, and the cheerleading squad to go with, so it was the hardest thing for both of us." His gaze found Mazey again. "You coming here is a miracle."

CJ snapped like a pit bull on a chain. "Stop." She put a hand on Mazey's leg and squeezed, in case she was tempted to forget her promise. "You could be feeding us a total line. You've had an entire day to concoct this story."

"You're right. I could. So how are you going to know that I'm telling the truth?"

CJ only knew of one way. To somehow get the truth from Patsy. "We need some time."

He stood. "I get that. But CJ—" He spoke to her, but his attention was on his daughter. "Please give me a chance. Give us a chance. This means more than you can know."

She glanced at her sister. "You're not the only one with high stakes here. I only want what's best for Mazey. Mazey's all that matters."

He nodded. "I agree. I'll wait to hear from you."

"Come on, Punk." CJ stood and put a hand down for her sister. Holding hands they walked to the bike, Mazey looking over her shoulder now and again to where her father sat, gazing after them.

When they got to the bike, CJ stopped. "Thank you for following my instructions. I know it must have been hard for you."

Mazey looked up at her, eyes swimming. "What now, CJ?"

"Let's get out of here first." She drove out of town and pulled off at a picnic table on a quiet stretch of road overlooking the Rio Grande as it wound lazy through the desert landscape. The only real green evident was the thirsty vegetation at its edges.

"Let's sit there." CJ pointed to the picnic table, and they shed their jackets and helmets.

CJ pulled out her phone and dialed a Facetime call. She wanted to see Patsy's face and wanted her to be able to see Mazey's.

"Cora Jean, you better not be calling to tell me you're not coming home." She looked tired, the lines around her mouth deeper.

"Hello, Patsy. I have Mazey here, and we just met with her father. We have questions."

"You what?" she screeched.

"We need to know what happened. Why he left." CJ kept her voice even, despite wanting to reach through the phone and shake her mother. "Please tell the truth. It's important."

"Well, that was a long time ago. I don't see what differ-ence—"

"Please, Mom?" Mazey's voice wobbled, and CJ patted her sister's leg.

"We have Beau's side. We need to hear it from you."

"Oh, for Christ's sake. It was a bar fight, okay? I hardly remember, only I ended up with a black eye the next day. Beau got hauled in, and did time. That's all I know."

"How did it start?"

"It was so long ago. I can't be expected to remember—"

"I know you were doing drugs that summer," CJ prompted.

"I wasn't—well it was nothing hard, just something to…." Her eyes darted. "Look, I don't owe you an explana-tion."

"You do, but we won't go there," CJ said. "Please, Patsy. Just tell us the truth. It's more important than you know. Were you friends with the guy who started it?"

"He was an… acquaintance."

"Was he a supplier?"

"Dammit, CJ! I will not sit for this cross-examination. I am your mother, not a witness." Her chin went up, her eye-brows came down. The picture of righteous indignation. "Now, when are you leaving to come home?"

CJ sighed. "When you said. We'll call you later." She hit 'end'.

"CJ?" Mazey's voice held hope and dread at the same time. Her bottom lip trembled.

"Yeah, she didn't say it, but we know it. Beau told the truth."

"Okay." The air from Mazey's exhale brushed CJ's face. "What now?"

"I don't know." She'd sensed that Beau was being honest but didn't want to trust such flimsy evidence. How would they know if the rest of what he said was true?

They sat and watched the dirty water drift by.

"I have an idea." She pulled up the internet investigation site, plugged in her credit card number, and the name and information she knew about Beau's partner from the auto body shop in Albuquerque.

In ten minutes, they had the answer. The trail ended at the lawsuit. There was no information after that—his partner was in the wind.

Mazey slapped her hand on the table. "I told you, CJ. He told the truth. He's a good guy."

"So far, Punk. So far. Let me think on this a while." He hadn't lied, but there was no way was she letting down her guard until she knew more. The future of the only innocent in the entire equation was on her shoulders, and CJ didn't intend to make another devastating mistake.

But then, she had never intended on making the first one.

Chapter 15

That evening, CJ sat once again at Murph's picnic table while he dug into her offering of the day: a pimento cheese sandwich. She was glad to see him eat — his color was better, and he was more alert than when she'd stopped by before.

"Dang, that's good. Haven't had one of these in decades." He took a sip of the energy drink she'd brought. When he'd finished half the sandwich, he put his elbows on the table. "I promised to tell you about this." He held up his right hand, displaying the missing one and a half digits.

She wasn't sure she wanted to hear the story.

"I'll save the rest for later." He wrapped up the remaining half to keep the flies off and set it aside. "You ever hear of Heartbreak Ridge?"

She shook her head.

"Big battle of the war. We'd been over there twelve months, and my unit had been in some hairy situations. We were tight. We watched out for each other. We were taking heavy fire coming from a machine gun nest upslope. I was closest so I pulled the ring on a grenade, took two running steps... and tripped." He rubbed his forehead. "Stupid. Too busy imagining myself as a hero to watch my footing. Luckily, I fell with my arm was extended or I wouldn't be here to tell about it."

CJ winced. "Damn."

"I argued with the surgeons, told them there was no reason I couldn't get back out there, but turned out Uncle Sam didn't want a right-hander with only two and a half fingers."

"I'm so sorry. That had to be hard to leave your buds."

"I was so ashamed, and I had no one to blame but me. They sent me to Walter Reed for physical and occupational therapy."

"Did it change the career you wanted to go in to?"

"That's the important part. I loved drawing all my life. Planned to be a draftsman, you know, buildings and such? Figured that dream was over. They made me do group head-shrink while I was recovering. Can you imagine? Sitting in a circle with amputees, blind guys, burn victims, and here I am, maimed by my own stupidity? I didn't talk for weeks, until they made me. Funny, though; once I said it out loud, it stopped tearing up things inside. Nobody judged me or thought any less of me, but it took me time to not think less of myself.

"In the meantime, the occupational therapist told me I could still be a draftsman if I could learn to use my left hand. He threw it out like some kind of challenge."

"Is that even possible?"

"Well, it wasn't easy. But it gave me something to focus on besides hating myself. I figured if I could do that, I'd have done something to be proud of."

"You did it, didn't you?"

A glint came to his eye when he smiled. "Thirty-five years. Ended up a Master Draftsman."

"Holy wow." She loved happy endings, even if they only happened to other people.

"But that's not why I'm tellin' you this." He waved a hand. "Point is, I was really down when I came back. Thought I had no choices—it felt hopeless. But I found that when I felt like I was out of options, I just needed to look on the ground for the ones I had discarded because they seemed impossible." His bushy white brows came together, and his faded blue eye lasered into her. "It might not be easy, but it *is* possible. You hear what I'm saying, girl?"

She swallowed to ease the tightness in her throat. It didn't help. "I hear you, Sarge."

CJ headed back to the cabin. Sarge sure was amazing. No one would know looking at his worn, dusty clothes and food-stained beard that he was a hero. He sure wouldn't claim the title, but CJ had a close-up view of how he'd felt back then and what it would take to get past it. Yeah, Hero with a capital 'H'. She could never be that strong. She hadn't had the guts to even consider what would happen when this trip was over and Mazey was settled back home. How do you reach out and grasp a future, when you didn't deserve one?

She stepped into the cabin to find that Mazey had fallen asleep reading at the table, her head resting on her arms. CJ couldn't help her smile any more than the pain spreading from her heart. God, she loved that kid. Mazey really was a miracle — so bright and beautiful and clean, despite where she'd come from.

CJ'd come from the same home yet turned out so very different. Even before Afghanistan, she hadn't had the… whatever Mazey had. Hope? Innocence? Sparkle? She guessed she couldn't blame everything on the war. But if you're not born with the ability to see the good side of things, how can you develop it later?

Probably about as likely as a guy with two and a half fingers making a living at drawing.

~~~

"So? Can we call my dad now?" Mazey shoved the last forkful of pancakes in her mouth.

She'd been up since dawn, and CJ'd taken her to an early opening restaurant for breakfast, to delay the inevitable question she wasn't any closer to having an answer to. CJ still didn't trust Beau, but didn't know how she'd get closer to trusting him without… getting closer. "I guess so, Punk." She took a sip of coffee, then pulled her phone out and dialed.

He picked up on the first ring. "CJ?"

"Yeah, and Mazey. I checked with Patsy last night, and it appears you're telling the truth about the past. But I've gotta be honest, I'm still not comfortable and I'm not sure how to do this."

"I am," Mazey stage-whispered.

"Well, you never did drop your bike off so I can paint it. Why don't you bring it by this morning, and we'll start there?"

"Okay, what time?"

"We're not open now, but I'm here, so if you come now, we won't be disturbed.."

"We're ready!" Mazey said

CJ held up a warning finger. "Okay, we'll be by in a bit." She hung up.

Mazey punched her fists in the air. "Let's go."

"Okay, but you need to know that I'm not letting down my guard. And you'd better behave."

Fifteen minutes later, they walked into the body shop.

Beau came around the counter. "Let's sit down and talk for a bit. I have questions, and I know you must, too." He walked to the next room and returned with three chairs. "I have water or soda."

"Soda, please," Mazey chirped.

"I'm good." CJ dropped her leather jacket on the floor, turned one of the chairs around, and straddled it.

Beau stepped behind the counter where he apparently had a compact fridge, because he came back with a cold soda he gave Mazey, then he sat.

"I waited *so* long to meet you," Mazey exclaimed.

"My wife and I stayed up talking for the longest time last night. She knew about that summer, but neither of us could have imagined you."

Mazey tucked her hands under her thighs in the first sign she was nervous. "So, it's okay? That I'm here?"

"Now that I've had a chance to get over the shock, it's more than okay. It's as if a prayer just walked in the door."

Claxons rang in CJ's brain. Sure, it *appeared* Mazey's dream had come true, but CJ knew that's not how dreams worked. "Hold up a minute. Moving kinda fast, here."

Beau turned his attention from his daughter for the first time since they'd walked in the door. "I'm sorry, CJ. This must be hard for you. I know you're trying to protect your sister."

And if she only knew how to do that, she'd feel a lot better.

"I have a question for you two, and I know it's a big ask." He sat. "Would you come to dinner at my house tonight? There's a lot to catch up on, and Linda so wants to meet you." He took a breath and glanced to CJ. "But if you're not comfortable, we could meet for dinner somewhere."

Shit. Mazey's biggest life event, and the decision is left in the hands of an incompetent. This is exactly why she hadn't wanted to take Mazey on this trip, in case it came down to something like this.

On one hand, it seemed a no-brainer. He was decent: on paper, according to his employee, and, if she were honest, in her dealings with him as well. No alarms going off, no red flags. But hell, she'd missed red flags before and look where she ended up.

Mazey didn't move, but the yearning in her eyes bored into CJ. The kid never complained about her lot in life, never asked for anything to be given to her. She kept her head down and worked for what she wanted. Whether this turned out good or bad, could CJ really kill Mazey's one hope?

Nope.

She snatched her jacket from the floor and stood. At least she could check out the Browns' house — get more clues to what kind of people they really were. "What time do you want us?"

"Seven. I'll get you the keys to the loaner, then I'll write down the directions on how to get there."

Chapter 16

They wouldn't be home for dinner, so CJ left Mazey reading on the cabin porch and she walked to Murph's campsite, bag of uncooked hot dogs in hand.

He was sitting at the picnic table, looking to the road, as if he'd been waiting for her. She swallowed her worry, but it came right back up. She knew he wouldn't be deflected this time, but he had to eat, and beans were not a stable diet for an old man. "Hey, Sarge. You like hot dogs?"

"Is a frog's ass watertight?"

"I'll take that as a 'yes'." She handed over the bag.

"Sit. This'll just take a minute." He poured lighter fluid on the coals in the metal grill box and lit it. "Now, tell me what you came here to say."

"I-I didn't. I only came to bring you dinner, because—" Her knees went wobbly, so she sank onto the bench. She should have anticipated this. After all, she knew no good deed went unpunished. She opened her mouth to deflect, and if that didn't work, to refuse. But his focused gaze held her: open, accepting, non-judgmental. Electricity gathered under her skin, like just before a static shock. It was a feeling she knew well — and the only thing that released it was cutting. But what if confessing to this random soldier did that, without all the blood?

He was an old man — she'd bet he'd take her admission to his grave. A soldier's promise.

She couldn't watch him watch her, so she closed her eyes and fell into the past.

Night. The lights of Bagram airport off to the right, the razor-topped wire to the left. The hot, gritty wind whipped her hair back. The Humvee growled, eating up sand. She had precious cargo onboard. Logan in front, Mateo and Eddie in the back, laughing their asses off.

They were at the edge of the base, past the runways, where the blast walls were farthest, apart when she took her foot off the gas and the Humvee died. The guys went quiet. The only sound was the wind hissing through the razor wire. Except in her head, she was screaming. *Fuck!* She clenched the wheel, thinking furiously. She'd cannibalized the fuel injection system from a rear-end wreck so it should be fine…wait. She snatched a bottle of water from between the seats and jumped out before the vehicle stopped rolling. She ran to the front and fumbled for the hood latch. Odds of the enemy watching at that exact moment were statistically small, yet her flesh prickled with premonition.

Boom. Hissssss.

They all knew a shoulder-launched missile when they heard one.

She'd screamed, *Get down!*

A blast of red heat slammed her, then a concussion of sound. She stood frozen with panic. The truck flipped, the back of the blazing Humvee getting closer… All went black.

Her eyes flew open to the old man sitting across the picnic table. She took a few panting breaths.

"I woke in an Army hospital. They didn't." Her biceps hurt. She loosened her fingernails' grip.

After sitting silent for more than a minute, Murph said, "I'm so sorry." He shook his head. "Survivor's guilt is the worst. The VA can help, you know. It may take time to get an appointment, but it'll be worth it."

Yeah, take appointments from soldiers who needed it? Deserved it? No way, even if she had benefits, which she didn't. She pushed to a stand. "I've got to go. Can't be late to dinner." She stepped out from the table and walked away fast, head down.

"You come back sometime. We'll talk."

She didn't turn, just waved a hand. She'd hoped for release, but instead the pressure had built with the telling, focusing the cutting edge of the past so clear it was more vivid than the burnt grass around her. She jogged back to the cabin, for the blade that would make the pain bearable — for now.

~~~

Two hours later, dressed in the best of their clean but road-weary jeans and T-shirts, they climbed into Beau's loner, a bilious green ten-year-old Korean beater.

Mazey slammed the door. "Kinda nice not to worry about helmet-hair when we get there."

"You worrying about your looks? What're you growing up on me, or something?"

"Stop. You know this is important."

CJ reached to ruffle her sister's hair, but she ducked. "He already thinks you're all that tied up with a bow. What we're finding out tonight, is if *they* are all that." She put her hand on the keys in the ignition but waited until Mazey looked at her. "We're interviewing them, not the other way 'round, Punk."

"Yeah, okay." But she put a fingernail in her mouth and worried it.

Fifteen minutes later when they pulled into the drive, the lights of the house were blazing onto the perfect lawn. She turned off the engine.

Mazey didn't move. "Wow. Nice house."

"It is." But money didn't make the man. She was staying on guard-dog duty. It was easy to say the right things. Tonight she'd see if he walked the talk. "Come on, Punk. I'm right beside you the whole way."

The door opened before they made it to the porch. Beau stood backlit in the doorway. "Right on time. Come on in." He held the door. CJ stepped in first, Mazey on her heels.

The blonde she'd seen working in the garden stood in slacks and a loose white blouse, hands clasped before her, chewing off pink lipstick.

"CJ, Mazey, this is my wife, Linda." Beau closed the door.

CJ reached a hand to shake, but the woman stepped forward and wrapped her in a hug. "I'm so happy to meet you. Thank you for coming." Her Southern accent was pure honey.

CJ went tight and stepped back probably sooner than was socially acceptable.

Linda held her arms out for Mazey.

She paused and, frowning, looked up at her sister.

"She doesn't look like she'll bite, Punk."

They all chuckled, and Linda hugged Mazey tight. "I couldn't believe it when Beau told me." She let go but still held both of Mazey's hands. "You're really real, aren't you?"

It was such an awkwardly sincere declaration that Mazey smiled, and her shoulders lost some stiffness. "Um. Last I checked."

"Oh, what am I doing? I'm sorry. You'll think I'm a weirdo." Linda clasped her hands in front of her again, knuckles white.

Beau stepped over to put his arm around her. "They'll think you mean it, love." He kissed the end of her nose.

Sweet. CJ wanted to think they were faking it to look good, but couldn't make herself buy it.

"Come, dinner's ready." Linda ushered them into a formal dining room with gold brocade drapes and a table set with pretty china. She pushed open the swinging door to the kitchen.

CJ took a step forward. "Let me help."

"You're guests. Sit." Beau pulled out two chairs on one side of the table that would seat six easily, before pushing through the swinging door to help his wife bring out plates.

Mazey looked down at the formal china, and too much cutlery.

CJ smiled to calm the panic on her sister's face. "Just watch me for which fork to use."

Beau and Linda brought in platter after platter until the table was covered, then sat across the table.

"Wow, it's Thanksgiving!"

"I couldn't help it," Linda said. "I had to do something to keep busy so I wouldn't be so nervous."

"*You* were nervous?" Mazey whispered.

"Of course, silly. This is a big day for us, too." They all took turns loading their plates with turkey, mashed potatoes that were too creamy to be from a box, rolls, vegetables, and salad.

Mazey looked around the room. "This is a really great house. Have you lived here long?"

Linda passed the creamed corn in a tureen to CJ. "We started out in an apartment and saved every penny to buy a house. This had been a rental, and when the last tenants trashed it the owner had enough and put it up for sale, 'as is'." She rolled her eyes. "We're eating, so I won't go into the details, but trust me, it was disgusting. But we wouldn't have been able to afford it otherwise, so I'm not complaining."

"Now," Beau said, "I seem to remember a lot of complaining at the time, from both of us."

"Yeah, but you have a Barbie dream house now," Mazey said, and dug into her cranberry sauce.

Linda smiled. "Never thought about it that way, but yeah, we kinda do. This place is a palace compared to where I came from."

CJ stopped chewing. This perfect runway housewife came from the same type of place they had? Hard to imagine.

Linda must have noticed. "Yeah, I grew up on the bad side of Memphis. We were what you call dirt-floor poor. I was the last of eleven kids." Her smile wobbled. "So it never occurred to me that I wouldn't be able to have a houseful of them."

Beau touched her arm in silent support.

They weren't faking it for their audience. She was sure of it. These two had overcome huge problems through hard work, luck, and fate. Guess it did happen for some people. She smiled, listening to Mazey firing questions between bites. She was so glad this might happen for *her*. CJ finally sat back and rubbed her taut belly. "I can't remember the last home-cooked meal I had. Thank you."

"You're more than welcome." Linda pointed her fork at Mazey. "Be sure you leave room for dessert. I made a lemon meringue pie."

"To Patsy — our mother — home-cooked tends more toward beanie-weenies," CJ said.

"You don't cook?" Linda looked surprised.

"Before this, she was in the Army," Mazey chirped. "She was in Afghanistan. Until she got hurt and had to come home."

CJ's cheeks burned. "Mazey, hush. They don't want to hear about me. They want to get to know you."

"Thank you for your service." Beau's somber gaze fell on her. She ducked out from under it and hopped up. "I can't cook, but at least let me wash the dishes."

Linda stood. "You'll do no such thing. We'll dump the dishes in the sink, then go to the living room and chat."

Within ten minutes she and Mazey were ensconced on a comfy couch in the living room, coffee and hot chocolate on the coffee table before them. Beau and Linda sat in high-backed chairs on either side.

"Now," Beau said, "Mazey, tell me all about yourself. What hobbies do you have? You're in what, third grade? What's your favorite subject? Do you like sports? What—"

"Honey," Linda laughed. "You have to give her time to answer."

Mazey sat back. "I'll be in fourth when I go back to school. My hobbies are astronomy and geology. No on sports, my favorite subject is science. I'm going to be a Lunar Geologist when I grow up."

The couple looked a bit gobsmacked. Mazey had that effect on people.

"I don't even think I know what that is," Linda said.

While Mazey gave them a lecture, CJ studied the Browns. They listened, lightning flashes of emotion flicking across their faces. Even being critical, CJ couldn't find a hint of insincerity or duplicity in them. Could they really be as good as they seemed? She'd never been around a 'normal' family before — she'd half believed they only existed in TV shows from the '50s. Maybe Beau and Linda had time travelled. That would explain—

"CJ, answer their question." Mazey elbowed her.

"Sorry?"

Beau smiled. "I asked you what you plan to do next, now that you're out of the Army?"

Her cup rattled in the saucer when she set it down, spilling a few drops. "I haven't really thought much past this trip."

"She's going to go to college," Mazey said.

She raised an eyebrow at her sister. "I am?"

"She wants to be an EMT. Maybe even a Physician's Assistant someday."

Wow, the kid had a memory. CJ had mentioned that a couple years ago on a Facetime call. "We'll see. I'm just working on enjoying the trip right now."

"Yeah, she needs to." Mazey shook her head. "She gets really sad sometimes."

CJ glared. "Let's stick with you, Punk."

"We're interested." Linda gave CJ the pitying look she'd hoped to avoid. "Easy to see that Mazey is devoted to you."

"Well, the feeling's pretty mutual." She bumped shoulders with her sister. "When she's not being a brat, anyway."

"I'm not a...well, I guess I am, sometimes." She bumped back.

They chatted for an hour, 'getting to know you' things. CJ was careful to keep the spotlight off herself. She learned that Beau had been in the baseball minor leagues but had to quit when his dad died. Linda was a master gardener, played tennis and Bunko, which she explained was a dice game, but more of an excuse for women to get together and drink wine. All four parents were dead, and they had no siblings.

It was past dark when the girls finally made it to the front door.

"Well, what now?" Beau asked. "I mean, how long are you in town for? We'd really like to get to know you both better."

CJ told them she'd promised Patsy they'd be on the road back to California a week from tomorrow.

"In that case, look, I don't want to overstep, but can we do some things together?"

CJ looked down at Mazey's, 'oh please?' look. "Okay, but I'm not comfortable with you just taking Mazey."

"Oh no, you misunderstand," Linda said. "We'd want you there, too."

Yeah, she knew better than that, but it didn't matter. Only Mazey mattered. And CJ would be there to be sure things with this family were as good as they looked. "Well, I guess that's okay then."

Chapter 17

Four days later, CJ drowsed in the sun by the pool, only half listening to the rousing game of water polo. She and Mazey had spent time with Beau and Linda every day. They'd visited the Arboretum, Republic of Rio Grande Museum, and of course the Planetarium. The Browns proved to be more normal than anyone CJ had ever known, and they were clearly enamored with her sister, so when Linda asked to come swim with Mazey, CJ couldn't find a reason to say no. Mazey's instincts had been right. CJ could take her back to California, knowing that she had an emergency exit. If things got bad, or weird, she could call her father.

CJ had put off thinking about her own future for too long. Problem was, she still couldn't see through the past to whatever was ahead. Like a black towel thrown in a hot wash — everything came out gray. She knew that living in the past wasn't really living at all, but how could you leave the past when it held everything and everyone who mattered? She could never embrace a future she didn't deserve. And no matter how many times she time traveled back, there was no way to change the outcome. So she lived in purgatory, temporarily distracted by her sister's precarious situation. But when that was resolved? What came after purgatory? Sure wasn't heaven for the likes of her.

She squinted at the slanting sun. It was getting late, and she had to think about dinner. "Hey Punk! Time to get out."

"Oh no," Mazey whined. "Just ten more minutes?"

"Nah, we've gotta get showers and figure out dinner."

Both teams groaned, knowing the game was over.

Linda and Mazey swam to the edge and climbed out. Linda wrapped a towel around Mazey, rubbing her dry before getting one for herself. Linda pulled off the purple bikini like few women in their forties could. CJ spent a minute wondering if her boobs were real, then gave it up as mean. Hey, if they had the bucks, and it made them happy, who was she to judge?

CJ realized with a start that she'd kinda miss the Browns when she and Mazey headed for California. She'd maintained a space separate from the happy family, but Mazey was going to be bereft. "Hey, Linda. How about you call Beau and have him meet us here? Pizza's on me."

"Whoop!" Mazey threw a fist in the air. "That's my favorite sister, right there."

Linda smiled. "That'd be nice, CJ, thank you. I'll run home, grab a shower, and have Beau pick up a pizza, then pick me up when he leaves the shop. We should be here in an hour and a half or so."

"That'll work, but only if I can pay him back."

Linda winked. "You're going to have to fight that out with him." She slid into shorts, a tank top and sandals, and walked to her car.

CJ put an arm around her sister's shoulders, and they strolled back to the cabin.

"You having fun, Punk?"

"The best." She looked up, a frown clouding her features. "It's Tuesday."

"That it is."

"Mom said we had to leave by Saturday."

"Yeah, but you know where Beau lives now. Maybe you can spend some time here in the summer."

Mazey's eyes got big. And shiny. "I don't even know where Mom lives now. What if the school doesn't have advanced classes? What if..." She took a halting breath.

"What're you saying, Punk?"

"I just wonder if maybe Mom would let me stay. Here in Laredo."

Wow. Mazey had always been such a staunch Patsy defender... Maybe she had more survival instincts than CJ had given her credit for. She winced at the heartache her sister was in store for down this road. "You don't even know if Beau and Linda would want that."

"You know they'd love it, CJ."

"Neither of us knows that. Taking responsibility for a kid full-time is way different than being a week-long, 'Disneyland Dad'. Even if that's what they wanted, you know Patsy wouldn't go for it."

"Can we call Mom and ask? We don't have to tell my dad about it."

CJ knew her mother. Patsy would react like the dog in the manger to keep what she had. Even if she didn't *really* want it. "That'll be a hard sell, Punk."

"Okay." She turned away.

If CJ hadn't been listening, she'd have missed Mazey's small sob. "But hey, let's get showers then call her and see which way the wind is blowing today."

Mazey's gaze was trusting. "I call first dibs."

"Just don't use all the hot water again, and don't forget to rinse out your bathing suit."

After they showered, CJ looked around. "Punk, this place is not fit for company. I'll clean the kitchen and the bathroom if you'll make the beds, put stuff away, and sweep the floors. Deal?"

"Can we call Mom first?"

CJ sighed. She'd been hoping to put off what would likely end up in a showdown, but it had to happen eventually — Mazey wouldn't let this go. She pulled out her phone, hit speed dial, and set it on the table.

Patsy's smoke and sandpaper voice came over the speaker. "Don't even tell me you're not leaving, Cora Jean."

"Well, hello to you, too."

"You never call to say hello. You always have an agenda. Usually one I'm not going to like."

"Hi, Mom." Mazey chirped.

"Hi, Gracie. Are you having fun?"

"A blast. We went to the planetarium here, and they have the most amazing telescope—"

"That's nice. You're not going to believe what happened, girls. Are you sitting down?"

Mazey took two steps to the table and sat. "Yes."

"Yeah, right." CJ wiped down the tiny kitchen counter.

"A man came up to me after my performance last week. Turns out Ralph owns four bars, and he thinks I'd be a good draw for them! I'm going to keep my gig, but four other nights I'll be traveling to his places to sing. Do you believe it? Finally, after all these years, I'm on my way!"

CJ snapped to guard-dog mode. "Where are these bars?"

"Oh, all over. Victorville, Lake Arrowhead, Wrightwood, Silver Lakes. Can you imagine the exposure?"

"Patsy, some of those are a hundred miles apart. Have you forgotten that you have a nine-year-old at home?"

"Do you really imagine that I didn't think this through? She'll stay here with Arlo while I'm working. I'll be home the other two nights, and—"

"Who's Arlo?" she and Mazey said together.

"I told you about him. The songwriter? He works from home, so it'll be great. I told you he can't wait to be a dad, right?"

Patsy had blown right past dreams straight to crazy-town. CJ hit mute on the phone. "Punk, you want to go buy some sodas at the camp store for all of us? You really don't want to hear this."

Mazey's jaw went tight, even as her bottom lip loosened. "I'm old enough. This is my life. I'm not leaving."

CJ shrugged and unmuted the phone. Patsy was still gushing about her change in fortunes. "Earth to Patsy."

"What, Cora Jean?" Her voice went flat. She knew this news would be met with the enthusiasm of smoking roadkill on the dinner table.

"You're suggesting that Mazey come back to a place she's never been, a school she's never seen — to basically live with a guy she's never met? Are you so self-centered that you can't see where this might be a problem?"

"Of course it will take some adjustment. I told Ralph I wouldn't be able to start for two weeks. That should give Grace plenty of time to acclimate."

Nothing short of a bomb was going to get through to Patsy, so she pulled out the Fat Boy. "We met Mazey's dad."

"You did *what?*" Each word increased in volume and pitch.

"Yup. And guess what? He's a nice guy. Settled, married, a business owner, Little League coach." She couldn't believe *she* was making a Beau Brown pitch, but put up next to Patsy's life he freaking walked on water. "He loves Mazey. And she loves him."

"I do, Mom." There was a quiver in Mazey's voice. "He's amazing."

"And *I* am your mother."

"I know, and I love you, too. But what if I stayed here, instead of coming home?"

The pleading in Mazey's voice ripped into CJ's gut.

"Are you out of your mind? I am not—"

"Patsy, think about it." CJ let a bit of Mazey's plead leak into her voice. "You could go and pursue your career, knowing Mazey was safe and happy."

"Are you insinuating that she would not be safe or happy here, Cora Jean?"

Given the conversation so far, any sane person would know the answer to that, but CJ wasn't going to say so.

"You will leave there on Saturday as planned. And when you get home, we are going to have a talk. A very frank talk, about the way things are going to be."

Mazey's expression imploded and a fat tear fell to the table. "But Mom—"

"Amazing Grace Newsome. Do not argue with me. You will come home, and that's the end of this discussion. Goodnight."

Click.

Mazey buried her head in her arms on the table and sobbed.

CJ stepped over, squatted and put her hand on her sister's back, rubbing circles to soothe. "We'll give her some time to think about it, Punk. We'll call and ask again in a day or two."

"We'll be leaving then, and I'll never get to come back!"

Her muffled wail made CJ want to slap Patsy senseless. If they'd been in the same state, she would have.

A knuckle rap came on the door. "Pizza delivery!"

Shit. CJ hesitated, but then decided Beau should see what's beyond Disney Dad. "Come on in."

He stepped in, a plastic grocery bag hanging from his pizza-box-laden arms. "We come bearing — what's wrong?" He strode to the counter and set down his load. "Mazey, hon, what's wrong?"

CJ stood. "We just had a tough phone call with Patsy."

Linda came in and closed the door behind her. "Oh, I'm sorry."

"Come on, Punk, let's do pizza." She tapped her sister's back, a hint to pull it together.

"I'm okay." Mazey sniffed. "Thank you for the pizza."

Beau cocked his head. "I guess we're not going to talk about the elephant in the room, then?"

CJ took a quart of soda from the grocery sack. "Let's eat it instead."

Mazey pulled a blanket from the bunk bed. "We can have a picnic." She spread it on the floor.

Beau opened his mouth, but CJ shook her head. Better to let Mazey calm down for now. In a few minutes they sat in a circle on the floor, eating. Mazey's ruddy face the only hint there'd been drama.

When they were done CJ gathered the paper plates, but Beau touched her arm before she could stand. "I know this might not be good timing, but..." He reached for Linda's hand, his face holding a question.

Nodding, she took his hand.

"We wanted to ask what you would think about staying."

CJ frowned at him. "We've got to leave on Saturday."

"No. We mean for good." His soft gaze fell on Mazey. "We'd like you to live here, with us."

Mazey's jaw tightened, her brows furrowing.

"I know it would depend on your mom's permission, but we can't even think about that until we know what *you* think of the idea."

"I can't."

"I know you'd miss your mother. But I'd fly you to California when you wanted, even if just for a weekend. And you could spend the summers with her."

Linda squeezed Beau's hand. "We have a wonderful gifted program, and in high school you can take courses that will count for college credit."

She stood, hands fisted at her sides. "It's not that I don't want to, I can't!" Chin stuck out, she paced.

CJ recognized the signs of a Mazey Meltdown.

"I called Mom, and asked if I could stay, and she said no," She stopped in front of Beau and Linda. "I know I shouldn't have without talking to you first, but…" Her hands tightened to fists at her side. "I worked so hard to find you. CJ thought I was crazy. But I *knew* I could do it. And I did! But now it doesn't matter, because Mom is making me go home." She was practically spitting the words. "I don't know where that is, I don't know who the guy is I'll be living with when Mom is on the road, where I'll be going to school, and…I can't stand it!" She stopped pacing, and hands fisted and face scrunched, and stomped her feet. "I always make do, and don't expect things. Because then you get hurt when it doesn't happen. But for once, just for this *once*, I wanted something. Something important. Something big. But as usual, the kid has no say and I'm so sick of it!" She ran for the bathroom, her exit punctuated by a door slam that shook the windows.

Followed by a shocked silence. Beau and Linda both turned to CJ.

Well, that pretty much ended Disney-Dad time. Beau was getting to see what a kid was really like, tantrums and all. Though she didn't blame Mazey for this one. "Mazey floated a trial balloon. Patsy shot it down."

"Well, we'll see about that." Beau's jaw turned to granite. "Fathers have rights, too. CJ, would you give me her phone number? I'll call her tomorrow."

CJ shook her head. "I wouldn't do that. You pushing would have the opposite effect. Unless you want to get into DNA tests, attorneys, and court dates."

He glanced at Linda.

"I'd trust what CJ says, hon. She knows Patsy."

Yeah, too well.

"You can trust me to tread lightly."

"Yeah, but…" But she could see from his iron gaze he wasn't letting this one go. "Okay." She sent her mother's contact to Beau's phone.

Linda walked over and knocked on the bathroom door. "Mazey, come on out now."

Silence.

"We need to talk, hon."

Nothing.

"Please?"

The door opened and Mazey emerged, eyes red from crying but her jaw still set.

"Come on." Beau waved her over. When she stood in front of him he put his hands on her shoulders and leaned down so he was at her level. "Just breathe a minute."

"But it's not *fair*! This is all I want and—"

"Breathe first, then we'll talk." He waited while Mazey took a few deep breaths.

"Okay. First. Life isn't fair. You've lived long enough to know that, right?"

She nodded, head down.

"Your mother will always be your mother. I will *always* be your father. If your mother doesn't want me in your life, we'll have to live with that."

Her head snapped up. "You're giving up that easy?"

"I'm not giving up. I'm thinking about you. Custody battles can get really nasty. It would make your life hard, and that's the last thing I want. If I have to step back and wait until you're old enough to make your own decisions, I will."

"But—"

"I don't want that either. It's the last thing Linda and I want. Especially after getting to know you the past week. But Mazey, things can change. Tomorrow, next month, next year, your mother might cool off and change her mind. We just have to be patient, and not give up hope. Can you do that?"

CJ could see the war going on behind Mazey's eyes. She knew how hard this was for a headstrong kid to accept. Finally she nodded and buried her head in Beau's shirt.

When the Browns had left, CJ put Mazey to bed. Exhausted by the day's emotions, she was asleep in minutes.

CJ had to admit, tonight convinced her that Beau and Linda could be way more than Disney parents — they were the real thing. They'd shown both patience with Mazey's snit fit, and even more importantly Beau was willing to sacrifice what he wanted more than anything for Mazey's well-being. Something her own mother wasn't capable of.

She stepped out on the porch, closed the door gently behind her, and pulled her phone to check the time. Odds were good that, on a Saturday night, Patsy would be at some bar by now. She hit speed dial, grateful when it went to voicemail. "Patsy, It's CJ. I know we kind of pitched you a heater out of left field today. I don't blame you for reacting. But think about it for a minute. Your career is moving ahead. You'll get four times the exposure now, and word will spread. Who knows what will happen next? Nashville isn't out of the question..." CJ knew better, but Patsy was always desperate for validation. And coming from the most critical person in her life, she'd lap it up. "Beau wants time with Mazey. He'll do a DNA test if you force the issue, but once I hang up, I'll send you a recent photo — there's no doubt he's her father. All I'm asking is that you not make a long-term decision on a short-term reaction. Think about it. This could be a really good deal for you." Best end this before she laid it on too thick. "Okay we'll talk later. 'Night." She hit 'end', hoping logic and common sense wasn't totally lost on her mother.

Chapter 18

The next day, Beau and Linda picked up Mazey to go to Wednesday church service with them. They'd invited CJ, but she declined. No need to spend an hour of her life asking for forgiveness that she wouldn't buy even if some minister offered. Like using a Sharpie on a white board, some sins couldn't be wiped clean with a prayer.

Beau had said the bike was done, so when they returned from church she and Mazey would pick it up, settle the bill, and drop off the loaner car. CJ felt like she was at the beginning of the end of the trip, with all that entailed. Now the weight of Patsy's ultimate decision hung over all their heads. When Beau had called, Patsy said she would 'think about it'. CJ'd heard that all the time, growing up. It meant Patsy was delaying a 'no'.

CJ made the beds, took out the trash, then decided to stop and take the leftover pizza to Sarge.

She was surprised to see him up, nursing a cup of coffee at the picnic table. "Hey Murph, you're up early."

"Storm coming." He flexed his damaged hand. "I always know."

"I'm sorry. You need some aspirin? I've got some at the cabin."

"Nah. If I took something for every ache, I'd be an opioid junkie by now. Sit, girl."

"Do you eat cold pizza?" She settled the box on the table and sat.

"Is there any other way to eat it?" He flipped the top and took a piece. "Meat Lover's. My favorite."

"We're heading home in a couple days."

"Yeah, you said." He took a bite.

"Sarge, I'd feel a lot better about leaving if I knew you were going home, too."

He raised an eyebrow. "You wouldn't be worrying about an old soldier, would you?"

"Hell, yes." From what she'd seen, he had to be about out of money, and without the food she brought he probably wouldn't eat at all. "You said you wanted time alone, out in nature, and you've had that." She sighed. "All good things come to an end."

"You talkin' about me or you, CJ?"

Her mouth pulled to a lopsided smile. "Both of us, I think."

He nodded. "I've been thinking it's about time I headed back."

"Good."

"And you?"

"I'll take my sister home to California."

"And then?"

Her gaze flitted over the trees, the road, the field beyond. "Then we'll see."

"You're tough, girl. Too tough to give up."

"Yep."

"You're going to be fine. I know it."

"Yep." She nodded.

"Know how I know?"

"How?" When he smiled, she realized she shouldn't have seemed interested.

"Because you're not so good at letting go."

She smiled with half her mouth. "Can't argue with that, Sarge."

His forehead crinkled. "Everyone has regrets, girl. We do the best we can with the load we have to carry. But just be sure you're not carrying weight that isn't yours. See what I'm saying?"

"I sure do, Sarge."

His rheumy eyes turned steely. "You're saying it, but you're not believing it. That's because your brain is in the way. See, it's your brain's job to find answers. But some answers aren't all facts and figures and logic — they take a leap of faith. That's when you gotta see with your heart." He tapped his chest with his mangled hand. "Your heart already knows you're going to be okay. It's small feeling, and it's hard to feel it over your brain's banging around. But when you feel it, you have to grab on with both hands and make that leap. Because that's what's going to save you." He nodded. "Take it from somebody who knows."

He sounded like Mazey, with her 'little voice', but it was all too woo-woo for her. She believed they believed it, but... "I appreciate you taking the time, Sarge. I've got to get back." She pushed up from the table. "When do you think you'll be heading out?"

"No tellin'. But if you come by and I'm gone, you'll have your answer."

In that case, I'll say goodbye now." She snapped to attention and gave him a smart salute. "It sure was good meeting you. Thanks for everything." She reached out to shake his hand.

Instead of taking it he stood, edged out of the bench, and hugged her. "It's me should be thanking you. Not many people take the time to notice an old man, much less worry if he has what he needs." He backed up but didn't let go. His bright blue eyes assessed her. "You are a good person. You stay strong. And don't forget what I told you about choices — if you don't think you have any, look at the ones you threw away. Y'hear?"

"Yessir." She patted his back, stepped out of his arms and walked away, thinking that everyone who made it out of a war zone carried scars — some on the outside, some inside. Some soldiers recovered, others couldn't.

~~~

Beau stood in the door of the body shop when they drove up. "Come on in."

CJ and Mazey followed him to the paint bay. Lola lounged in a sunbeam — scrubbed, shiny, sexy. Mazey ran over to check out the paint job. "Oh my gosh, this is the sweetest!"

CJ had to admit it was. The claw marks were below the bear paw in a cream circle, and he'd chosen a bold font for the words. "You do great work, Beau." She reached for her wallet. "What do I owe you?"

"Nothing."

Her head snapped up.

"You're family."

"No, Mazey is. This is my bike. I'll pay." The words came out clipped from between her clenched teeth.

He studied her face and must have realized he wasn't going to win this one, because he led the way back to the lobby. He walked behind the counter, made out a sale slip for an amount that was at least a third too low.

But studying his face she knew she wouldn't win *this* one, so she handed over her credit card.

"I missed Lola," Mazey said. "It felt weird to be in a car. When I grow up, I'm going to get a bike just like her."

Beau handed over the receipt. "Would you two come to the house?"

"I don't know, we should probably—"

He touched her hand. "Please, CJ? I have something I want to show you." He turned to Mazey. "And Linda wants your help making cookies. Would you like that?"

"Yes." But she looked to CJ for approval.

She couldn't deprive her sister time with the Browns. If Patsy didn't change her mind, Mazey might not see them for at least a year. "Sure."

They'd left their riding gear at the shop, so they shrugged into it and followed Beau's car to his house.

Linda stepped out the back door in an apron, one hand behind her back. "There you are. Are you ready to bake, Mazey? I have something for you." She displayed her surprise: a white apron with, *I keep hitting the space bar, but I'm still on Earth* across the front.

"Oh, way cool!" Mazey slid off the back of the bike, stripped off her helmet and jacket and handed them to CJ. She stepped over to Linda, who dropped the apron over her head and turned her around to tie it. "Neat, huh, CJ?"

"It's you, Punk."

Mazey followed Linda up the back steps to the kitchen. The screen door slapped behind her.

CJ dismounted and unbuckled her helmet. "That was really thoughtful of Linda. I know she couldn't have run down to Walmart and picked that up."

Beau stood, hands in the back pockets of his jeans. "I think she ordered it online. She's got something for you, too."

"Oh, no need to go to trouble for—"

"Why do you always do that?" He cocked his head to the side, like he could maybe understand her better that way.

"Do what?" She set her helmet on her seat and laid both jackets on the rear seat.

"Assume that we only care about Mazey. You're Mazey's blood, too, and it's clear what you two mean to each other."

"Yes, but—"

"Have you never had someone who did things for you, not because you're related but just because they liked you?"

Logan's laughing face appeared in her vision, and she shifted her focus to the driveway. "Yes. But it would have been better if he hadn't."

Beau's silence finally brought her head up. He was still looking at her like she was an unsolvable puzzle. She shifted her feet. "What?"

A red tint crept up from his collar to splash his cheeks. "Can I show you something?"

The weight in his voice was a siren blaring, warning her to say no. But she owed him, if only for being so good to Mazey. "Okay."

He led the way to the side of the white clapboard garage and climbed the wooden staircase beside it. He paused at the small landing at the top, pulled keys from his pocket, found the correct one and unlocked the door. "Come on in."

When she stepped in, she was met with the smell of stale dust and cut wood.

"Haven't been up here in a while. Let me get some windows open." He strode to the picture windows that overlooked the driveway and wrestled them up.

It was a small apartment, and unfinished. The floors were new but unvarnished, the walls were particle board, and the kitchen to her left had cabinets but no countertop or sink. She walked across the room to a short hallway. What was to be a small bath opened on the left, and at the end a bedroom, also unfinished. She walked back to the main room. "This is going to be real nice when you're done with it." She leaned against the wall beside the open door to the stairs, wondering why he'd brought her.

Beau stood, head down, hands in his pockets.

The sirens in her head went off. "What is it?"

He looked up. She'd heard the phrase 'his face was a mask of pain', but this was way worse. There was no mask. It was as if pain had detonated inside and shot out of him. His face contorted in a silent wail of grief.

She wanted to flee down the stairs. She wanted to cover her ears. Because she knew she didn't want to hear whatever had caused the level of hell she saw in his eyes. But she owed him, even though she sensed that bomb of pain was going to tear through her, too. "Tell me."

"I'm sorry," he choked out. "After all this time, I thought I could do this…" A sob cut off the rest.

She stood on shaky knees while he pulled himself together, palming his eyes and taking big gulps of the fresh air blowing in the windows.

"This was to be an apartment for my little brother. He was on a carrier off the coast of Libya—" He grabbed her elbow when her knees gave out. "Whoa. Are you okay?"

She slid down the wall and her butt hit the floor with a sad plop. *This.* This is what she'd run from at Logan's house. What she'd dreaded in the pit of her stomach since hitting Stateside. She was barely managing to hang on after what happened to the guys, but seeing the families — there had to be a more accurate word than 'pain', but her tortured mind couldn't conjure it.

"Go on." She tried to ignore the stream of babble in her head, focusing instead on breathing. In. And out.

"Denny was going to settle here when his tour was over. I was waiting, so we could finish this together."

The dead in his voice ate through her skin like acid, and bit into the softer layers beneath. "He didn't come back."

He slid down the wall to sit beside her. "Nope. You lost someone, too." It wasn't a question.

Pressure built under her ribs, constricting her organs, bowing her bones. Fear sent cold shivers racing across her skin. The babble in her head got louder, faster. *Shoulda-beenme —Ican'tIcan'tIcan't!* She clamped her hands to the sides of her head to keep it from shattering.

"I can't anymore." It leaked out of her like the last squeak of air from a wrinkled balloon.

"Tell me."

Her head shook without an order from her brain. She'd just told the story to Murph and the pressure was worse, not better. Besides, he was there for Mazey, not her. She didn't want a reason for him to be closer. She didn't deserve that. "This trip Mazey and I were on? It was supposed to be me and three of my good friends." She swallowed. "They didn't come back, either."

"I'm sorry."

They sat, listening to the wind and pulling themselves together.

The pressure surged, pushing her skin taut. There had to be a way to relieve it besides cutting. That was only temporary, and she didn't have enough skin to make it through the rest of her life. She thought about what Murph had said, about picking up choices she'd discarded. But she'd tried everything. A still photo of lights from Logan's house, shining on the porch, drifted through her mind. Except maybe...

Chapter 19

Beau heaved a sigh and she jumped. She'd half-forgotten he was there.

"I'm so sorry. I didn't bring you up here to make you sad. I'd hoped the opposite, in fact."

"Why did you bring me then?"

He looked around the room. "Whether Mazey can live with us or not, I wanted to offer this to you. As a place to live. A place to settle. A place to heal. If you wanted."

It took a few heartbeats to find her voice. "Why would you do that?"

The deep calm she admired was in his gaze. "Because..." He hesitated, as if tasting his words before he said them, "because you seem kind of lost. It might help to have a home base, with people nearby who care about you."

"Come on. You met me a week ago."

"You're right, I don't know you well. But I know you're caring. And kind. And I don't know the whole story, but I'm thinking there's a reason you took your sister with you on this trip, and it wasn't because you'd be lonely." He looked over at her. "I know Patsy, remember?"

"She's almost no trouble, and we've gotten even closer the past weeks."

"See? Caring."

The icecap around her heart started to melt. But she couldn't take shelter she didn't deserve. "Thank you for the generous offer. It means more to me than you could know. But I'll have to say no."

Well, let me know if you change your mind. As you can see, it's been free for some time."

"I'm so very sorry about your brother."

He stood, gave her a hand up, and they headed back to the house. They walked in on a cookie assembly line. Linda rolled out dough, Mazey used a variety of cutters, then arranged them on a baking sheet and put them in the oven. The kitchen smelled of warm memories that CJ wished she possessed. She picked up an overly browned reindeer and took a bite. "This is good. But Christmas cookies in summer?"

"Since I most likely won't be here for winter, we decided we'd do this now." Mazey didn't look up.

Linda glowed with happiness, and maybe a bit from the heat of the oven. "Stop eating and start frosting. I've got to start dinner soon."

CJ and Beau sat at the table, slathering the cooled sugar cookies with icing and sprinkles. When the last tray was in the oven, Linda and Mazey joined them.

"Okay, it's a contest," Mazey said, choosing a snowman cookie. "Prize for the most beautiful cookie."

"What prize?" Beau asked.

"It's a secret. But it'll be worth it." She frowned, choosing a jar of red sprinkles and one of small silver balls.

CJ laughed. "You all might as well concede right now, because I am so gonna win."

"Really? You've made these before?" Mazey asked.

"Nope. But I'm gonna make a Santa that will make the real one cry."

Linda picked out a cookie shaped like a Christmas tree. "Bring it on, girl. I'm a professional."

They laughed, joked, and trash-talked their way through the next hour, finishing frosting the last cookie amid a minor sprinkle fight.

Linda surveyed the table littered with dabs of frosting and cookie crumbs, sprinkles everywhere. "Okay, you three to clean up. I need to start dinner."

Beau stood. "We will. But first, we have to decide the winner of the contest."

They walked to the counter where the four entries sat on a plate, spotlighted by a sunbeam.

"These are all pretty epic," CJ said. "Who's gonna judge?"

"My prize. I get to decide." Mazey moved the plate in quarter turns, to study each cookie closely.

Beau leaned a hand on the counter. "Come on. The suspense is killing me."

CJ stood back and watched them. She'd worried so much about Mazey's father, but anyone could see he was a good guy. They'd already bonded in the week since they'd met, like a real family. It made her so happy that, no matter what Patsy said, Mazey would always have this.

"Okay, I've decided." Mazey reached into the pocket of her jeans.

"Who won?" Linda asked.

"CJ!" She broke into a huge smile and held out CJ's prize — a tiny rock.

"Wow. Thanks." CJ ruffled her sister's hair and took her prize.

"Hold it up to the light and look at it close."

In the light CJ could see it was a translucent orange-gold, and in the middle a bug that looked like a mosquito, only smaller. "This is amazing."

"It's amber." Mazey pointed. "That's a hundred million years old."

"Oh Punk, I can't take this. It's valuable."

"So are you, CJ, and I want you to have it. Keep it in your pocket, and when you feel down you pull it out and remember to look for the good stuff." Mazey's eyes glistened.

"Ah, I love you, Punk." She pulled Mazey into a hug while Linda and Beau applauded.

"Okay, now you guys really need to clean up." Linda retied her apron strings. "I'm starting dinner."

CJ turned Mazey and swatted her butt. "You guys get started. I'll be in in a minute." She stepped out the back door and into the yard, then hit speed dial. It was time for Patsy to do the right thing.

"Yes, Cora Jean?" She heard Patsy exhale — cigarette smoke, no doubt.

"Patsy, listen. Please let Mazey stay. You don't have time for her, and she's so happy here. Beau is a really nice guy, and his wife—"

"Are you trying to tell me again what a horrible mother I am?"

"No. This has nothing to do with you. It's about Mazey, and what's best for her." She knew she should slow down, build a case, but she rushed on, hoping to bulldoze Patsy with logic. "There are good schools here, and they live in a nice house in a decent neighborhood. They aren't rich, but they're good, decent people. She'd be cared for and loved."

"All things she won't get here, am I right?" There was the rattle of a cigarette being pounded into the lopsided ashtray. "I know you don't think much of me. You've been clear on that since junior high. Miss High and Mighty, pointing out faults and flaws like a queen, looking down your nose at the little people. You've got all these opinions about what I should do. Who I should be. But you know what? You're not so perfect yourself, Cora Jean."

"This isn't about me, either. It's about—"

"I'll tell you what. I may be pathetic to you, but at least I try." Her voice grew strident. "What about you? You come dragging ass home, tail between your legs, not a word about why."

"I'm not—"

"No. Don't tell me. I'm not in your circle of trust, obviously. Never have been." She took a breath. She was on a roll now. "But you know what? At least I have a goal. It may be a joke to you, but it makes me happy, and I'm going after it with everything I've got. How about you? What do you *want*?"

CJ opened her mouth, then closed it.

"That's what I thought. No dreams, nothing to look forward to. You think I can't see that you're dead inside? What are you going to do about *that*? You know what? You're like that song, 'Dead Man Walking'. You need to straighten out your own sorry life before you come at me with what I need to do."

Realization slammed into CJ. She'd have never guessed Patsy could look past herself long enough to see into anyone else. Heat crawled up her chest, recognizing the truth in Patsy's words. "I'll call you back, Mom." She hit end, realizing after the hang up that she'd used Patsy's title rather than her name.

The world shifted under her feet and, dizzy, she sat in the grass to keep from falling.

Hell, she might as well have made this a one-hundred-dred-percent memorial ride — she'd been almost as dead as Logan, Eddie, and Mateo. She followed the bread-crumb trail back, seeing her actions from a different angle. Yes, she'd brought Mazey along to save her from the sleaze. But he hadn't been in the picture for weeks, and she knew that before the memorial ride fell apart. So, with the reasons for being out here gone, why had she kept going? Oh sure, Mazey would have been disappointed, but she'd have gotten over it.

But it hadn't even occurred to her to do that. Why not?

The only logical answer was... somewhere on the road to Laredo she'd outgrown some small part of the load she carried. The floodgates opened, deluging her with wants.

She wanted to make a million more memories with Mazey, wanted to watch her grow up. But it was more than that. She wanted things for herself — she wanted a future. She glanced up at the picture window over the garage. She even wanted to take Beau up on his offer. She wanted the solace of belonging to the cobbled together family they were forming, even if she would be the fourth wheel. She wanted to go to college. Maybe even become an EMT.

She wanted so much.

Was there a way past this black cloud she lived in? She knew she couldn't erase the past, but maybe the boulder she carried could be broken up a bit so she could somehow manage to carry it. She'd never move past it, but could she move on *with* it?

She hit speed dial again.

"Yes, Cora Jean." Her voice had softened a bit, like butter in a spring sun. She must have noticed CJ's slip at the end of her call.

"I'm sorry, Patsy."

"For what?"

"For constantly being critical. You're right; I have no right to judge anyone. My life is messed up, but I'm going to start doing something about it. Thank you for pushing me to see that. It was like the last penny just dropped."

A cigarette lighter clicked. Then silence.

In for a penny — today was a day of taking impossible chances. "You are Mazey's mother. You get to say where she lives. And you may not be perfect, but you did something right because she's a great kid. She's someone we both can be really proud of."

Exhaled smoke was her only answer.

"Well, I just wanted to tell you that. We'll be heading back on Saturday, so—"

"Wait. I have something to say." Patsy took another drag on her cigarette. "I'll admit, it pissed me off to hear that Gracie loves Beau. I was jealous. He called me yesterday. He actually called her a treasure."

CJ held her breath, fingering Mazey's stone in her pocket.

"You were right, too. It's not fair for me to travel so much and leave Gracie home with someone she hardly knows. Beau was always a good guy — it was me who messed up back then. I'm going to trust your opinion that he's a good man. She can stay there for now. We'll see how it goes. But she'll need to call me every week, and I want her here on school holidays no matter what. You hear me?"

It was as if the sun had beamed into CJ's chest, warming her cold heart. "That is awesome. It'll be so good for you both, you'll see." She stood and brushed grass off her jeans. "I gotta go tell her, but Patsy?"

"Yeah."

"Thanks."

"You could call me 'Mom' once in a while you know. Wouldn't kill you."

"Maybe not. 'Bye... 'Mom'."

Chapter 20

The evening turned into a celebration. Beau broke out a bottle of wine for the three of them, and sparkling cider for Mazey. CJ sat back and sipped, thrilled that Mazey would be safe, settled in a normal, loving home. They discussed plans, told Mazey about the school she'd be attending, and the zillions of details that relocating would require.

At ten o'clock, tired but content, CJ stood. "Time to go, Punk."

"Oh, not yet, please?"

Linda stood. "You two are welcome to stay the night. We've got a spare room with two single beds."

CJ needed time to process everything that had happened. "Maybe some other time. It's been a long, eventful day."

"Would it be okay if I stayed?" Mazey asked.

"Well sure, if you want to." She ignored the small pinch in her heart. This was a dream come true for Mazey. If she were jealous, she'd be as bad as Patsy.

Mazey's grin was her answer.

"I'll pick you up in the morning. We can go to the library if you want."

"I'll make breakfast," Linda said. "Say nine?"

She was a little worried about being sucked into this blended family vortex. Besides, she had a lot of thinking to do. "Thanks, but I've got food at the cabin I've got to use up."

The ride back was colder without Punk at her back. She unlocked the cabin door, flipped on the lights, and sat at the tiny kitchen table. Her mind was like a landscape after a tornado, littered with waterlogged thoughts and whirlwind emotions.

She didn't deserve the future she so desperately wanted. But what if there was a way to *earn* it?

"Just calm the fuck down, Maxwell. There's got to be a way." She wove her fingers into her hair and held on. Sarge's wrinkled face appeared in her mind, and she remembered his words: *If you don't think you have any choices, look at the ones you threw away as being impossible.*

What had she discarded that she now so desperately needed?

It seemed her mind cleared for the first time in forever. She sorted through the mess and picked up one of the impossible choices she'd discarded back in Wyoming.

~~~

That night she dreamed of the desert but, for a change, not the bad one. It flipped times and places, as dreams do, but the subject stayed constant. She and the guys were planning this trip. They researched online what bikes they'd buy: Eddie wanted a crotch rocket, Mateo had a Gold Wing picked out, and Logan, a cruiser with ape-hanger handlebars. Endless discussions of where they'd go, what they wanted to see, and the fun they'd have. She woke with drying tear tracks and a smile.

She glanced up at the ceiling. "Okay, I'm listening, guys."

She fixed strawberries and a bowl of oatmeal for breakfast. She'd finally settled on the only choice that could possibly help — both her and the guys. And the fact that it was the hardest really didn't come as a surprise.

She was going to finish what she set out to do to — visit the guys' families. She'd tell them the whole truth and let the chips fall. After all, she deserved whatever they'd heap on her. She couldn't live with this any longer. She didn't hold much hope that it would help her, but if there was a God maybe it would help *them*. And if it didn't work? She'd burn that bridge when she came to it.

Her spirits lifted. Not on hope — this was too uncertain for that — but on at least a glimmer of a *chance.*

Now that she had a plan, she was anxious to get started. Get it over with. The thought of riding Lola all that way seemed too slow. Too much time to change her mind, to lose courage. Plane tickets and rental cars would be faster, and if she added up the hotel rooms, meals and gas involved in a cross-country motorcycle trip, it probably wouldn't be much more expensive.

On the way out of the campground she cruised past Murphy's site, to find it empty. A pang loosened her grip on the throttle, and the bike slowed. "Hooah, Sarge," she whispered. "Thank you."

She collected Mazey at the Browns' and they rode to the library.

Her sister climbed from the back and took off her helmet, chattering the whole time.

"Hang on, Punk," CJ said when Mazey headed for the sidewalk. "We need to talk."

Mazey looked at her shoes. "I know I shouldn't have stayed last night. I just got so excited."

"What? No." She smoothed her sister's shiny hair. It was getting long. She'd have to tell Linda to get it cut. "I'm glad you did. You needed time with them, and I needed time to think."

She squinted up at CJ. "About what?"

"I'm leaving, Punk."

Her brows came together. "Wait, what? Where? You can't go without me!" Her voice got higher and louder as she went, like an ambulance siren getting closer.

"Calm down. I'm going to go see Mateo, Eddie, and Logan's families. I need to talk to them."

"But we're a team. I can help. I've been there from the beginning, and I'll be there for you. We can leave in the morning. I won't be in the way, I promise."

"I love you for offering, Punk. But I think this is something I have to do alone." She smiled, and hugged her amazing little sister. "And you have things to do to get settled with your dad and Linda."

Emotions flashed across Mazey's face, each too fast to catch before another replaced it. "I'm worried about you."

"But Punk, it's not your job to worry about me. I'm a grownup, in charge of my life. You're a kid, and you haven't had much time to get good at that. Focus on *that*. Not worrying, but having fun. Doing kid stuff, just because it makes you happy."

"I don't like this." She sighed. "But I can see you're not going to give in, so... I'll try." Then she relaxed, and the corners of her lips curled up. "Told you you were brave."

CJ snorted. "Yeah, as evidenced by the night I ran away from Logan's."

"I know this is really scary for you. But it's gonna be okay, CJ. I know it."

"Yeah, thanks."

"Hey, I was right about my dad, wasn't I?" She put her hand over her heart. "I don't know how I know, but I feel it here." She lifted CJ's hand and put it to her chest. "If you listen real hard, you can feel it, too."

It was so close to what Murph had told her that, in spite of herself, CJ tried.

"You have to listen hard. It's a tiny thing, buried under all the being scared and confused. It already knows you're going to be okay. You have to trust that feeling."

Everything in her went still and silent, waiting, wanting...but there was nothing. "I'll take your word for it, Punk."

"It's there, CJ. You've just told it to shut up so often, it won't talk now. Keep listening. You'll hear it, I promise."

"How do you know that?"

Her face transformed from a sage to a child with her smile. "Because you're here. You survived the war. No one could do that without that little voice."

"Your mouth to God's ears, little one."

"When are you leaving?"

"As soon as I can get flights. Will you be okay here?"

"Of course."

She wished she had Mazey's courage. And surety. She slung an arm around her shoulder. "Ready to go learn something?"

"No. If you're leaving, I don't want to spend the day reading. Can we go for a ride instead?"

She smiled down at her sister. "I love you, you know that?"

"Yeah, I know." She ducked CJ's noogie.

They spent the day exploring. The land here was fairly flat and brush-covered. To most it would seem drab, just a place to be ridden through. But to them, it was beautiful in an oh-so-subtle way. Tiny flowers on the sage, pads of prickly pear sprouting everywhere, a huge cerulean sky dotted with white cotton-ball clouds. CJ stayed in the moment, enjoying this last ride with her sister before life changed and she'd have to share her.

By the end of the day she was windblown, sunburnt... and content. It felt good to be moving again — and not only physically. Tomorrow would be the beginning of putting her plan into play, but she wasn't letting herself think beyond it. What would come, would come.

The sun was a red fireball at the horizon when she pulled into Beau's driveway.

Linda stepped out and waved when CJ shut down the bike. "Beau got home early, and I'm fixing tacos. Come on in."

CJ removed her helmet but kept her jacket on. Beau was in the kitchen, opening mail. "How was the library?"

Mazey walked over and hugged his neck. He closed his eyes and leaned his head against hers. "We didn't go. We've been riding all day."

"Should have known," Linda said. "You both have sunburns. Let me get—"

"Hang on just a minute, Linda, will you?" CJ stepped forward. "I'm going to try to fly out in the morning, and I wondered if I can leave Lola and my stuff here. I shouldn't be gone more than a week."

"Of course you can." Beau studied her like a hawk watches a mouse. "Where you going?"

She held his gaze. It wasn't easy. "Going to visit my friends' families."

He nodded. "I think that's a good plan."

"Okay, I'll go get our stuff and check out of the cabin."

Mazey tugged her sleeve. "I want to help."

"Why don't you two take my car?" Linda said. "It'll be easier than loading down the bike."

"It would. Thank you."

Cleaning out the cabin only took a half-hour; they were old hands at packing up.

"This is kinda sad." Mazey scanned the empty space. "So much has changed since we moved in here."

"Yeah. But you're starting a wonderful new part of your life."

"So are you."

If she could get through the next week, maybe. "Hope so, Punk. Hope so."

The next day, Beau and Mazey drove CJ to the airport and she boarded her plane for Omaha. Linda had bought Mazey a cell phone, and after extracting CJ's promise to call every night she punched the number into CJ's phone.

During the flight CJ's stomach jumped from more than just turbulence, but it felt good to finally being *doing* something instead of running. Was that the little voice that Mazey spoke of? CJ didn't know.

The land out the window on their approach was about as far from Laredo landscape as possible — a showy beauty, with lots of old gnarled trees and green pastures. She picked up her duffel and an economy rental car and headed out.

Mateo's family farm was outside Morse Bluff, about sixty miles from the airport. She rolled through the small town not far from the wide, lazy Platte River. She took a succession of ever-smaller roads, the last being gravel. She pulled up in front of a mailbox that looked like a white barn with red accents. The number on the side told her she was here. She turned off the engine, rolled down the windows and sat a bit, trying to calm the frantic drum-line cadence of her heart. Cornstalks taller than her head nodded in the breeze. The cawing of crows and the wind rattling through the corn were the only sounds.

Peace stole in as slow as the Platte's current and she sat a while longer, reveling in it. But when she turned the key, panic ignited with the rumble of the engine. What would she say? Could she force out what she'd held in for so long? "You can do this. You *will* do this." She shook her head to purge the doomsday scenarios then turned into the corn-walled driveway.

The corn curtain parted to reveal a whitewashed clap-board house with a small yard bordered by fields, as if the corn begrudged the space. By comparison the barn was huge, a mammoth twin to the mailbox. Easy to see what was most important here.

She forced her hand to the door handle, took a deep breath, and stepped out. Whatever she was setting in motion would be over soon. No one answered her knock at the front door, so she followed the tire track past the chicken coop and rusty swing set in the back yard to the barn.

Standing outside the massive open doors, she peered into the gloom. "H-h-hello?"

A tall, rangy, middle-aged man stepped from behind a tractor, wiping his hands on an oily rag.

No going back now. "Mr. DeLeon? I'm CJ Maxwell. I knew Mateo—"

"Name's Carter. Bruce Carter."

"Can you tell me where Mr. Deleon is?"

"This is my farm."

What? Could she have put the wrong house number into her phone when Mateo gave it to her? "Do you know where the DeLeon farm is?"

"This used to be theirs. I bought it a month ago."

"Oh." She was so ready to finally do this, it took a moment for her sluggish brain to change tracks. "Where are the DeLeons, do you know?"

He walked over, squinting into the light spilling into the doors, still wiping his hands. "The father passed away of a heart attack, from what I understand. Mrs. DeLeon said she was taking the two youngsters to live with her family in Costa Rica."

"Oh no." Had the shock of Mateo's death brought on the heart attack? Was she responsible for *another* life? Dizzy, she stepped back, grateful when her back touched the solid presence of the door. "Do you know when?"

"When he had the heart attack?" He glanced out at the corn. "No one said."

Her brain chugged, processing like a 1980 Commodore. "Do you have a forwarding address?"

"No. Why would I?"

"How about their realtor? It would be on your paperwork."

"Look. I don't know why this is so important to you, and I don't mean to sound uncaring, but as you can see..." He tipped his chin to the corn. "I have a crop to get in, and not much time to do it. So..." When she didn't move, he made shooing motions with the oily rag.

"Yeah. Okay." She turned and walked to her car, trying to suck air back into her lungs. Of all the scenarios she'd conjured, this one had never occurred to her. She opened the car door and fell in. Mateo's poor mother. She lost her son, then her husband, her farm... her country.

In the quiet, Murph's voice whispered, *"You only bear the blame that is yours."*

She didn't know when Mateo's dad passed, or what caused it. It couldn't be too hard to track down the realtor in a small town, but to what end? Even if she was able to contact Mateo's mother and discover the timeline, what would it do besides give her another whip to flog herself with?

"Let it go," a tiny voice whispered.

The breeze pulled it out the window and into the corn.

Chapter 21

CJ reversed her route and checked into a cheap hotel next to the airport, feeling like a three-day-old helium balloon — drooping, dispirited, and deflated. What she'd discovered at the farm hovered at the back of her mind like a kamikaze mosquito. She tried to ignore it, but it wouldn't go away. The only thing she could think to do was stay busy. She went for a run, took a long bath, then walked across the parking lot to the Pancake Palace for dinner.

It was dark by the time she got back to her room. Sitcom reruns on TV didn't hold her interest, so she picked up her phone and dialed Mazey.

"I've been waiting for you to call, CJ. How did it go? What's it like there? Were they nice to you? They'd better have been nice to you. Tell me everything."

"Punk, you've gotta stop worrying about me. I'm the grown-up, remember?"

"Don't change the subject. What happened? I'm dying over here."

"Nothing happened. Mateo's mom sold the farm and moved to Costa Rica."

"What? Why?"

Talking about it was like pushing her thumb into a deep bruise, but she knew Mazey wouldn't let it go. "Mateo's dad died of a heart attack, and his mom took his little brother and sister to live with her family. That's all I know."

"That is not your fault."

Damned kid was too smart. "I know."

"No, really. It isn't."

"I'm working hard at believing that, Punk." She was so tired of being in her own head. "What did you do today?"

"I went shopping with Linda. She wanted to get me more clothes, even though I told her I had enough."

'Enough' in Mazey's experience was threadbare minimum. "What did you get?"

"Way too much. I tried to stop her, but she about bought out the store. And now she's talking about redecorating my room. She's going crazy, CJ, and I feel bad about it."

"I'll bet she's having a blast."

"She *is*. I thought her face would crack from all the smiling."

"They've wanted a kid for a long time. I know it makes you uncomfortable, but just try to think of it as you doing them a favor. It'll get easier, I promise."

They talked for another half-hour about Mazey's thoughts and impressions of her new home, and when they hung up CJ felt more herself. Less alone.

She tried calling Patsy but got only her voice mail. "You're probably on your way to your gig. I just wanted to say hi. Break a leg, Pats — Mom. Talk to you later." She hung up smiling, thinking how shocked Patsy would be to get a casual call from her eldest.

~~~

She'd read somewhere that Boston had cut down the hills to fill the bogs, and seeing it from the air she believed it. The tall buildings seemed to lean over the water, yearning for more land. Coming in for a landing the plane almost skimmed the waves, and CJ glanced around to be sure no one else was alarmed. They weren't, but she didn't relax until the wheels touched tarmac. There she rented a car, threw her duffel in the back and headed for Fish Pier, where Eddie had said her his father's fishing boat was moored.

When she arrived the *Working Girl* wasn't tied at the dock, so she wandered the pier, watching the vendors lay out the morning's catch on ice-filled bins and letting the salty breeze tangle her hair.

She stood at the edge of the pier, watching the fishing boats come in. Just beyond the dock skyscrapers loomed, and a new building was going up right across the street. The smell of fish on the breeze was making her stomach flip. From the way Eddie talked, his dad was a hard man. Mateo's family being gone was now feeling more like a reprieve. Maybe she could go get coffee and come back when he wasn't busy unloading the day's catch.

No. She had a plan. She pushed her guts down where they belonged. The only way out was through.

A boat's engine roar was deep and guttural, like a giant clearing its throat. Two men jumped from the *Working Girl* to the dock. "What the hell — You're leaving me *now?* You told me you'd be onboard all summer!" A short, bandy-legged man in a watch cap was shaking his fist at a tall skinny dude. That had to be Eddie's dad. Her feet wanted to head for the parking lot, but she forced them forward.

"Yeah, and the semester starts in two weeks."

"Then you owe me two more weeks."

"I've got to get home and see my parents. I've got to get ready—"

"What the fuck is wrong with you young people? Is your word as shitty as your work ethic? The hell am I supposed to do?" He waved at the boat. "I can't run this bitch shorthanded!"

The kid appeared calm in the face of the little man's fury and flying spittle. "Cap'n, we never discussed end dates.

I have other obligations. I took your crappy wage and the dangers of the job because I wanted real-world experience to go with my marine biology degree. But I have plans and—"

"Screw your fucking plans! What about mine?" His shout rolled out across the water, but none of the men on the dock or the boat paused in their tasks. "No, you know what? You go home to mommy. I don't need you, or your whining. Get the fuck away from me." He turned and bent to check the dock lines.

The college kid walked to where CJ stopped, unable to push herself farther. The fear raging inside must have shown, because as he passed he said, "His bark is bad, but he never bit."

"Until now," she muttered. *Stick with the plan.* She forced herself on. *Stick with the plan.* She reached the side of the bobbing boat. One of the oilskin-clad workers scuttled beneath the nets and the other worked to open a hatch in the deck.

"What *you* want?" Eddie's dad looked her up and down. "You're sure not applying for a job."

"Um, no. Sir." Her throat worked, but no more words could get past the wad in her throat, hanging like a chunk of tar but tasting like rotting fish. "Could I speak with you?"

He squinted from the deck. "Ain't that what you're doin'?"

She glanced around. "I mean, can we go somewhere and talk privately? For coffee maybe?"

His red face squinched tight. "Do I look like I got time to sip tea? I got to get these fish unloaded and sold. And now I'm a hand short." He rolled his eyes to the sky. "Jaysus, why you makin' it rain idiots today?"

She stood with her mouth opening and closing, like the fish flopping on the deck.

"Go already." He turned his back and took a step.

"It's about Eddie."

His body froze, all except his shoulders. They rose to ear level, but it looked more like a turtle pulling its head into its shell. He turned, slow and measured. Pain flicked in his eyes before his mask of disgust fell once more. "Follow me."

He walked fast to the back of the boat, where the nets pulled splashing squirming silver fish from the hold. She hopped onto the deck, slipped in water, and grabbed the edge of the wheelhouse until she steadied.

Eddie's dad marched around the corner and she followed, teeth gritted, a death-grip on the bobbing railing the whole way. Trying to ignore the workers' sidelong looks, she followed him through the open door and up four steep stairs.

He sat at a small, anchored table in the tiny room. At the front, the horizon bobbed past the dirty windows. A wooden steering wheel sat amid dials and gauges.

"Sit."

She edged into the plastic seat across from him and took a closer look while trying to put words together in her head. His skin, ruddy and rough, spoke of his career and the broken veins on his nose were a map of what he did at night in place of sleep. A week's growth of beard surrounded thin lips. But Eddie's ice-blue eyes bore into her with an intensity that made her breath stutter in her chest.

"Dante Amanto. Who the fuck'r you, and how do you know my Eddie?"

Her throat clicked with her swallow. Fighting her flight reflex, she stuck out her hand. "CJ Maxwell. Eddie was my close friend..." She couldn't edge the word out of her locked jaws. "...over there."

The steel in his jaw and his eyes softened, and he shook her hand in what probably was for him a gentle grip, then let her go. He said nothing, but the questions in his glance screamed.

She pulled her hand back, hoping he hadn't felt the shake that ran through her. "I wanted to tell you how much your son meant to me. He was one of the happiest, funniest people I've ever met. I loved him like a brother."

He took a sharp inhale. "Don't need you to tell me what my son was."

You knew this would be hard. Suck it up and say it. "Yessir. I just wanted you to know what he meant to me. See, I was there. At the end. I was driving the vehicle." She looked down at the table. No way she could say it, looking at him. She took in a short, ragged breath which all her seized lungs would allow. "The accident... it was my fault." Those words pricked the bubble in her chest and the contents rushed out, eager to be free. Turns out, what was in there were words. All the words she'd never said. Trapped there in the dark, they'd gone rancid, fetid, putrid. They rose to her throat and out of her mouth, into existence. Into reality.

"See, I'd replaced the fuel injection system in the Humvee. It started fine. I ran a field test and it ran a bit rough, but that wasn't unusual with the sand..." *shutupshutupshutup.* "I never thought to replace the PMD — it never showed any inclination to fail in the test drives. We were headed for a poker game, out where the blast shields are far apart, when the damned thing died. I realized what was wrong." She tried to stop blabbering, but the words were as unstoppable as vomit. "All I needed to do was cool it off...I grabbed the water and was at the hood when the RPG hit." There were more words about what happened next, but she'd spare him that, even if she had to bite her tongue off to do it. "I came to tell you how incredibly sorry I am."

She lifted her head. She'd never seen a cow shot with a bolt gun to end its life, but she now knew the look. His eyes filled with confusion, then pain, before anger swept them away. "You came here. To tell me that?" His tone was low and deep, the warning in a wolf's growl. "What the fuck is *wrong* with you?"

"Most everything, sir." She wanted to look down, away, anywhere, but his gaze wouldn't release her.

"So you came here to make yourself feel better? Because you couldn'ta thought it'd help me to know that I've lost my son, and everything that matters, because you're a fuckup and a useless excuse for a human being?"

His words did worse than cut. They burned like a lit cigarette pushed into her skin. Why *had* she come? It seemed so clear in Texas, but in this lion's den she couldn't remember. *This* is why she hadn't knocked on Logan's family's door, but she just now understood that, soul-deep. What had she been thinking?

Erosion made inroads in the craggy lines of his gray-tinged face. "Eddie'd'a been home by now. I'd be turning over the business to him. I'm the third generation to fish these waters, and now it ends with me. You destroyed my family. My business. My legacy. My son." His voice thickened. "Did ya get whatever fucked-up absolution you wanted outta this? Huh? Did ya?" His yell bounced off the metal walls to batter her ears.

Anger flared. Eddie had no plans to take over the business, but he'd obviously never had that last phone conversation with his father. After meeting the man, she understood why. It would feel so good to throw the truth in his face and walk away, having faced her worst fear and come out at least having scored a punch. "Sir, Eddie wasn't—"

"Hey, Cap'n." One of the workers stood on the stairs, looking at her with a worried frown. "Everything okay here?"

"Get back to work!" Dante half stood, and when the guy scuttled down the stairs he plopped into the seat and turned his attention back to her. "Well?" His rheumy eyes shone with moisture. His wobbly whisper hurt more than his shouts.

Grasping for the right words to spew, she glanced around the tight quarters. Rust peeked through the chipped paint and several gauges were cracked, condensation fogging the glass, rendering them useless. A patina of decay covered everything. Despair hung with the smell of long-dead fish in the air. Looming skyscrapers bobbed in the windows. How long before the city usurped the tiny fishing fleet? From the encroaching construction, not long. When she met the worn old man's gaze, it hit her. There was only one thing she could do for Eddie. And his destroyed father. She heaved a breath, her anger dissipating with the exhale. "I came to tell you the truth. And how sorry I am about it, sir."

"God may forgive you, but I sure'n shit won't." His face crumpled and he growled, "Now, get off my boat."

~~~

She didn't remember stumbling to the rental car, falling in, or slamming the door behind her. Nightmares she hadn't even thought to dream had become real. She rammed the key in and cranked the engine.

This plan was a disaster. Mateo's dad was dead, his family scattered. Possibly — no, probably — her fault.

She squealed out of the parking lot, sending a pedestrian scooting down the crosswalk.

Eddie's father's business was sinking out from under him, leaving him drowning in booze and despair. That part was partially Eddie's fault, but she sure hadn't made it any better.

She barely managed to keep the car between the white lines the few miles to the hotel without killing herself or anyone else.

She parked, jerked the key. The cacophony in her skull making her brain throb, she ran for her room. Once inside she ran the water in the tub, pacing the dingey carpet while she waited for it to fill. When steam rose off the water a few inches from the top, she stripped and sat, ignoring the sting of heat on her skin.

It was time for Plan B.

She reached for her trusty razor, screwed off the top, and withdrew her ticket out of hell. Her gaze fell on her thighs, to all those triple-stripe scars. If each had helped release the pain, surely peace would come with three deep ones across her wrists. She allowed herself to savor the ecstasy it would be to let go of all the blame. All the shame. Like after two shots of tequila, her body would go slack. And when the water was dyed a deep ruby she'd slip under to finally sleep, undisturbed by dreams.

Blade poised over the blue rivers under the skin of her wrist, a familiar smile flitted across her mind. *Mazey.* Pictures flashed: Mazey flying into her arms in the kitchen in California. Their heads together on the sleeping bags as Mazey pointed out constellations. Riding the mountains on Lola, Mazey's trusting arms around CJ's waist.

It would be bad for her.

But she had Beau and Linda now, and they'd help her deal. CJ thought about leaving a note, but what could she say? It would take a small book to explain to Mazey how much CJ loved her, how much she wanted the best for her. But most of all, about how CJ couldn't live with the pain anymore.

But she didn't have that kind of time, and words on hotel notepad wouldn't convince Mazey anyway. She'd probably hate CJ for this. "She'll be first, behind me." She ran the blade feather-light over her skin, not hard enough to leave a mark.

She was so tired. The weight was crushing her. The emotions she'd pushed down over the past few days erupted, hitting with the force of an IED blast. She dropped her head in her hands and hung on as all the fear, pain, and regret rained down like razor bits of shrapnel. A mewling whimper escaped, escalating to the howl of a wounded animal.

She couldn't have said how long it lasted, but when it had passed she sat listening to the unnatural silence within. What could it mean? She felt around inside, looking for clues, but all there was just a hollow space, like a huge underground cavern.

Her worst fear had come true. She had not only heard the condemnation from Dante's lips, but she'd witnessed the physical, mental, and emotional devastation Eddie's death had wrought in his father.

Woul• the outcome have been •ifferent if E••ie ha• come home? came a whisper from the void.

Aside from his grief? No, it wouldn't have.

And you didn't tell him. That was a good thing to do.

What kind of bullshit logic was that? She'd caused his pain to begin with, and she should take credit for not making it infinitesimally worse? "And who the hell are you, anyway?"

Probably the little voice they told you about.

She lifted the blade again. This was the best option. The only option left.

You haven't gone to Logan's yet, the small whisper came again.

And subject another family to what she just doled out to this one? Logan's family didn't need anything she could tell them.

You don't know that. You haven't tried.

She looked up at the tile ceiling. "Haven't tried? I've done nothing but try since I got home! Shut the fuck up." Fantastic. Now she was splitting into multiple personalities, officially tipping the scale to batshit crazy.

You don't want to do this.

She sat for a long time, weighing options and casting around for solutions she'd discarded as impossible.

The voice was right. She didn't want to do this. And not only because of Mazey. Turns out Sarge had seen her clearly when he said CJ didn't let go easily.

She wanted to *live.*

But Patsy had reminded her that there was several light-years difference between not wanting to die and actually living. It would mean she'd have a future — a whole life ahead of her. The potential blew through her like the first warm spring breeze after a brutal winter.

This felt like the end, but what if it didn't have to be? She'd lived long enough with her mistake to know it would only be possible if she could find a way to put the weight of the past *down.*

The water cooled enough to raise a shiver. She stood and pulled the chain to empty the tub.

It was time to finish Plan A.

Chapter 22

No wonder Logan had loved it. Casper, Wyoming from the air was travel-brochure eye-candy. A wide green valley surrounded by mountains with a river running through it. CJ's stomach buzzed with anticipation. Whatever happened, today was the end of the trip. It couldn't have been more different than the one they'd all planned, but it was the end.

And for the first time since the trip began, the cold tide of dread wasn't rising in CJ's chest. She didn't know how she'd manage to live the rest of her life. But for now, anyway, death was off the table.

She'd called Mazey last night and told her of the Boston meeting, giving it as positive a spin as possible without lying. Despite her best efforts, Mazey's voice wobbled with worry by the end of the story. The poor kid had grown up fast, living in Patsy's orbit, and CJ hated that she'd been the cause of putting any more worry on those narrow shoulders. But kids were resilient. Maybe, given enough time at Beau's, Mazey would be able to relax into kid-dom. Where she belonged.

Once outside the terminal, she picked up a rental and began the hour and a half drive to Medicine Bow — the last stop on this long road. She drove into the mountains, appreciating the conifers' beauty that she hadn't been able to last time, due to fear and darkness — outside as well as in. Not that she wasn't concerned about the outcome today. She was closest to Logan, so in a way this was the most important meet of all. But today she felt lighter. Stronger. More alive. She rolled down the windows, letting the spruce-scented air swirl in, bringing with it a smile.

Being alive was a choice. And today the choice felt glorious.

She drove over the mountain ridge, then down into the valley, down progressively smaller roads until she stopped once more in front of the sprawling, deep-porched log home. She sat a moment, taking in the house and the fact that there were no cars in the drive. If there was no one home, she'd hunt them down — she wasn't leaving until she'd done what she came to do. Heart beating like a hummingbird's, she shut down the engine and opened the car door.

She'd steeled her heart for the last two confrontations, but the sandpaper experiences of the past weeks seemed to have worn through her flimsy armor. She tried to gather it to cover her fragile core, but it was as gone as yesterday's sunrise. She strode up the drive. She was going in naked. Exposed. Vulnerable.

And maybe that was the way it was supposed to be.

She climbed steps to the porch and, before she could stall, knocked on the door.

Steps came closer. The door opened. The woman who stood there reminded her of June Cleaver. If June had a closetful of plaid, denim, and hiking boots. There were lines around her striking blue eyes (Logan's eyes), and a red bandana around her wild, reddish-blonde curls.

Her brows came together. "I know you."

"No, ma'am. But I—"

"You're CJ Maxwell."

CJ opened her mouth, but no words fell out.

A brilliant smile broke over Logan's mom's face. "Well get yourself in here!" She pulled the door wide. "We've wanted to reach out to you, but the Army wouldn't pass on your contact information." She closed the door behind them. "I'm so happy you're here. Do you want some coffee?" She set off down the slate-floored hall at a brisk pace.

CJ followed.

"The guys took a group of fly fishermen into the mountains, and they won't be home for hours. We can have a nice girl talk before the bulls barrel back into the china shop. Have a seat."

She waved to a distressed, round wood table in the middle of the large, sunny kitchen.

CJ sat, trying to absorb the woman's welcome and her surroundings at the same time.

"Oh, I'm sorry." She stuck out a hand. "I'm Doris."

CJ's hand was grasped in a strong grip. "H-how did you know who I am?"

"Logan sent us photos, and his emails were full of you. The others, too, but mostly you." She turned to a coffeemaker. "Coffee?"

Her storm-tossed stomach nixed the idea. "No, thank you, ma'am."

"I'm just Doris." She poured coffee into a purple stoneware mug, stepped to the table, and sat.

This had wandered so far off the script CJ had imagined that she was off-kilter, almost dizzy, and not sure how to proceed. "I need to talk to you, ma' — Doris."

The woman's brows came together again. "Best you tell me what's on your mind."

"I don't know how much you know about what happened out there — when Logan was…when Logan died. I've come to tell you."

"I can see you need to say it." She set down her mug and squared her shoulders, and a muscle in her jaw flexed. "Go ahead."

It seemed she'd done nothing but tell parts of this story since the trip began. It didn't get easier with the telling. But she didn't tell it to make it easier — she told it because it was the truth, and the truth *had* to be told to the people it would matter to. She took a breath. "It was my fault. I made a huge mistake. No, two. See, I'm a — I was a mechanic. I'd replaced the fuel injection system on a Humvee, test drove it, cleared it. It was due to be picked up in the morning. I let the guys talk me into driving them to a poker game." She looked down at her hands in her lap. She pulled a strip of cuticle off, putting a finger over it to stop the bleeding. "I found out too late when it died in the absolute worst place possible, that I should have replaced the PMD, too."

She forced her gaze up, to Logan's mother's face. She didn't want to, but she owed the woman at least that. "We were between the blast barriers and the razor wire, flying along when the engine died. We were in no-man's land, spotlighted by security lights on poles. Ducks in a shooting galley had a better chance." She pulled air into the space that the words had taken up. "I was trying to get the hood up when we were hit." She swallowed and pushed out the rest. "I woke up in the dark. I crawled, feeling my way, and found them, one by one. They were..." She shuddered, remembering the feel of sticky pieces beneath her palms. "Gone."

"What happened after, to you?"

"There was an inquest. My commander interceded on my behalf, though I don't know why. I got an OTH — Other Than Honorable discharge. I have no access to VA benefits." She huffed a chuckle that was close to a sob. "But still they gave me a Purple Heart." She made herself still, ready to accept whatever came next. She was done running. Done dreading. What would be, would be. "I wouldn't have had this happen for anything, ma'am. See, I found the first real friends I'd ever had in the middle of a war zone. People who *knew* who I was deep down, and loved me, even knowing it." She shook her head, still not able to believe it. "It was like the world shifted and I saw things, ordinary things, different. Like my world had been black and white, and suddenly everything was in brilliant color. And surround sound. It changed me." She looked down. Blood smeared her fingers. "I'm not telling you this for sympathy, or for you to go easy on me. It's only so you understand what your son meant to me. I loved him like a brother."

"I know you did." Her shoulders rose on a deep breath and she swiped a tear fast, as if angry for letting it escape. "I know God is in charge and, for a reason unknown to me, He wanted my son. It's just that I struggle sometimes to accept it." A wan smile lifted the corners of her mouth. "You've portrayed this as all your fault. It's not."

"But, ma'am, I told you—"

"And I heard you. But I think you've forgotten some things about my son." She set her elbows on the table. "Logan came into this world fighting to have his way. It was his strength. And his greatest weakness." She stood. "Come, I'll show you."

CJ had no choice but to follow her up the stairs, to the last room on the left. CJ stopped at the doorway, unwilling to take the step that would crush her — seeing the room he grew up in, and would never see again. A photo stuck into the edge of the mirror caught her eye. She only glimpsed the edge of Logan's grin, but she knew the rest because she had the same photo buried in the bottom of her duffel. The four of them in camo, arms around each other's shoulders, laughing their asses off. A fierce wave of longing rattled through her, stronger than it had been in months. But this was a part of her penance. She squared her shoulders to bear it.

Doris walked in without hesitation. "He was our high school's pitcher. You probably knew that."

CJ nodded, keeping her eyes trained on the bookshelf of trophies across the room.

"He broke every record the school had, and most of the league's. He was all-state and was accepted to four good colleges on full-ride scholarships. But he turned them all down. He wanted to serve his country. His father and I tried to change his mind, but when we saw he was determined we gave it up as a lost cause." She turned to CJ. "That's what you've forgotten — when my son's mind was made up, nothing could change it. And from what he told me, the other two were pretty much the same."

CJ nodded. She couldn't deny it.

"You've been beating yourself up for a long time, haven't you?"

She couldn't talk, so she continued to nod.

"Then it's time to put it down. You had a part in that horrible night. So did they. But the biggest blame is at the feet of the people who fired that weapon." Doris stepped over and put her hand on CJ's shoulder. "Logan is fine, hon. It's us left behind who aren't. But with God's help we're working on it, and you must, too."

How wonderful would it be to believe in this woman's God? To be comforted by the belief in a higher power? But faith was something you had or didn't. And she didn't. "Ma'am, I'm not religious."

"Oh, my religion isn't even the first reason I know my son is fine." A smile broke on her face like when clouds clear, letting sun through. "He told me."

She'd taken Doris at face value, but what if Logan's death had unhinged her?

"I can see you don't believe me. Come, I'll show you."

What, tarot cards? A seance? Wary, CJ followed Doris as she retraced her steps back to the kitchen. She kept walking through the back door, the groomed back yard, and into the meadow beyond.

"Where are we going?" CJ watched her feet for snakes.

"You'll see."

The meadow took a gentle slope downward, toward a thick line of trees about a quarter-mile away. They walked in silence, tall grasses shushing against their jeans.

They walked into the dappled shade of the huge trees, their steps quieted by last fall's damp leaves, raising scents of decay, fresh oxygen, and growing things. Doris followed a faint trail between the trunks. As they walked deeper the burble CJ took as hushed conversation turned out to be water, tumbling over rocks.

"We're here." Doris stopped at the side of a stream. Or maybe a river; it had to be forty feet across, and at least six feet deep. The water was crystal clear — she could easily see the topography of colorful stones scattered across the bottom. Startled silver fish darted upstream away from them.

"This was Logan's place. He came down here almost every day. Always with fly rod in his hand, but he never brought dinner home. I think he more just sat and daydreamed."

"Good place for it. I've never seen anything so pretty." The trees at the edge trailed branches, as if stooping to drink.

"You sit for a spell. Logan will come to you." Doris smiled, then turned and walked away, calling over her shoulder. "Come back to the house when you're done."

CJ watched until she disappeared into the trees. What a sweet, odd lady. CJ dearly hoped that grief hadn't forced her poor mind to conjure her dead son. A huge flat rock extended over the water. She stepped to the edge of it and sat.

A stray breeze set the branches swaying, leaves rustling like distant applause. The glassy surface of the river moved like liquid mercury, shifting but never breaking. The water over the rocks made a deep sound, like an old man's chuckle. She breathed in the smell of dank cold places, even as the dappled sun warmed her skin.

There was something different, but it took her a while to recognize what it was.

She closed her eyes, and the restless antsiness that had chased her for months faded. Quiet stole in to fill the space.

Reveling in the change, she waited.

In time, peace inched into her bloodstream like a heavy dose of Valium, releasing her muscles from their constant tautness.

She didn't mind the waiting.

Her legs swung, her chest expanded on deep inhales and slow, gentle exhales. How long had it been since she sat still, and just *was*?

Had she ever?

Thoughts came and went like the puffy clouds over the sun. Mind quiet for maybe the first time in her life, she felt at harmony with herself, the world, and her tiny place in it.

She happily waited.

But the change in the slant of light on the water and the stinging nerves in her butt reminded her she couldn't stay forever in this place.

Logan hadn't spoken to her. Even Mazey's small voice had been silent. But one thought had flickered in and out of her mind, flashing and darting like the small birds that swooped down to catch bugs on the water's surface. What if you didn't have to pay forever for a mistake, even a bad one? What if the forgiveness she'd chased across the country wasn't something that could be granted by others, but something only *she* could give herself?

It had never occurred to her in all her thinking that *she* could be the answer.

She scooted back from the edge and stood, waiting for the needles to fade before stepping away. "I love you, Logan. I always will." She spoke to the trees. To the river. To this amazing space that belonged to her best friend. "I'm leaving here, but I'm not leaving you behind. I'm taking you with me. Because life without you doesn't work. I know, because believe me I tried. I don't know what happens next, but if you're with me I know I'll be okay. Okay?"

Only the sounds of nature came back.

She stepped into the trees, but then turned back to glimpse this charmed place once more. Her heart thudded in slow, strong beats, pushing the newfound sense of ease to all her hungry cells. Perhaps a pardon of sorts?

And it felt... possibly... permanent.

Could it be that her best friend had spoken to her in silence, in the way she needed the most? Maybe not, but it made her feel good to believe that. So she would.

She walked slowly back to the house, trying to absorb what just happened. It was like she'd been trying for months to climb a fifty-foot wall. And when that didn't work, beating and clawing at it. Now the wall had vaporized, and the wide-open space in front of her was so big she couldn't take it in.

And as if they'd been behind the wall waiting, realizations hit her one after the other.

She could let go of her friends. She didn't have to be afraid to lose them, because she'd carry them with her, a part of her, always. Maybe what she had to let go of was who *she* was — that tormented ghost, living some in the present, some haunting the past. She now had a future. No, it was bigger than that, because she never believed she had much of one to begin with.

With a start, she realized that *she* had built that wall. She'd wanted to be a medic, but when the Army said they knew better she followed without complaint, wanting to find a place to fit in more than she wanted her own dream. She did the same with the guys, and she could finally admit they *all* had paid a heavy price for it.

She'd blamed Patsy for her lack of choices. Blamed her for what she was — for what she wasn't. CJ'd spent so much energy making her mother the bad guy. Why?

The answer hit with the slap of shame.

Because it was easier to blame her mother than taking a chance on a dream and possibly finding she wasn't smart enough. She wasn't good enough. It was a safe path, because despite Patsy's lax, self-centered parenting, CJ knew her mother wouldn't give up on her and walk away.

Mazey was right. It didn't matter if her mother ever made it past singing in dive bars, because it was the dream that was important. And chasing it made Patsy happy.

That made her braver than her oldest daughter.

Ouch.

Even little Mazey was brimming with dreams. When CJ tried to protect her by standing in her way, Mazey plowed right past her. And her little sister was just getting started; she'd achieve many more big dreams before she was done.

CJ didn't know what hollowed out the black hole of insecurity in her, but she was starting to realize it was big enough to suck in any aspirations she had the temerity to hope for. That was going to take time, and maybe even some professional help to figure out.

But now she *had* time. Freedom came on the breeze that lifted her hair, and she raised her hands and did a little twirl, dancing with the meadow grasses. She had a lifetime of days stretching ahead, gleaming in the sunshine like some kind of crazy yellow brick road.

She'd been given a tremendous gift today. She couldn't wait to start exploring it.

Her feet flew the rest of the way to the house.

Chapter 23

CJ tapped lightly on the kitchen door. When Doris opened it a few seconds later, CJ felt the older woman's regard on the skin of her face.

The older woman broke into a smile. "He spoke to you, didn't he?"

"No. But I felt..." CJ shuffled through all her words, but couldn't come up with one that fit. She just shrugged.

"Come in and we'll chat. I fixed us some lunch." She turned and walked into the room.

CJ wiped her feet on the sisal mat and stepped in. "I don't want to put you out. I'll just head out and grab some lunch in town."

"Oh don't be silly. Matt called, and his clients are having so much fun they've booked extra time. He and Luke won't be home until tomorrow." She tossed the salad in a cut-glass bowl, then carried it to the table. "Do you want iced tea or water?"

She should be on her way, but Doris had been so nice she didn't want to be rude. "Wow, this looks great. Tea, please."

"Sit, sit." She poured two glasses of tea and brought them to the table.

CJ sat in front a plate with a thick sandwich on it.

Doris sat. "Chicken salad. Made it this morning."

"How do you find the time? Keeping up this big house, the business and all?"

"Oh, I've had practice. Been doing it for twenty years, since Matt decided to give up the corporate world and come back to do what he'd always wanted to do."

"Wow, that was a big dream." CJ bit into her sandwich. It was chunky, with cut grapes, walnuts, and was that tarragon? "This is wonderful."

"I love to cook. We'd planned to have a brood, at least six kids. But God only gave us the two, so we fill the house with hunters, fishermen, birders, and nature-lovers. I keep them fed."

"Was this your dream, too?"

Doris chewed and swallowed before answering. "*Matt* was my dream. He was two years ahead of me in high school, and hardly knew I existed. But when I saw him in the halls as a freshman, I knew I was going to marry him." She chuckled. "It took me a while to convince him, however." She glanced around the huge room. "We married when we finished college and went to the city. He got a job as an attorney and I was a buyer for a large corporation. We made it work, but we came to hate the noise, the crowds, and the anonymity. We were parched for nature. So when he said he wanted to come home, I was overjoyed. I'd be happy never to leave it again."

"I can see why. It's so beautiful here."

"What's your dream, CJ?"

It would feel weird to say it out loud, especially since she'd been disloyal to that dream for so long. But maybe it was time. "I wanted to train to be an EMT. Maybe go back to college and become a nurse. I'd love to work in an emergency room someday."

"Oh, what a good dream — a career helping people."

"Yes, but..."

"But what?"

"What if I made a mistake, and someone else paid for it?" Again. There was no law that your worst nightmare couldn't repeat.

She put down her fork and grasped CJ's wrist. "Oh, hon. Big dreams come with big risks. The question is, are you going to let this fear, which may never happen, keep you from helping all those other people, whose lives you may save?"

She'd never thought of it that way. Maybe there was a softer way of judging herself. One more thing for her to figure out.

"This may sound strange, but if you have the time I'd like it if you'd consider staying a few days with us. I know Matt and Luke would love to meet you, and we'd love to know more about Logan's life over there."

"Oh, I couldn't—"

"This place is healing. I have a feeling you could use some of that."

The empathy in the older woman's eyes pulled out the question CJ had wanted to ask from the beginning. "Ma'am, why are you being so nice to me?"

Doris' grip tightened. "Logan loved you. From what I've seen today, his judgement was sound. It would be a crime for you to go through life crippled by the past. He wouldn't want that. There has been so much loss, so much heartbreak, for all of us. It's time we started living the rest of our lives." She shook CJ's wrist. "Time for you to start, too."

A startled, sharp sob broke from CJ's throat. "I miss him so much."

Doris slid out of her chair to her knees beside CJ and wrapped her arms around her.

CJ leaned into the comfort, drinking in what felt like redemption.

The next day, Logan's father Matt and his brother Luke came through the door, laden with fishing equipment and chattering away. Seeing CJ drinking coffee with Doris in the kitchen, they stopped still.

Doris hopped up. "You're home." She stepped over to kiss her husband and hug her son.

"Mom, those guys were really nice and they picked up casting fast. Good tippers, too."

"That's nice. Don't you dare drop those muddy boots on my kitchen floor, Luke. Take all that stuff to the back porch, then come get coffee and I'll introduce you to our guest."

They smiled as they walked by. CJ didn't expect that would last long when they found out who she was. A shimmer of jitters ran under her skin. Dammit, she should have left at dawn. But she'd wanted to go out and say goodbye to Logan first. She sat on her hands to keep from fidgeting.

When they were settled, steaming coffee mugs before them, Doris introduced CJ.

Luke looked confused. His father's brows came down and stayed there.

She gave an abbreviated version of why she was here, along with her part in the accident. It didn't come out as harsh and stark as the first time. Could that mean she was beginning to step back from the edge? Kinda felt how she'd imagined that would feel. Doris took Matt's hand, and when CJ finished Luke spoke first.

"You're the one who came up with the motorcycle trip idea. Logan really liked you."

"Yeah." She cut a glance to Matt, whose expression hadn't changed. "And he told me you're going to be next year's star of the high school football team."

He blushed, and ducked his head. "If I could be half as good a quarterback as he was a pitcher, I'll be doing okay."

She addressed Matt. "Sir, I can't begin to tell you how sorry I am—"

Doris stood, stepped behind CJ's chair, and put her hands on her shoulders. "We know you are. No more recriminations, no more regrets. We go forward from here, remember?"

CJ was sure that was aimed at her husband as much as her.

A muscle in his jaw worked, hard and fast. "If you'll excuse me, I've got to put up the gear." He stood and walked out the back door.

"I'm going to run up to my room for a minute," Luke said, and was gone.

"Ma'am, I should go now." CJ tried to stand.

Doris patted CJ's shoulder. "You're fine. Sit tight. I'll be right back." She followed her husband out the door, closing it behind her.

CJ couldn't hear the words, but the tone came through well enough. Doris' calm murmur, his louder; deeper, urgent. She had to find a way to make a quick, graceful exit. Maybe she could lie about a call asking her to come back to Laredo. It'd have to be lie; Mazey told her to stay as long as she wanted.

To stop trying to eavesdrop she walked to the great room, perching on a leather ottoman in front of the tall, well-used fireplace, hands between her knees.

Luke bounded down the stairs, and when he saw her he came over and thrust a photo into her hands — the photo of the four of them, arms around each other. "He sent us this. I should have recognized you." He flopped onto the overstuffed plaid couch. "Tell me about Logan over there."

He didn't seem angry but, still, she picked through her memories like sorting through a munitions dump, trying to choose the least dangerous one. "He was the most loyal, moral man I've ever met. He saved me from a bully, and even got into a bar fight when someone called Mateo a wet-back." She chuckled. "We were lucky to get out of there just before the MPs showed up. The next day wasn't fun — we were all bruised up and even I had a black eye." She sobered and looked into Logan's true-blue eyes in the photo. "He was the brother I never had."

"He was the brother I had for a while. I miss him bad."

She sniffed and set the photo on the heavy glass and wood coffee table. Time to deflect. "Tell me about fly fishing."

"You've never done it?"

She shook her head.

"Oh, you have to learn. It's the best. We mostly catch and release — unless we're going to prepare lunch for the clients." He glanced to the kitchen doorway. "I'm not a fan of killing things. I'm glad I'm in school during hunting season. But don't tell my dad."

"I won't. We're agreed on that one."

"But fly fishing is different. It's your skill against the fish, and they're smart. You have to know where they hold in the stream, what they're eating, try to imitate it, then lay it out gentle and with perfect drift. It's light tackle so you have to be careful, but when you do it all right and tie into a big rainbow, cutthroat, or a brookie, you've got a fight on your hands." He thought for a few moments. "It's like a combination of instinct, knowledge, luck, and skill. You'd be hooked from the first time you did it."

"You make it sound romantic."

Red spread up from his T-shirt. "It is, kinda." The brothers didn't resemble each other much, but she saw Logan in Luke's smile.

The back door opened and closed. Doris and Matt came around the corner.

Luke turned. "Hey Dad, can we take CJ fishing for an hour or two?"

From his scowl, Doris hadn't had much effect on Matt's opinion. "Son, we just got back, and we have work to do."

"Aw, the next group won't be in for three days, and CJ has never been. The car is still packed, so it wouldn't be a hassle. Please?"

CJ stood. "Thanks, but I really have to be getting back to Laredo."

Luke stood, too. "You know Logan would want us to teach her. She was his best friend over there, and he loved fishing more than all of us put together."

Doris took her husband's elbow. "I think that would be lovely. You're right, Luke, that's what Logan would have wanted."

Matt's face showed the battle going on behind it.

She had to get out of here. "No, really I—"

"We'll go for a couple hours." Matt said, jaw tight. "But then you owe me chores, son."

"This is going to be epic." Luke turned to CJ. "Come on, we'll find a pair of waders and boots for you in the garage."

If the kid could get his dad to do something he clearly didn't want to, her flimsy arguments would have no effect. She followed him out the door.

Less than an hour later they were in a big, muddy SUV stuffed with fishing equipment, bumping down a dirt road.

Luke turned in the front seat. "We're going to the Miracle Mile. Best chance to hook you into a nice rainbow, maybe even a brown."

A deep pothole jarred her tailbone. She shifted to her other cheek. "Even if I don't catch a fish, the scenery will have been worth it." She'd gotten a peek through the trees to the broad Platte River as it meandered through a sage brushy meadow.

"Nah, we're good guides. You'll catch a fish. Right, Dad?"

"No one out here better."

She'd noticed several turnouts, but they'd passed every one. "What's wrong with these spots?" She pointed.

"Too many fishermen. You can't have a crowd to appreciate fly fishing."

Ten minutes later Matt took a barely perceptible track through the grass, and five minutes later stopped under the trees at the edge of the river.

Matt eyed her in the rearview mirror. "You don't mind a bit of a hike, do you? Best fishing is upstream a bit."

"Sure, I'm up for it."

They piled out and pulled rods, vests, and nets out of the back. Loaded like a rented camel, she followed Matt's broad shoulders down a dusty wandering path. Luke brought up the rear.

"There are snakes, but with the waders and your boots, unless you step on one you shouldn't have a problem."

"Snakes?" From then on, she skipped the scenery and kept her eyes downcast.

She was sweaty and hot by the time they stopped, probably a mile from the car. It looked as though this area flooded routinely. Just back from the sandy bank was littered with downed saplings like pick-up-sticks lying on top of mud.

Matt stopped. "Stay close to the water here. Easier walking."

Luke checked her rod. "You've got a cicada on. Should be good about now."

Matt stepped into the water. "First, we have to teach you how to cast. Come on out."

He led her to knee-deep water and positioned her facing upstream. "Okay, you move the rod forward and back, stopping at ten and two. It's slow and easy, see?" He demonstrated, the bright green line snaking out and back. On the last forward swing, he dropped the tip of the rod and the fly drifted, to land soft as a leaf on the surface of the water.

"Wow, that's beautiful."

"Now you try."

She tried.

"Slow down, you can't snap it. You have to give the line time to get out behind you. Here, see?" He demonstrated, and she saw this time how the loop behind him unfurled.

She tried again. And again. About the tenth time she was starting to get the hang of it, but her line still slapped the water in the front. A half-hour later, she was feeling pretty good.

Luke had been fishing upstream. He stepped out of the river. "I'm just going to get by you guys and go downriver a bit."

"Okay," Matt said, but he was focused on her cast. "Now, drop the rod tip on the next one."

CJ did, and though the fly hit harder than his it was her best cast yet. The fly drifted a few feet, then a fish exploded up and snagged her fly on the way down. "Yikes! What do I do?"

"You got him! Keep tension on the line but don't pull — let him wear himself out." Matt stepped to her side. "Don't worry about getting him on the reel. Just pull in line with your other hand. Rod tip up, keep the tension!"

It was like she was connected to the fish through the taps and tugs on the line. Excitement burst like a glitter bomb in her gut. Heart galloping, she pulled the line in slowly, taking it in as the fish allowed.

"Hang on, CJ! Bring him to me. Gentle now." Matt extended a net, and when the fish slid in he hoisted it out of the water. "Nice rainbow. Well done!"

Hands and knees shaking, she took a step to him. The fish flopped, the rainbow stripe on his side flashing. "Oh, he's beautiful!"

"Ahhhhh, shit!" The shout came from behind them.

They turned. Luke pitched forward and fell on his hands, one foot in a hole. "Help! Dad!"

Matt handed her the squirming net and ran.

She pulled the hook out of the fish's lip, then let it go. She followed, stumbling out of the water, dropping her rod and the net on the shore.

"Stop, CJ. Don't come any closer," Matt said.

She glanced down at the muck crisscrossed with branches.

"Dammit, Luke, you know better than to walk in this mess."

"I had to pee. Dad, my leg is broken." Arm around his father's shoulder, he pulled his leg from the downed timber and fell to a sitting position. His left toe pointed up, his right flopped to the side in a position that shouldn't be possible. "Agh, that hurrrrts!"

CJ's stomach lurched. Both bones broken. Tib-fib fracture. Had to be.

"Jesus, son." Matt knelt by Luke, staring at his leg.

CJ tightrope-walked on the branches, being careful where she put her feet until she reached the men. "Hang on, Luke." She sat on a mat of grass beside him. "Matt, can you get a cell signal out here?" She'd left her phone at the house.

Matt just stared at his son's leg.

"Matt!" She waved a hand to break the tractor beam.

"Huh?" His face was whiter than Luke's.

"Can you get a cell signal?"

"Um." He fumbled with the top of his waders until his shaking hands emerged with his phone. "No bars."

"Okay." CJ's mind worked hard and fast. It didn't look like an open fracture, but she couldn't see through the waders. "Do you have a knife?"

Luke moaned.

When Matt produced a jackknife, she slit the leg of Luke's waders.

"These are my new pair, shit. I'm sorry, Dad. Goddamn, that hurts."

Matt just patted his shoulder. "We'll get you out of here, son, don't worry."

No exposed bones, but the leg below the knee was ballooning, his jeans already tight. CJ slid her hand down to his ankle, being careful not to touch the leg. She found only a thready pulse. That was not good — with the adrenaline, his heart had to be slamming. She should feel a bounding pulse. "Matt, you're going to have to double-time it back to the truck. If you can't get a signal there, you'll have to drive until you do and send help."

"We can carry him out."

"No! Dad, it hurts so bad. I'd pass out."

"We can't move him. It would be dangerous."

"I'm not leaving you, son."

"Matt." She waited until his head came up. "I don't know how to get back to the truck. You have to go."

Matt shot panicked looks around. "I can make a travois out of branches and our vests. We can drag him—"

Luke's eyes rolled back in his head. He was out.

Probably better he didn't hear this. "Look, Matt. This is a bad fracture, and I'm not getting much of a pulse at his ankle, which probably means there's damage to veins or arteries. He could lose his leg. We don't have much time. You have to go right now."

"How do you know? You're not a doctor. Maybe it's not as bad as you think. We could try." His eyes darted, nostrils flared like a panicked horse. Shock was setting in — for both of them.

But he was right. Who was she to say? She'd had first aid classes, and read everything she could in high school, but what if she was wrong? Again. Panic crashed in, muscling coherent thoughts aside. Matt was Luke's dad. Let him make the decision. She'd be off the hook, and not be responsible for more damage. She couldn't live with more guilt.

She glanced at Luke. The pain had left his face with consciousness, smoothing his forehead, easing his jaw, stripping the years, leaving him looking about thirteen. He was a good kid — he had a big life ahead of him. She couldn't let his father make a mistake that could endanger that. And if she was wrong, at least he wouldn't have to live with the crushing weight of guilt that she already bore.

"Matt." She spoke soft and calm. "We can't take the chance of me getting lost. This is the only way — we'd do more damage trying to get him out of here. You have to trust me." Her stomach squirmed, realizing she was asking this man to trust his only remaining son to the woman who'd killed his first one. She bore down, forcing herself to hold his gaze. "I'm right. I know it. Now go."

He stared at her for long moments, deciding.

Then he lurched to his feet and ran.

She sat holding Luke's hand, willing him not to wake.

Ten minutes later, he did. "Wha — Nggghhh!"

Her hand was crushed in his grip, knuckles grinding together. "Don't move. Hang on, Luke. Your dad has gone for help. We'll have you out of here soon."

"God, I'm such an idiot." He moaned. "This could ruin my football career."

"How did this happen?"

"I went to the trees to pee. I was on my way back when I heard you yell that you caught one. I looked up, and stepped in that damned hole. There was a branch across the front of it, my heel caught on the back, and it just snapped." His face drained of what color had come back.

She squeezed his hand. "You're going to be okay, I know you will. It shouldn't be long — your dad took off like a charging buffalo."

"Dad knows first aid. He must have just panicked." He looked up at her. "Thank you for not letting him move me. I owe you."

"Owe me?" A choking sob burst from her and she clung to his hand. "You should hate me."

"What, for Logan? Anyone can make a mistake. God knows I just did."

"Yeah, but yours only hurt you." The tide of oily guilt rose in her, swirling faster and higher than it had since her hours in the bathtub.

"That's was just luck. It could happen to anyone, anytime." He shifted and moaned.

"Here. Let's lay you back. You'll be more comfortable." She shifted until she was behind him, one leg on either side of him, and slowly eased his torso onto her chest. "A little better?"

"Yeah." He grunted. "Logan wouldn't want you to suffer like this, you know."

She sniffed. "I know. But I don't know how not to."

"I know. I don't, either."

She felt his chest hitch against her chest, and she wrapped her arms around him, laid her cheek against his hair, and they cried, sharing their pain.

Chapter 24

The view out the window of the plane on Sunday was very different from her last flight — could it only have been four days ago? But that was okay, because she felt different. By the time the life flight helicopter showed up they'd pulled themselves back together, but the pieces came together in a new pattern. A bond had formed between them.

CJ and his parents had sat in the waiting room for hours, waiting for Luke to come out of surgery. The paramedics told Matt things would have been much worse if he'd moved his son. When he gushed, thanking CJ, she lost it again, her regret and apologies flowing out with the tears. They shared a group hug.

Luke would carry a plate and screws in his leg, but they said he should be well enough to practice by October.

The next day she spent time at Logan's spot on the river, absorbing nature's peace and having one-sided conversations with him. Doris was right. It helped. The load was still there on her shoulders, but something had shifted. It felt easier to carry now. Lighter. She would always cherish her experience in Wyoming — and the family who hadn't judged. Before she left, they extracted a promise for a return visit, and she was so looking forward to that. But for now, she was looking ahead for the first time since Afghanistan.

The plane came in for a landing on the flat brown land, and as soon as the seatbelt sign dinged she snatched her duffel and stood shifting foot to foot until she could get off the plane. She trotted through the stream of people in the Laredo terminal until she burst out the doors to find the Browns with Mazey, standing on the sidewalk with balloons and a poster board sign emblazoned, *WELCOME HOME*, in red magic marker and a liberal dose of glitter.

Mazey made a flying leap into CJ's arms, her too-long legs locking around her. "I'm so glad you're back!" Then she whispered, "I told you it would be okay."

CJ laughed and spun her sister in a circle. "Amazing Gracie, my very own fortune-teller."

"Nah, I just know you."

CJ set Mazey down, and Linda was the next hug. "We're so glad you're back, safe and sound."

Instead of stepping back, she leaned in. It felt good. "Thanks."

Beau had been watching. He stepped forward, but instead of a hug extended his hand. "Well done."

Mazey had obviously shared their conversations, but CJ couldn't be mad about it. She took his hand. "Thank you."

Mazey grabbed her other hand. "Let's go home. I want to show you my room!"

Home. That was one thing she'd done right. Her sister was safe, with people who loved her — a reminder to balance her mistakes with her wins.

Back at the Browns', Mazey dragged her into a room very different from their old room back in California. It was roomy where the old one was cramped, and instead of nasty shag carpet the hardwood floors were scattered with colorful throw rugs. A queen-sized bed took the place of the narrow single. But in the ways that mattered, it was the same. Rocks graced every spare surface and constellations covered the ceiling, proof that Mazey lived here.

"Mom sent my stuff. Cool, huh?"

"Way cool, Punk."

"Oh and look!" She lifted the geode CJ remembered from the bedroom in California. She pulled the two halves apart, revealing purple crystals inside. "I told you I'd open it when something special happened."

"It's beautiful. And finding your dad sure was a special occasion."

"It was. But I'm talking about our trip together."

CJ couldn't help it. She reached out and tucked Mazey's hair behind her ear, and trailed her fingers down her cheek. "Yeah, that too."

"Wait, you haven't seen the best part." Mazey walked to the window and pulled the heavy drapes. "Turn on the knob below the light switch."

When CJ did a globe on the ceiling lit and turned, spilling stars, comets, and planets across the walls in a revolving diorama. "Ohhhh."

Mazey threw herself on her back on the bed, patted the comforter next to her, then laced her fingers beneath her head.

CJ walked over and laid down beside her, and they watched the heavens turning above them.

"CJ?"

"Yeah?"

"Is it okay that I'm here?"

She turned her head to take in her sister's sharp features. "What do you mean?"

"I feel kinda bad about abandoning Mom."

"Oh, Punk." She slid an arm under Mazey's neck. "Mom is fine. She's doing what she loves, and you'll go visit her at Christmas."

"I know, but I'm afraid of what she'll get into if I'm not there to watch out for her."

She wanted to argue that none of her mother's poor decisions were Mazey's responsibility.

But she also knew from personal experience that it didn't matter what anyone else thought. If you felt responsible, you were. And the thought of Mazey suffering made CJ's soul ache.

Maybe the way watching CJ's suffering hurt Mazey? Probably.

"You know what I learned at Logan's?"

"What?"

"That when bad stuff happens, you look for your part in it and blame yourself. And if it is your fault, that's a good thing to do — so you learn not to do it again. But you have to be careful not to take any more than your share of blame. Because you can only fix your part. You can't fix someone else's piece. It eats at you because you really want to fix it, but you can't. It messes you up. Know what I mean?"

"But how do you know where your part ends, and someone else's starts?"

"Yeah, that's the hard part." She pulled her sister's head to her and kissed her cheek. "What do you say we work on that together?"

"I'd like that, CJ."

"So would I, Punk. You're a pretty smart kid, you know that?"

"Well, duh," she said with a smug smile.

"Oh, really?" CJ tickled her sister until she screamed with laughter.

~~~

CJ treated them all to pizza that night to thank them for... well, everything. They sat at the picnic tables outside, and when their number was called Beau went inside to pick up the order.

"This reminds me of our trip out here on Lola." Mazey pulled napkins from the dispenser and passed them out.

"Yeah, it kinda does." CJ dealt the paper plates.

"You two are lucky. You made so many memories together." Linda put the flimsy napkin in her lap.

"CJ, can we ride Lola to see Mom next summer?"

"We'll see, Punk. But I'd sure like that."

Beau returned with a huge metal pan of Hawaiian pizza.

After their first pieces had been eaten, hers was still on her plate. "Um, I have a huge favor to ask."

"Need another ride to the airport?" Beau asked.

Mazey stopped, mid-reach for another slice. "You're not leaving me again, are you? You said..."

"No, no, it's not that." This was Mazey's family, not hers, no matter how nice they'd been. She had to push the words out. "I've done some research. Laredo College offers EMT training, and they also have an RN program. There's nothing special in California for me, and I'd like to stay close to Mazey—"

"Well, of course you do," Linda said. "And you should."

CJ stared at the table. Why was asking so hard? "The apartment above the garage... if I helped you get it in shape, and paid rent, would you—"

"Yes," Beau said. "I offered it before, but I didn't think you were interested."

"Well, I had some stuff to work through, but now it's time for me to get moving on a career."

"We don't need your rent. You're free to—"

"I couldn't stay unless I was paying."

"Okay, then you're going to need a job." He wiped his mouth. "I happen to know that the Ford dealer next door to my shop is looking for a mechanic, and they like to hire veterans."

"Thanks, but no." She shuddered. She was never working that career again. "I've researched, and the Red Cross teaches a ten-week program in Phlebotomy."

Linda cocked her head. "Okay, I'll bite. What is that?"

"Drawing blood." Mazey's gaze bounced between them like a spectator at a tennis match.

"I figure I can do that when I'm not in school, and it'll be good experience for later, and I have enough left in my savings for first, last, and deposit on the apartment. What do you think?" She looked to Beau.

"You don't need all that. I can't picture you having wild parties. We'll work out what's a fair rent later, okay?"

Mazey jumped up and ran around the picnic table to hug CJ's neck. "You're staying!"

"If you don't choke me to death, first." She chuckled, extricating herself. "I need to get myself together, and this would be the perfect place." Her voice wobbled to a stop. "Look, I want you two to know how grateful I am."

"We wouldn't have it any other way." Linda nodded at the pizza box. "Now, you gonna eat or what?"

"I wondered if I was asking God for too much." Mazey sat down beside her sister. "But my second wish came true, too!"

CJ hugged her sister's neck "You and me, forever and always, Amazing Gracie."

Afterword

Four years later ~

The soccer field was knock-your-eyes-out green. Not an easy feat for Laredo summer grass. The groundskeepers must have put in the time, water, and love to make it nice for today. A stray breeze lifted the edge of her maroon gown, exposing the hem of the white dress beneath. CJ couldn't remember the last time she wore a dress, but today warranted it. She just hoped she didn't trip, crossing the stage in these danged heels.

Commencement speeches were always dry and predictable, but today she'd be happy to sit as long as they wanted to drone on.

Cora Jean Maxwell, RN. Who could've imagined such a thing? Well, besides her family, who had been cheering her on since she started down this road. It hadn't been easy, but her life was so much better than before, and she was grateful. Her therapist had helped a lot, but she was still learning to forgive herself. The hardest was getting past the fear of making a mistake that could hurt someone. But she wasn't sure that having someone's health in your hands should ever come easy.

She wasn't over that horrible mistake the four of them had made that night in the desert. Humans are so proud of their big brains. They think it puts them above animals. But if an animal makes a mistake — a deer not being watchful when she takes a drink, a possum crossing the road... If they live, they learn and move on. It's only humans that bear the pain of past mistakes — the price to pay for big brains. She'd managed to work her way through, one experience at a time, and now she saw in every day a new chance to prove herself worthy of forgiveness.

They had the graduates stand and the first row walked to the stage, waiting to be called. It gave her the chance to scan the crowd. Patsy and Arlo were halfway up. Who would have guessed that her mother's songwriter boyfriend was a decent human, *and* still around after four-plus years? He'd even sold a song or two... nothing you would've heard, but still. He was a good influence on Patsy, too. She'd toned down the makeup and was wearing more age-appropriate clothing. She waved frantically. She was still headlining dive bars, loving life.

And wasn't that what everyone aspired to?

Her row was called and she followed the line to the stage, her stomach jumping like it was full of crickets. She hadn't heard from Laredo Medical Center yet, but had hope that even if she didn't get into the ER right away she'd have a job there. Hopefully soon.

Logan's family had wanted to come, but summer was their busiest time, so instead she promised to visit. Lola was packed and waiting, and she and Mazey would leave in the morning. Mazey loved Medicine Bow as much as CJ. It would be so good to get out on the road and let the wind blow the school-year stress away.

Mazey, Beau, and Linda were in the front row, Mazey looking so grown up in her sundress, her hair pulled back in a high ponytail. She'd finally grown into her legs, and though her thick glasses and angular face may keep her from being beautiful CJ could tell she'd be a handsome woman. She would start Harmony Science Academy High in the fall and was already researching colleges. CJ blew her a kiss.

She was so proud of her Amazing Gracie — the girl who taught her to notice the beauty all around, and to be grateful for it.

The girl she set out to save, who ended up saving *her*.

At the base of the steps to the dais, she was up next. She straightened her cap, tugged the tassel and took a deep breath, letting it out slowly to calm her runaway heartbeat.

"Cora Jean Maxwell."

She climbed the three steps and walked to where the dean held out a hand — and her diploma.

She thanked him, and at the cheer turned to the audience, moving the tassel to the other side. High up in the bleachers, three guys in fatigues were whistling and stomping. Black spots danced across her vision, and when she stumbled the dean caught her arm.

"Are you all right?"

She glanced back to the stands, but of course the top row was filled with regular families — no camo.

"I'll be fine. Thank you."

She walked to the other side of the stage and down the steps. "Stay with me guys, this dream is just getting started."

Acknowledgements

Soldier/Afghanistan research: Thank you all for your service:

- Paul Elderfield
- Raleigh Stahl
- Kyle Mohr
- Eileen Saunders

And thanks once more to Bruce Rauss, my "god of all things automotive." This time for Humvee maintenance tips.

Thanks to Cyndi D'Alba who, when I was searching for something, told me to use the experience of my own broken leg. Hey, at least the pain went for *something* good!

As always, my faithful critters/editors: Fae Rowen, Donna Hopson, and my amazing beta reader, Miranda King.

Thanks to Lou Aronica, for being patient while I hammered out the bugs. They were legion.

And, as always, to my dedicated readers. Thank you for "getting" me.

About the Author

Laura Drake is a New York and self-published published author of Women's Fiction and Romance. Her debut, *The Sweet Spot*, won the 2014 Romance Writers of America® RITA® award. She's since published 13 more books. She is a founding member of Women's Fiction Writers Assn. and Writers in the Storm blog.

Laura is a city girl who never grew out of her tomboy ways. She gave up the corporate CFO gig to write full time. She realized a lifelong dream of becoming a Texan and is currently working on her accent. She's a wife, grandmother, and motorcycle chick in the remaining waking hours.